# The
# Granddaughter's
# Irish Secret

# BOOKS BY SUSANNE O'LEARY

Susanne O'Leary

# The
# Granddaughter's
# Irish Secret

bookouture

Published by Bookouture in 2024

An imprint of Storyfire Ltd.
Carmelite House
50 Victoria Embankment
London EC4Y 0DZ

www.bookouture.com

ISBN: 978-1-83525-581-0
eBook ISBN: 978-1-83525-580-3

This book is a work of fiction. Names, characters, businesses, organizations,
places and events other than those clearly in the public domain, are either the
product of the author's imagination or are used fictitiously. Any resemblance to
actual persons, living or dead, events or locales is entirely coincidental.

# 1

The invitation was lying on the doormat when Rose came home, laden with shopping bags. Dublin was dull and dreary in early March, and she was tired after a long day at work followed by grocery shopping. But she forgot all that when she saw what the postman had brought. Excited, she dropped her bags, picked up the bright pink envelope and opened it. Here it was at last. The invitation to the wedding of the year, which was bound to be extremely glamorous. Smiling, Rose read the brief text.

*Louise and Aiden are pleased to invite Rose Fleury and Gavin Lynch
to their wedding in St Mary's Church Killarney, Co. Kerry, on May 2,
at 3pm, and to the dinner after the ceremony at
Aghadoe Heights Hotel.
Black tie
RSVP before April 20.*

Rose's smile widened when she saw where the wedding was taking place. Aghadoe Heights was where all the posh wedding receptions took place. Killarney was also a short drive away from Magnolia Manor, where she had spent all her childhood summers. She couldn't wait to tell Gavin about the event and show him the invitation. She knew he'd be delighted to go. Perhaps they could extend their stay for a few days, if the weather was nice. It was the perfect time to go to Kerry and enjoy the beautiful landscape around Killarney, then perhaps travel further to Dingle town with its wonderful views over the Atlantic Ocean.

As the wedding was on a Saturday, she and Gavin could go and visit Rose's grandmother at the manor. They could see how the building work on the old house was progressing. Gavin hadn't seen it all yet, but this was a perfect opportunity to introduce him to some of the family. Rose put the invitation on the mantelpiece and went into the kitchen with her shopping. Tonight was a very special night, and the wedding invitation would add to the celebrations. She couldn't wait for Gavin to come home so they could make plans for the wedding and their trip to Kerry. It would be so lovely to go there in early May, when the spring sunshine made everything look so beautiful. She was sure he would fall in love with her hometown.

Gavin was the managing director of Murray & Fitzpatrick estate agents, and they had met when Rose started working there. Her degree in marketing and her diploma in real estate was more than enough for her to be hired straight away. She had been so excited to work at such a prestigious firm, the largest estate agents in the country. She had had no plans to fall in love, but a few months after her arrival at the office, she had felt someone's eyes on her as she walked to the copying machine. Looking around, she spotted a tall, dark-haired man staring at her across the expanse of the reception area. She knew who he was but had never spoken to him directly – he was one of the partners in the firm and she was still a junior agent. But he wasn't technically her line manager, so he had asked her out very soon after that first encounter. They had connected immediately. Everything happened so fast after the first few dates. He told her she was different to any of the girls he had met before, and she felt the same. He was handsome, fun, flirty and absolutely irresistible, always made up in a perfectly pressed suit. It was as if their meeting was written in the stars. After a short period of dating, Rose had moved into Gavin's plush apartment in one of Dublin's smartest areas.

Rose knew that dating her boss was not ideal, as her sister Lily often warned her. 'Having a relationship with one's boss is a very bad idea,' Lily had said many times, to which Rose had just shrugged and rolled her eyes. Lily was so old fashioned. The fact that Gavin was her boss didn't have any impact on their relationship, good or bad. And they didn't actually work together; he was technically *everyone's* boss because he was so senior. At home they were just a couple like any other. 'A gorgeous couple', many people remarked when they were out together, and Rose silently agreed. Gavin was handsome, glamorous and well-off, a heady combination that attracted many women. But he had chosen Rose, not only because of her blonde hair and bright blue eyes, but also because she was clever and fun. At least that's what he often said.

They had been together four years, and that's what they were going to celebrate tonight with dinner. She wasn't the best cook in the world, but she'd do her best to serve up something special, like she did every year on their anniversary. She had been to the posh deli around the corner where she'd bought a ready-made potato gratin and fillet steak from the butcher, all of which she was sure she could manage to cook to Gavin's liking. The gratin just needed twenty minutes in the oven and the fillet steak was easy enough – he liked it rare. They would have a tomato salad, then a Camembert that was ripe enough to be slightly runny, just the way Gavin liked it. Then profiteroles with extra chocolate sauce. All this served with a lovely Beaujolais, Gavin's favourite, and half a bottle of champagne that she had bought as an extra treat.

Rose had just put the gratin in the oven and laid the table when she heard the front door slam. Gavin was home just in time. Her face glowing, she turned around and smiled as he came into the kitchen.

'Hi, sweetheart. You're home early. Dinner won't be long. You'll have time to shower and change beforehand.'

'Not yet,' Gavin started, with a strange look in his eyes. 'I have something to tell you.'

'Oh?' Rose closed the oven door. 'Is it about that house in Rathmines? Did the sale fall through?'

'No, it's not about that.' Gavin put his keys in his pocket, still standing in the door, looking at her.

'What is it then?' Rose asked, busying herself with the steaks. 'Oh, by the way, Aiden and Louise's wedding invitation is on the mantlepiece. They're getting married in May in Killarney. They never did a save-the-date thing, so it was quite a surprise. But it'll be lovely, don't you think? And we can go to Dingle afterwards and stay with Granny, she should be home from France by then, and—'

Rose stopped as she looked at Gavin. He stared at her as if he had never seen her before. 'What is it?' she asked. 'You look as if... Has something happened? Something bad?'

'Sit down, Rose,' he said.

'Okay.' Her knees at once weak, Rose sat down at the table. 'Tell me then,' she urged. 'I can't stand you looking at me like that.'

Gavin sat down opposite her, his face pale. 'I don't know quite how to put it, so forgive me if this sounds harsh.'

'Go on,' she urged.

Gavin cleared his throat. 'The thing is, I'm leaving.'

'Leaving?' Rose asked, bewildered. 'Quitting your job?'

'Yes and no.' Gavin looked down at the table, then met Rose's worried eyes. 'I'm going to New York. The firm is setting up an office there and I've been asked to head the new team.'

'Oh, wow, that's exciting,' Rose exclaimed, relieved it wasn't anything worse than that. 'So we're moving to New York? When?'

'*We're* not,' he corrected. 'I'm not taking you with me.'

'Oh,' Rose said, trying to understand. 'So you want me to come over a bit later?' she asked, even though she felt in her gut what was coming.

'No.' Gavin paused, looking awkward. 'It's not easy to say, but the thing is...'

'You're breaking up with me?' Rose whispered, finally acknowledging what he was trying to tell her.

He nodded, looking miserable. 'I feel... I have felt lately... That we're not getting anywhere really. I mean... there is so much you want that I can't give you. I'm not ready to commit to having a family, or even to make more of a commitment.'

Speechless, Rose stared at him. 'What?' she croaked. 'What do you mean?'

He shrugged. 'What I just said.'

Rose couldn't believe what she was hearing; Gavin had never said anything like this before. If he wasn't sure about the relationship, he had kept those feelings well hidden.

'You can't commit?' she asked incredulously. 'Or is there someone else and you're too chicken to tell me?' Anger rose in her chest like red-hot lava. 'How can you do this to me? And this way? This horrible cowardly way, tonight of all nights, when I've cooked dinner for you and we were going to celebrate, and—' She stopped, unable to go on. Her whole world seemed to crumble, the world she had built up while she thought they had something that would last forever. But here he was, telling her he was leaving her. 'You're forty-two, Gavin. If you can't commit now, you never will.'

'Maybe not.' Gavin rose from the table, looking at the plates and cutlery, the two candles, the little bouquet of flowers in a silver vase and the napkins folded into hearts. 'I'm so sorry,' he said. 'But all this is not what I want. I just can't stay.' Then he walked into the bedroom.

Rose sat there as if paralysed, wondering if she was dreaming. It could not be true. Could it? Then the door opened and Gavin came out rolling a suitcase behind him. He stopped in the doorway. 'You can stay in the apartment as long as you like,' he said. 'I'll leave a forwarding address at the office as soon as I'm settled.'

'You packed that suitcase so quickly,' she said, ignoring his remark. 'Or... was it already packed?'

'I made sure I had everything organised,' he said. 'I'm catching the early flight to New York tomorrow morning. I'll stay in a hotel near the airport tonight.'

'You had it all worked out,' she said bitterly, getting up from the chair. 'How convenient.'

'I thought it would be easier.' There was a hint of sadness in his eyes as he came forward to kiss her cheek. 'Goodbye, Rose. I'll be in touch. I'd like us to stay friends. You've been wonderful and I'm sorry if I hurt you.'

Rose backed away. 'Bye then,' she said stiffly. 'Don't bother to call me. You can forget about being friends. I don't think I want to see you ever again.'

Gavin sighed. 'Okay. I know you must be angry and upset. But I think you're better off without me, to be honest.'

'Please, just go,' she said under her breath. 'I can't stand listening to you.'

He stood there, looking at her for a minute. Then he slowly walked to the front door and left.

Rose stood there for a moment, staring at the door, trying to take in what had just happened. She looked at the steaks waiting to be fried, the gratin cooking in the oven, the beautifully laid table, the flowers and the bottle of wine, feeling foolish to have made such an effort. It had all been for nothing. Stunned, still not quite believing he was gone for good, Rose sank down on a chair, staring into space. The phone on the kitchen island suddenly rang and startled her out of her misery. She grabbed it without thinking and whispered, 'Hello?'

'Rose?' a voice said. 'Is something wrong?'

At the sound of her grandmother's familiar voice, Rose burst into tears. 'Oh, Granny,' she sobbed. 'Something terrible has happened.'

'What? Are you ill?' Sylvia Fleury sounded alarmed.

'No, it's not me, it's Gavin,' Rose said.

'*He's* ill? What's wrong with him?'

'Nothing. But I wish he had something seriously wrong, something that causes a lot of pain,' Rose said angrily. 'He has just walked out on me. Right now, this evening, when I had cooked him a lovely supper. Told me he was going to New York and that he wasn't taking me with him and that he was breaking up with me.' Rose started crying again.

'That's horrible,' Sylvia exclaimed. 'Well, I didn't like him at all, to be honest.'

'You only met him once,' Rose remarked, blowing her nose.

'Yes, when he very reluctantly came to stay and didn't seem to like anything in Kerry,' Sylvia countered. 'And he looked as if he couldn't wait to get back to Dublin. I didn't say so at the time, but I thought him more than a little bit stuck up.'

'I know what you mean,' Rose mumbled. 'And you're right, even though I couldn't see it at the time.'

'Is there another woman involved?' Sylvia asked.

'He said there isn't,' Rose replied. 'He went to take up a job in New York. He's leaving tomorrow morning,' she added, tears rolling down her cheeks. 'And I'll never see him again.'

'Good,' Sylvia said sternly. 'You're better off without him, darling. You'll see that in time. Wouldn't it be worse if you had been planning a wedding and he left you at the altar or something?'

'Maybe,' Rose said, dabbing at her face with one of the

napkins. 'Oh, Granny, I don't know how I'll cope without him. What am I going to do? I can't go into the office and face all the pitying looks and whispers behind my back. And please don't say I should have known dating my boss was a bad idea. I'll get that from Lily as soon as she finds out.'

'I won't say it, even if it's true,' Sylvia promised. 'You're very upset and I don't want to rub salt into the wound. Maybe you should take a break and come down to Kerry for a few days?'

'Are you there now?' The thought of going home to Magnolia Manor, the place that had always been a haven to her, made Rose feel calmer. The mellow stones of the old house, the lovely gardens, the wonderful views of the ocean from the top windows, drifted into her mind. The balmy salt-laden air and the smell of woodsmoke and lamb stew... Oh, to be there and forget about all this misery. She imagined her grandmother there to meet her, looking after her the way she used to when Rose was a little girl, making her hot chocolate with marshmallows that she called 'a hug in a mug' and wrapping a blanket around her.

'No, I'm in France and I'll be here for at least another month.' Sylvia paused. 'I initially called to ask you to...' She stopped. 'But now is not the right moment. I'll call you back in a day or two, perhaps.'

'No, please, Granny,' Rose pleaded, wanting to stay talking to her grandmother and listening to her warm voice. 'Tell me why you called.'

'Well,' Sylvia started, 'the apartment project is well under way and Arnaud and I are working remotely on it. But we need someone to help out. Someone with marketing experience and a bit of know-how in real estate.'

Rose nodded. Magnolia Manor was being converted into apartments. It was too big for anyone in the Fleury family to maintain as a home any more, but a plan was underway to make it into living spaces for senior citizens, with shared gardens and facilities. Sylvia had told Rose about the plans two years ago. 'We thought we'd hire someone and pay them a salary. The gatehouse is empty, so that might suit whoever we hired. It's a nice place to live and so convenient to the house. So I wanted to ask if you knew of someone who'd be suitable for the job? But now you're too upset to think about that, so we'll leave it for a while.'

'No, don't,' Rose said, suddenly excited. 'I have the perfect candidate for the job. Someone with the right qualifications, who'd be delighted to live in the gatehouse and wouldn't ask for a huge salary.'

'You do?' Sylvia said, sounding doubtful. 'Who?'

'Me,' Rose said.

# 2

A month later, Rose was sitting on the little patio on the sunny side of the gatehouse of Magnolia Manor. It was a beautiful spring day. She was enjoying her breakfast when she heard Joe, the postman, pull up in his green van outside the front door. He waved at her as he put an envelope through the letterbox and shouted 'Lovely day,' before jumping back into the van and driving off. Rose smiled and turned her face up to the sun, listening to the birdsong and feeling the soft breeze from the sea against her face. Total bliss at last. The post could wait, like everything else on this warm spring morning.

She had come here last night, having left Dublin after a traumatic month that included the painful breakup with Gavin, a move out of what had been her home for a long time, and quitting her job at Murray & Fitzpatrick, which was also a huge wrench. But it had been impossible to stay on at the firm after what had happened. Gavin had dumped her and Rose knew everyone would find out. She was embarrassed and very sad. Her grandmother's phone call had happened at the right moment. Sylvia's suggestion to run the rebuilding project of the old manor had been like a lifeline.

Running the Magnolia Manor project was going to be fascinating. The senior apartments were going to have all kinds of amenities, like a spa, gym, pool, library and communal dining room – the first such concept in the country. And though Rose was worried about leaving her job so suddenly, she knew Sylvia's offer of employment would give her good experience. She would never have let a man force her out of a job, but it was the perfect opportunity to diversify.

Rose relaxed in her chair as the soft breeze brought with it a scent of the first roses mixed with the tang of seaweed, a smell so special to this part of Kerry in the springtime. Who could complain about being in this heavenly spot? The job of running the building project would be a challenge, with everything that was involved in getting the business off the ground. Giving up her career had been hard, but maybe this was the beginning of a new one?

Coming home had been the best remedy and here – in this cute little house in the middle of a lush garden, her family close by and a beautiful landscape to explore – Rose could heal and get her confidence back. The ugly scene with Gavin just before he left had slowly faded as she packed her belongings and moved out herself. And here she was, on the first morning of her new life, her bags not yet unpacked, enjoying breakfast in the sunshine.

As Rose sat there, she could hear the noise of the building work in the manor house. As the sound of hammering and drilling broke the peace, she got up and gathered her breakfast dishes, reluctantly going inside to get dressed and get ready to tackle her first day at work. The postman had brought a welcome home card from her sister Lily, and an invitation to the opening of a new boutique in Dingle that sold vintage clothes. That might be fun to go to. Rose propped both cards on the mantlepiece and went upstairs, carrying her tote bag and one of the suitcases she had left in the hall last night.

Her bedroom, the largest of three, with views over the tree-tops to the sea, was flooded with sunlight. The curtains with a print of tiny rosebuds were fluttering in a soft breeze. Humming a little tune, Rose put her tote bag and suitcase on the bed and took off her dressing gown. Then she went to the tiny bathroom on the landing and had a quick shower. Back in the bedroom, she slowly dressed in jeans, a shirt and trainers. She tied back her hair, thinking she needed a restyle. She delved into the tote bag for her makeup case, which she had stuffed there with some last bits and pieces before she left the flat in Dublin. As she pulled out the little case, she felt a wad of papers that consisted of assorted bills and a few letters she had forgotten about. She took it all out and glanced at it, noticing the pink envelope with the wedding invitation she had been so excited about the night Gavin had left her. She read the invitation again, feeling as if a cold hand was squeezing her heart.

Rose had been so happy when she first saw the invitation but now, after her breakup, it was like a dagger in her chest. She had wanted to go so badly. This would be a society wedding with everyone dressed up to the nines, champagne and caviar in the best hotel in Killarney.

Louise and Aiden wouldn't hold back on the bling. Louise loved glamour and they had saved up for the wedding for two years, ever since they got engaged. Louise and Rose had started at the firm at the same time, and become close over long lunches and drinks in the pub, and helped each other take the first steps in their careers. Aiden was friends with Gavin, so when Louise and Aiden started dating, they would often go out together as a foursome. Then Louise had left to work for another firm and they had lost touch for a while. And now Louise and Aiden were getting married, and had invited Rose to this wedding that was sure to be amazing. Louise had called Rose shortly after Gavin had left and offered her support. She said she wanted Rose to come to the wedding and suggested she use her 'plus one' on someone else instead.

Rose wasn't sure she wanted to go under the circumstances, but it would be such fun to be there, catching up with all the gang from Dublin, especially now that she needed cheering up. But then she had a feeling everyone would be looking at her with pity, whispering to each other how Gavin had left her to go to New York and take up a whole new career. 'Dating her boss,' they would mutter, tutting at the insanity of it, and how she had not only been dumped by her boss but also lost her job and run off to Dingle town to hide. And then they would comment at how she was staying 'in that run-down wreck in the grounds of a building site', when in reality she was living in a charming old cottage, newly restored and modernised. She had heard those whispers and insinuations in the ladies' loo in a restaurant in Dublin recently.

Rose stifled a sob as she remembered what she had heard and reached for her phone. She needed a shoulder to cry on, and there was only one person in the world who could provide it. Rose sat down on the bed and brought up the number.

It took a few rings before her sister Lily answered in hushed tones. 'Hello? Sorry, I have to speak softly. Naomi has just gone to sleep.'

'Oops. I forgot,' Rose whispered back, remembering that her two-month-old niece was difficult to get to sleep. 'Do you want me to call you back later?'

'No, it's okay. I'll go outside,' Lily replied. 'It's a lovely day. Hang on.'

'Great.'

'Right, the coast is clear,' Lily said after a while. 'She's still asleep. We had a bit of a rough night so, now that she's finally settled for a while, I can sit down here in the garden and look out at the sea while I talk to you.'

'Lovely.' Rose imagined Lily sitting in her front garden

looking out over the stunning view of the ocean, her trusty baby monitor clutched in her hand as it always was these days. 'You're lucky to live in that amazing house. Thanks for the card. So nice of you to send it.'

'I just thought I'd welcome you home. I'm so happy to have you nearby,' Lily said.

'Me too,' Rose replied. 'And I also want to thank you for not saying "I told you so" when Gavin did what he did.'

'Oh well, that wouldn't have been very kind,' Lily replied. 'Who wants to hear stuff like that when they're feeling bad?'

'I'm glad you realised that.' Rose paused, already cheered by Lily's voice.

'Was that why you rang?' Lily asked. 'To say thank you?'

'Yes and no. I was just feeling a little sad. I found Aiden and Louise's wedding invitation in my bag. I got that over a month ago but I haven't replied yet.'

'Do you want to go?' Lily enquired.

'In a way yes. It'll be one of those blingy affairs in Aghadoe Heights Hotel in Killarney. Everyone who's anyone will be there. And I'm desperate to see Louise and catch up. I don't want to let her down.'

'Sounds important,' Lily said. 'You should go.'

'I don't think I want to,' Rose said with a sigh.

'Why not?'

'I'll be the only one without a boyfriend.'

'Are you worried Gavin might be there?' Lily asked.

'No, he won't,' Rose replied. 'He's in New York, so I'm sure he won't travel all the way back just for this.'

'What's the problem, then?'

'Louise said to bring a "plus one", but I have nobody to bring and they'll all know what a loser I am.' Rose felt tears prick as she said it out loud.

'Don't be silly,' Lily snapped. 'Of course you must go. A Fleury woman can never be a loser. It just isn't on the cards. Pull yourself together and put on your blue dress and your gorgeous necklace you got from Granny, go to that wedding and smile. Did you have it cleaned like I told you?'

'Yes, I handed it into that jewellery shop in Killarney on my way through. They specialise in antique jewellery,' Rose said. 'Granny told me about them.'

The necklace was Rose's most precious possession. With large blue topazes and tiny pearls set in white gold, the necklace had been in the family for a hundred and fifty years. It had been a morning gift to a Fleury bride in the middle of the nineteenth century. Rose's grandmother had given it to Rose two years ago, just before the annual Magnolia party they had thought would be the last. It had all ended happily and the Magnolia party was still the event of spring in Dingle town. Rose had been allowed to keep the necklace and wore it occasionally to parties that demanded some dressing up. It matched her blue silk dress perfectly and brought out her deep blue eyes.

'Good,' Lily said. 'It's important to look after the old pieces.'

'Of course it is. So if I do go, to the wedding, who am I going to bring?' Rose continued. 'It has to be a good-looking, successful man who looks great in a tux. I can't think of anyone that fits the bill around here in the sticks. Oh, I wish Gavin hadn't dumped me just now. He looks amazing in black tie.'

'He wasn't the right man for you,' Lily stated. 'You deserve better.'

'It's too late for me to find anyone better or worse.' Rose sniffed. 'I'm a thirty-five-year-old spinster. Left on the shelf.'

'Oh please.' Lily sighed. 'You sound more like an eleven-year-old right now. Enough of the self-pity.'

'Yeah, okay. I'll try to perk up. But I don't want to go without a date. There's nobody around I can ask.'

'Why can't you go on your own?' Lily asked. 'Then you can be the beautiful single girl, and maybe meet someone and dance the night away with no worries.'

'And no boyfriend,' Rose muttered. 'But maybe you're right. If I go on my own, I'll look confident and independent like I don't really care. Hmm. I'll consider that.'

'You should,' Lily agreed. 'That's what a strong Fleury woman would do. And now that you're going to run the senior apartment project, it would also help your image as a business woman. Are you excited about it?'

'Yes. I think it'll be great,' Rose replied. 'I'll be using all my skills. Not only business and marketing, but also design when I do the furnishings. It'll be fun. Except the legal aspect, but then I can call on Wolfie. Granny said he's her solicitor now, he'll be dealing with all things legal, contracts and all that.'

'He's changed his name to Noel,' Lily cut in.

'He's Noel Quinn now instead of Wolfie? Why?'

'Noel is his middle name,' Lily explained. 'I actually suggested the name change because I thought Wolfgang was a mouthful for his clients. Hey, maybe he could be your plus one?'

'Are you joking?' Rose tried to imagine Wolfie – or Noel Quinn, Lily's former boss – in a tux. Not the kind of clothes she would associate with him, he was not the snappiest dresser in town, to put it mildly. Especially when he dressed casually in tracksuits that had seen better days, teamed with a Kerry foot-ball shirt. But when she thought about it, she realised Lily was right. Wolfgang – or Noel – might look good in black tie. Tall and good looking in a Scandinavian way, with light blonde hair, light blue eyes and a dazzling smile, he might do. But he wasn't exactly the man of her dreams.

'Nah,' she said. 'He's a bit of a nerd. He'll talk about bird-watching and hillwalking all night long and bore everyone to tears.'

'So what?' Lily said. 'He's also a solicitor and runs his own firm. Isn't that what you'd call successful? I bet your girlfriends coming down from Dublin will be impressed.'

'I can't pretend he's my boyfriend or anything,' Rose protested. 'It's too soon after... well, you know.'

'Of course not,' Lily assured her. 'He'll just be your plus one, your escort for the wedding. Your arm candy, if you like. That's what men do, so why not do the same?'

'Maybe,' Rose said, not quite convinced. 'But I haven't decided what I'll do yet.'

'Think about it, at least,' Lily urged.

'I'll consider him,' Rose promised. 'If I decide to go with someone and I can't find anyone else.'

'You won't. Listen, I have to go. Naomi seems to be waking up again for her next feed.'

'Give her a kiss from me,' Rose said with a fond smile. 'Don't forget my offer of babysitting whenever you want to go out.'

'Thanks, but right now I'm too tired to even think about going out. But maybe soon, when she's more settled. Dom and I could do with a night out. It seems like years ago.'

'Whenever you need me, I'm here. Bye for now, Lily-lou.'

'Bye, Rosie-roo. Don't forget to pick up the necklace from the jewellers.'

'I won't,' Rose replied. 'They promised to call when it's ready.'

'Great. See you soon,' Lily said and hung up.

Rose put her phone in her pocket, much cheered by her chat with her sister. Now it was time to go to the house and take a look at how far the builders had got.

As Rose locked the front door, the phone pinged with a text from Lily.

*You could always ask Henri to be your +one. He'd look fab in a tux... and that French accent... \*smiley face emoji\**

Rose groaned. Lily was teasing her – she knew the mere mention of Henri made Rose's teeth ache. When Sylvia had told

Rose about her plans to renovate Magnolia Manor, she'd also dropped the bomb that she was in a new relationship with a Frenchman called Arnaud. He was handsome and charming in that French way and Sylvia and Arnaud seemed so happy. They were even living together. Henri was Arnaud's son.

Rose couldn't forget how Sylvia and Arnaud had first met. For a time, Sylvia had thought Arnaud and Henri were going to take Magnolia Manor off her, due to some miscommunication their ancestors had many years ago. And it was Rose's opinion that Henri had made that situation worse. Arnaud was lovely, but Henri did seem a bit upset that they'd not ended up with the manor, just as investors in the renovation...

Henri wasn't difficult or rude, but he often tried to annoy Rose for fun. Everyone else seemed to find him charming. With his shaggy dark hair and brown eyes, he was a younger version of his father. But Henri didn't possess Arnaud's kindness and consideration or the warmth that everyone loved. Rose suspected those qualities were what had drawn Sylvia to him. And he loved her feisty nature, her controversial comments often making him laugh out loud. Rose smiled at the image of the older couple so happy together in a very unconventional way. They had just moved into the very first apartment on the ground floor of the manor that had been created, while the upper floors were being finished and would soon be put on the market.

Rose knew it would take a lot of work until all ten apartments were finished and occupied. She liked the way it was being developed – the outer shell of the beautiful Georgian house intact, the magnolia tree at the side of the big house untouched, in full bloom at the beginning of March every year.

All this was going through Rose's mind as she walked up the gravel path to the manor. Then her mind drifted to the wedding invitation and what Lily had suggested, which started to make a lot of sense. *Yes*, she thought. *I'll go on my own and look as if I couldn't care less about Gavin.* She would wear her light blue dress and the famous Fleury topaz necklace and laugh, even though part of her heart was missing. *Power dressing,* she thought, *in a glamorous way. I'll pull out all the stops and show them I haven't given up.*

As she reached the manor, Rose looked up at the ivy-clad façade, at the old windows glinting in the sun and the magnolia tree beside the front steps. She was yet again swept away by the history of it all and the thought that this house, centuries old, was part of her family history. The old stones spoke to her and whispered a welcome that only she could hear. Rose touched the magnolia tree before climbing the steps and entering the house through the massive oak doors that clanged shut behind her. She stood in the vast entrance hall – with its cavernous fireplace, tiled floor and walls festooned with antlers – and breathed in the smell of damp and old woodsmoke. This part of the house hadn't been touched yet, but she knew it would be a reception area with underfloor heating and sofas and chairs in front of the fireplace, which would have a small woodburning stove instead of a large open fire.

She had seen the drawings and loved how it would turn this cold space into something warm and welcoming – she could see urns with dried flower arrangements in her mind's eye. She put on a yellow helmet and walked through the long corridor. She glanced into what would be charming one-bedroom apartments, then into the ballroom that was being turned into a large communal dining room, then into the old dining room and drawing rooms, some of which were still very much a work in progress. Her own office would be in the attic, in one of the former servants' quarters, but that wasn't finished yet either.

Contractors were everywhere, hard at work, and she knew they were doing their very best to stick to the schedule. The foreman, a cheerful man with black hair called Kieran, showed her the plans and explained the progress they had made already.

As she listened to him, she realised that she would have to work from home for a while, until her office was ready. This didn't upset her as she was used to being flexible. She thanked him and walked back to the gatehouse, deep in thought. There would be much to do once there was more progress in the house and the apartments were being decorated and furnished. But as they all seemed to know what they were doing, there was no immediate rush. Relieved that she could relax for a bit, Rose was happy about what she had seen.

Once back at home, Rose looked at the wedding invitation again and decided what she was going to do. Going to the wedding alone seemed suddenly a very bad idea, so she sat down in the living room and picked up her phone to call Noel. Better to get it over with. She needed to know if he would agree to come with her so she could reply to the invitation. She didn't have his mobile number, so she called the landline to his office.

'Noel Quinn solicitors, Victoria Murphy here, how can I help you?' a soft female voice replied.

'Hi, Victoria, this is Rose Fleury,' she said. 'Would it be possible to talk to Noel, please?'

'Oh, hi, Rose,' Victoria said. 'I heard you were coming back to town and that you'll be running the Magnolia Manor thingy. Any news of Lily? Is she still going to be on a career break when her maternity leave is over? She said she'll be running the garden centre at the new senior place, but I didn't know if that was really going to happen.'

'Oh, yes, it is,' Rose said, trying her best not to laugh at the rapid delivery. 'Lily is determined to make a go of the garden centre when it's finished. You don't need to worry.'

'Oh great,' Victoria said, sounding relieved. 'Thanks for letting me know. And please call me Vicky. Everyone does.'

'No problem,' Rose said. 'So Noel...?'

'Oh yeah. Sorry, he's busy with a client right now. Can I ask him to call you back?'

'Yes please.'

'What's it about? Not being nosey, just to save time, really.'

'A private matter,' Rose said.

'Oh, right. Okay. I'll tell him.'

'Thanks.'

'No problem. Bye, Rose.'

Rose hung up with a smile. Vicky sounded like a fun woman. Rose decided to ask her to have coffee sometime soon. It was nice to know people who worked in the town instead of just childhood friends. She turned on her old laptop and looked through the files of the apartment project. There was a lot to get through, starting with the accounts and the design of the new website Henri had suggested. Sylvia had already told Rose that Henri had a lot of ideas for the project. When the phone rang, she was deep in thought. She picked it up, her eyes still on the screen. 'Rose Fleury.'

'Good morning,' a slightly familiar voice said.

'Noel. Thanks for calling me back so quickly.'

'You're welcome. So what's it about? All is well with Lily and her family, I hope?'

'Oh yes,' Rose replied. 'They're in great form, except Naomi keeps them awake at night, but I'm sure she'll settle down. I rang you about something else.' Rose paused, feeling suddenly awkward. 'Hey, can we meet for coffee? It'll be easier to explain to you in person.'

'That would be grand. We need to get to know each other better, anyway. How about a coffee at the Wild Atlantic Café in the harbour? It's a new place that I haven't tried yet.'

'Yes, it looks nice,' Rose agreed. 'Let's meet there in half an hour.'

'Perfect. See you then.' Noel hung up.

Rose turned back to her computer but found she couldn't concentrate. She had never been in this situation before, having to ask a man to escort her to an event. It felt strange and kind of miserable. She was so used to being asked out by men or having a boyfriend always by her side. But here she was, all alone, feeling oddly vulnerable without the security of a partner.

She shivered and tried to get back to work but it was too hard, so she touched up her makeup, got into her car and drove the short distance to Dingle harbour, where she managed to find a parking space. As she walked towards the café, she thought about what she was going to say. How on earth could she convince a man she hardly knew to be her fake date at a wedding?

# 3

The café was charming, all blue and white with dolphins painted on the inner walls, and outside a wooden deck with tables overlooking the bay. Rose bought a mug of latte at the counter and settled at one of the little tables on the outside deck. The salt-laden sea breeze was refreshing after a warm morning, and the sound of the waves so soothing. Rose took her sunglasses off her head and put them on against the dazzling sunlight. She looked out over the bay, spotting a rib laden with tourists going out to sea to spot whales and dolphins. She promised herself to join one of those tours soon – she loved watching the marine wildlife. She gave a start as someone touched her shoulder and turned to smile at the tall man standing there.

'Hi there,' she said. 'Long time, no see.'

Noel, dressed in a dark blue suit and a white shirt, grinned back at her. 'Hi, Rose. Yes it's been a while. But it's great to see you and have a chance to talk, now that I'm going to handle everything legal at the manor once it's up and running.' He paused. 'I'll just go and get a coffee. Won't be a tick.'

'Grand.' She watched him walk away and was, for a brief

moment, reminded of Gavin dressed just like that, in a suit and tie, all serious and businesslike. Rose mentally shook herself, feeling foolish for thinking the two men were alike at all.

He was back shortly and settled his tall frame on a chair opposite Rose, taking a sip of his mug of black coffee. Then he pushed back his shock of light blonde hair and looked at her, his bright blue eyes twinkling. 'I was just thinking how nice it is to have another Fleury girl back in Dingle. Lily and your grandmother must be delighted that you've moved here. What a stroke of luck that you decided to work for your grandmother.'

'A stroke of bad luck,' Rose said with a sigh. 'I had to get away from Dublin after a rather painful breakup.'

'Oh?' His eyes were sympathetic as he looked at her. 'I'm sorry. But why did you have to run away?'

Rose shrugged. 'I didn't have to run as such. But it was difficult to face everyone after it happened. We worked together and the office was rife with rumours and backstabbing. But what did I expect when I was in a relationship with my boss?'

'I'm sure that was not a calculation on your part,' Noel soothed. 'Even if the gossipmongers said so. You can't stop yourself falling in love, even if it's with the wrong person.'

'That's true,' Rose said, touched by his sympathy. His kindness was a great surprise and she suddenly felt he was someone she could confide in. Not only that, he made her feel so at ease that she was no longer nervous to tell him why she'd asked to meet him.

Noel crossed one of his long legs over the other. 'So, what was it you wanted to talk to me about? Do you need some legal advice?'

'No. Something personal. It's about a wedding that I've been invited to. The bride is a friend from work. We started at the firm at the same time. She was one of the girls I used to hang out with.' Rose stopped for a moment while Noel looked at her expectantly. 'Anyway,' she breezed on, 'I'm supposed to bring a "plus one" but I don't have anyone like that to go with, now that I'm single again.'

'Like what?' Noel asked looking amused. 'Okay, I know what you mean. I was going to joke about it but I see it's not a laughing matter.'

'No it's not.' Rose paused, not quite knowing how to go on. 'If I were in Dublin, I would have a number of male friends I could bring, but here, I don't know that many people. Oh, forget it,' she said, feeling stupid. 'I'm sure you wouldn't want to go to the wedding of a couple you don't know, with me, who you don't know that well either. It's okay, really. I'll go on my own. It'll be fine.'

'I see,' Noel said, looking thoughtfully at her. 'So you were going to ask me to be your date or something? At this wedding?'

Rose nodded, feeling awkward. 'Yeah, that was what I was hoping. Lily suggested it, actually. But don't worry about it. Let's talk about something else, okay?'

'No, let's discuss this.' He sat back and looked at her for a moment. 'I wouldn't have to pretend to be your new boyfriend or anything, would I? I'm not very good at faking stuff like that.'

'No, of course not,' Rose protested. 'That would be stupid. I just need someone...'

'To hold your hand, metaphorically speaking?' Noel filled in.

'Exactly. This "plus one" business is silly really, but I think it's to avoid having a bunch of single girls at the reception who would mess up the place settings. It's all about couples at those things.'

'As if two women sitting together would ruin the event,' Noel remarked. 'I know what you mean. It is a bit silly all right. Anyway, tell me where and when.'

'Second of May, Aghadoe Heights, black tie,' Rose rattled off. 'St Mary's Church beforehand.'

Noel nodded. He looked thoughtful, then he furrowed his brow. 'Okay. I think I'm free.' He picked up his phone and looked at the screen for a moment. 'Yes. I can do that. It's a Saturday and my dad is off to Cork to meet a gang of old legal eagles at some golf club.' He looked at Rose. 'I live with my father, you see. And I try to spend time with him at the weekend. He's a keen bird-watcher like me. And this time of year is very special, many birds come here to feed on their way from the Arctic to Africa. We often go out at daybreak to see them. But, as he'll be out with his old pals, the answer is yes. I'll go with you to that wedding. Could be fun, actually. I haven't been out much lately because of work.'

Relieved, Rose smiled. 'Phew, thanks. This is very kind of you, Noel. Makes me feel a lot better.'

'It would be a great way to get to know each other,' he said, looking at her in a strange way. 'As we're going to be working together from time to time, I mean. Sylvia said...' He stopped. 'Oh, never mind. She can be a bit bossy at times.'

Rose laughed. 'Oh yes, I know. She has a habit of ordering you to do things and, before you know it, you're doing it, even if you didn't really want to in the first place.'

Noel nodded. 'Exactly. But never mind that. Did you ever consider not going at all?' he asked, as he picked up his coffee mug. 'Saying you have something else on that day? That might be easier.'

'Yes, but then Louise would suspect the reason and think I'm a big chicken. And everyone would have a chance to talk about me behind my back. In any case, I want to go. Louise and I are still quite close. And I mean, Aghadoe Heights... That's an amazing place to party. The food is fabulous for a start.'

'I know.' Noel smirked over the rim of his mug. 'Why do you think I accepted? A free dinner at Aghadoe? I'd agree to escort Frankenstein's bride for that alone.'

Rose had to laugh. She had never seen this funny side of Noel before. She had always thought he was a bit uptight.

Perhaps he was just quiet. 'Oh, okay. I see now. And here I thought you were being so kind.'

He grinned. 'I'm not as angelic as I look.'

'That's a relief.' Rose finished her coffee. 'I'd better get going. I have several emails to send and I want to get started on the marketing and the website.'

'Yes, me too. I have to make sure the new girl doesn't mess up the filing system. She's great, but she's not Lily.'

'I think she's very nice. I'm sure she'll be fine once she gets used to everything.'

'She probably will. But she hasn't quite settled in yet. I'm afraid Lily spoiled me with her excellence.' Noel got up as Rose gathered up her bag and phone. 'We can make a plan for getting to the wedding nearer the date. And, of course, we'll meet soon again about the legal stuff for the apartment project.'

'Brilliant. Bye for now, Noel. And thanks again.'

'No problem,' he said, and walked away down the pier with a long-legged stride.

Rose stood there for a moment, looking at his retreating form. He was kind to offer to go with her to the wedding, and it had made her laugh when he said it was only for the chance to dine at a luxury hotel. She wondered briefly why he had accepted so quickly. Had there been a flash of calculation in his eyes when she told him about her conundrum? But whatever. She had her 'plus one', now she could accept the invitation and attend the wedding without having to be the odd one out. Her ringing phone interrupted her thoughts and she looked at the caller ID. It was her grandmother.

'Hello, Rose. Where are you?'

'At a café in the harbour,' Rose replied. 'How are you, Granny? I thought you and Arnaud were still in France? I was just up at the house but didn't see you there.'

'We just arrived about an hour ago. How are you settling in?'

'Great, thanks,' Rose replied. 'The gatehouse is very cosy.'

'Not getting a little lonely?' Sylvia asked.

'No, it's fine. I only arrived yesterday, I still have to unpack and then get stuck into the project. I'm quite happy to be on my own for a bit.'

'Well, don't be on your own tonight. Come to dinner,' Sylvia said, in a tone that sounded more like an order than an invitation. 'There is someone here who wants to meet you.'

'Who?' Rose asked, even though she had a feeling she knew who it was.

'Arnaud's son Henri. He came over with us. As you'll be working with him from time to time, we thought it would be a good opportunity for you to meet him properly. You've only met briefly so far.'

'The briefer the better,' Rose muttered.

'What did you say?' Sylvia asked.

'Nothing. I'll be there tonight,' Rose promised. 'I'm actually dying to see your new apartment at Magnolia. Are you pleased with it?'

'Yes,' Sylvia replied. 'It will take a little getting used to, but the builders did a great job. All we need to do now is decorate a bit more. Maybe you could give us some advice? You're so good at doing up houses.'

'It's more like doctoring old wrecks to get them sold,' Rose protested. 'But I'd be happy to help you with that and whatever else you need, Granny.'

'You're a darling. See you tonight. Seven o'clock for drinks. Don't dress up.'

'See you then, Granny,' Rose said, knowing the 'don't dress up' order was actually the opposite. She would have to put on something that her grandmother thought tolerable for a family dinner, or whatever it was. Arnaud was family, as he was Sylvia's fiancé, but Rose had decided quite a while ago that Henri certainly was not. It was true that they had only met a few times, briefly, but his superior tone during those meetings had annoyed Rose enough to get him into her bad books. That, added to the situation between the two families a little over two years ago, made him a real villain in her estimation. She still thought he wanted the manor for himself. Tonight would be hard, but she'd just have to grin and bear it. Hopefully she wouldn't have much to do with him in the future, apart from the odd business meeting. Everyone else seemed to have come to terms with Henri and accepted him as both a friend and business partner.

It seemed like a happy ending all around, except for Rose's resentment of Henri. She couldn't shake it.

# 4

Later that day, Rose was ready for dinner with her grandmother. Dressed in a paisley silk shirt and beige trousers, her hair newly washed and blow-dried, she walked up the gravel path to the manor. She touched the trunk of the magnolia tree again for luck, as she always did, before entering. Everyone in the family did this, as if not touching it would bring them bad luck. Superstition, they said, but it was also a way of connecting with the house and everyone who had lived in it for centuries.

Rose went around and into the courtyard, noticing that the back door had been newly painted a sage green. There was a series of buttons beside it with an intercom. Rose pressed the button to the intercom and waited for a reply.

A tinny voice said: 'Rose, is that you?'

'Yes, Granny,' she replied.

'Just a minute,' Sylvia said. 'I'm trying to find the... Oh, here it is.'

Then there was a buzzing sound, and Rose easily pushed open the door as she stepped inside a bright room. It used to be the utility room, but had been knocked together with the boot room, and now had two large windows letting in the evening light. Rose looked around in awe, at the newly sanded and polished oak planks, the walls covered in wallpaper with a design of tiny leaves and flowers. The back wall was hung with coats and jackets. Rose recognised the old umbrella stand bristling with umbrellas and walking sticks, which reminded her of the old boot room.

A door opened in the far wall and Sylvia peered out. 'Rose,' she exclaimed, stepping forward. 'How lovely to see you!'

Rose gave her grandmother a tight hug. 'Darling Granny. I've missed you.' She stepped back and looked at Sylvia. 'You're so tanned and healthy. And I love that yellow dress. It takes years off you. All that sunshine must be rejuvenating.' She couldn't take her eyes off her grandmother, whose brown eyes sparkled, her thick grey hair cut in a neat bob framing her only slightly wrinkled face. She was a few years over eighty but looked more than a decade younger.

Sylvia beamed at Rose. 'That, and the love of a wonderful man.'

'You're so lucky.'

'We both are.' Sylvia took Rose's hand and pulled her to the door. 'But come in and say hello to Arnaud and Henri.'

Rose followed Sylvia into a cosy living room, not much different to the old study, with the same oriental carpet, fireplace and sofa, flanked by two leather easy chairs. The windows had been replaced by double French doors leading out to a terrace, which allowed the evening sun into the room. 'How lovely,' Rose exclaimed, looking around. 'The old, new study.'

'Now the living room,' Sylvia filled in. 'We have a small office next to my bedroom, and Arnaud has a little cubby hole next to his. And we each have our own bathroom. We're very cosy here without getting in each other's hair. I always said that the secret of a happy relationship is separate bathrooms.'

Rose smiled. 'Yes, I think you're right. Maybe that's why

Gavin and I broke up. He always complained that I spent too much time in the bathroom.'

'That's not the reason. He wasn't right for you,' Sylvia said. 'He was what you might say stuck up. I'd call it having notions.'

'That too,' Rose said drily. 'But let's not go into all that. Where is everybody?'

'On the terrace,' a familiar voice called.

'Lily,' Rose shouted and ran out onto the terrace, where she found her sister and brother-in-law standing beside a pram. Their baby daughter was doing her best to disturb the peace with her loud crying. They both looked tired, especially Lily, who had dark rings under her usually lively brown eyes. Her hair hung drably, but her wide grin as she hugged Rose back lit up her face.

'Hi. Sorry about the noise,' Lily said. 'But Naomi is hungry. I have to go and feed her in Granny's bedroom.' She lifted the wriggling, crying bundle out of the pram. 'Won't be long.'

Rose laughed and turned to Lily's husband, Dominic. 'Hi, Dom. I haven't seen you since the christening. How are things with you?'

Dominic kissed Rose on the cheek, his green eyes twinkling. 'Wonderful to see you, Rose. We're fine, a little worn out with the new arrival. She's awake at the oddest hours. Sleep is optional these days.'

'Lily told me. Must be hard to have a baby waking up in the middle of the night. But isn't that normal at this early age?'

'Yes it is, I'm afraid,' Dominic said with a resigned little shrug. 'We'd give a thousand euros for a night's sleep right now, but we'll get there. We just need to figure out her routine. But what about you? How are you settling in with the new job and living in the gatehouse and all that?'

'Oh, I'm loving being back here,' Rose replied. 'Can't believe it's for good. The gatehouse is a little old fashioned but I'm sure it's character forming, doing the washing up and coping with the fire and the back boiler and all that. Just like the old days when we grew up in Magnolia.' She looked up at the façade of the large building, admiring the new plaster and restored windows. 'I love seeing the house getting repaired without ruining the period feel of it.'

'I agree. They did a good job,' Arnaud said beside Rose, handing her a glass of champagne. 'Good evening, Rose. So nice to see you again.'

'Oh thanks,' Rose said and smiled at him. 'Lovely to see you too, Arnaud.' He was, as usual, the epitome of elegance. Perfectly dressed for a spring evening in beige chinos and a white shirt, with a navy cashmere sweater over his shoulders. His white hair made his tan look even darker, and his brown eyes twinkled as he smiled back at Rose.

'I'm so happy to be back in this beautiful place,' he said, raising his glass. 'Cheers, Rose. Good luck with your new life here in Kerry.'

'Cheers, Arnaud.' Rose sipped the champagne and looked over the rim of the glass towards the end of the terrace, where she could see Henri walking up the steps from the garden path, looking unusually dishevelled.

He bounded up the steps and went to the small table to pour himself a glass from the bottle. Then he joined Rose, grinning at her. 'Hello, Rose,' he said in his part-French, part-American accent. 'You look a little tired. New job too much for you already?'

'Of course not,' Rose replied, smiling sweetly at him. 'Why would it be? And I'm not a bit tired. Feeling great, actually.' She glanced at his ruffled brown hair, wrinkly T-shirt, worn jeans and bare feet. 'You're not exactly dressed to impress. I'm sure Granny won't approve of you sitting down to dinner like that.'

He looked down at his clothes. 'Oh, you mean this? I've been surfing in the Maharees. Didn't have time to change. But I will as soon as I've finished this glass of champagne. I have my party clothes in the truck.'

'You have a truck?' Rose asked.

'He means his new Volvo SUV,' Dominic cut in. 'Great car, I have to say. Not something I could afford though.'

'Yes, I'm very happy with it,' Henri said. 'I can drive it across the sand on these beaches without having to worry.' He winked at Rose. 'Great for my image too. Perfect for pulling birds, as you say here.'

'How wonderful for you,' Rose said with a stiff smile, sidling away. 'Excuse me, I need to talk to Lily.'

'See you later at dinner,' Henri said as she moved away. 'Looking forward to chatting with you.'

Lily appeared through the French doors, carrying a sleeping baby, just as Rose was about to go inside. '*Shh*,' she whispered. 'I'm going to put her very gently into the pram and then wheel it away to the far side. I hope she stays asleep for a while now.'

Rose looked at the baby fast asleep in Lily's arms, her dark eyelashes fanned over her pink cheeks, the little mouth quivering into a near smile. 'She's adorable,' she whispered to Lily.

'Oh yes, she is. When she's asleep,' Lily whispered back. They both tiptoed to the pram. Lily put the baby down and started to push it away, Rose following behind.

When the baby was settled, Lily turned to Rose. 'Did you ask Noel?'

Rose nodded. 'I did and he said yes. So I have a plus one. Such a relief. It was so kind of him to accept just like that.'

'He's an absolute pet. And I think you'll have fun.'

'I'm beginning to think I will,' Rose said. 'Noel is better company than I thought.'

'Great. Then you're all set and can relax.' Lily looked across the terrace. 'Granny is waving us in. Dinner is served in the new kitchen diner. Wait till you see it.'

'So exciting. All the new rooms here are so lovely,' Rose said as they walked to the French doors. 'But can you leave the baby here all alone?'

'I'll make sure she's sleeping deeply, then Dom can wheel her into the living room while we have dinner.'

Rose nodded. 'Sounds good. How are the plans for the garden centre coming along?'

Lily sighed. 'Very slowly. But we're getting there. Could be ready in a month or so.' She stopped walking and looked at Rose. 'I have another plan for the walled garden, and I need your support. As you and Henri are working together, and he holds the purse strings, so to speak, I was hoping you'd put in a good word about it. At least vote for it if it comes to that.'

'He holds the purse strings?' Rose replied, surprised.

'Yes. I don't think Arnaud wants to be too involved, so he's shifted all of the responsibility for his investment to Henri,' Lily said.

'Great,' Rose replied sarcastically. 'Well, of course you have my support. And I have another little idea I'd like to put forward. Something I think Granny will love. I'll talk about it while we have dinner.'

'We'll support each other,' Lily said, putting her arm through Rose's. 'Just like in the old days.'

'But this time it's harder,' Rose declared. 'We're up against a stuck-up Frenchman who is in charge of the funds.'

Lily laughed. 'Yeah, but there are other investors,' she argued. 'They have to approve at the board meetings and they're all people we know. Henri will have his job cut out for him with Granny's feisty Kerry women.'

Rose laughed too. 'Yeah, I can just picture him at the next board meeting. He'll be less full of himself after that.'

They entered the new kitchen that was just off the hall. Rose stopped in the door and looked around in delight. The old country kitchen had been transformed into a bright room with tall windows, through which the evening sun shone on the polished floor tiles. There was a large round table in the alcove that had been created to separate it from the kitchen part, making it into a kind of dining room that overlooked what had once been the orchard, now overgrown. But the gnarled old apple trees were in full bloom – the canopy of white apple blossom cast a bright light into the room. There was a delicious smell of something cooking in wine and herbs.

'This is beautiful,' Rose exclaimed. 'What a transformation from the dark old kitchen that was here before.'

'Yes, isn't it lovely?' Sylvia said, beaming, as she sat down at the table laid with the best china, crystal and silver cutlery. 'And I have my very own chef,' she added, looking at Arnaud, who stood beside the large electric cooker.

'You are a lucky duck,' Lily said. 'What are you cooking for us tonight, Arnaud?'

'Coq au vin,' Arnaud replied as he ladled the food onto a large platter. 'Please sit down, all of you, then I'll bring it to the table. There is bread and wine, if you could help me out with that, Henri.'

'Of course, Papa,' Henri said. He had tidied himself up and changed into dark trousers and a light blue shirt, which made him look less a beach bum and more like a successful executive.

'He's making an effort,' Lily whispered in Rose's ear as they sat down.

'Maybe, but I'm not impressed,' Rose whispered back as she felt Henri's eyes on her. She met his gaze and smiled innocently as he approached her with a bottle of wine.

'St Emilion, grand cru 2005,' he mumbled in her ear.

'And the same to you,' Rose quipped, making Lily giggle.

'Very funny.' Henri looked less than amused.

'He was being polite,' Sylvia told Rose. 'The waiter always tells guests what wine they are drinking at posh dinner parties in France.'

'Well, we're in Kerry now and Henri is not a waiter at a posh party.' Rose raised her glass. 'Cheers, everyone, whatever the name of the wine.' With that, she took a huge swig, which went the wrong way, making her cough and splutter until Henri slapped her on the back.

'That's not the way to drink a good wine,' he chided. 'Especially one that costs fifty euros a bottle.'

'What?' Rose exclaimed. 'Fifty euros? That seems like a huge rip-off.'

'If you sip it slowly, you'll see why it's so expensive.' Arnaud came to the table carrying a huge platter with coq au vin and potatoes. He handed the platter to Lily. 'Please pass this around and save some for Dominic when he comes back. Where did he go?'

'He went to wheel the baby into the living room,' Lily said. 'If she didn't wake up, he'll be here in a few minutes. Fingers crossed and prayers, please.'

'I'm sure she'll stay asleep,' Sylvia said. 'Can you all sit down and enjoy this meal? Henri, please stop walking around muttering the name of the wine into our ears. We know what it is and we'd prefer to read the label ourselves.'

'Okay, Sylvia.' Henri put the bottle on the table. 'I just wanted to educate Rose a little.'

'Very kind of you,' Rose retorted. 'But I can read, you know, so that's not really necessary.'

'Stop this childish teasing,' Sylvia ordered. 'You're both old enough to behave at dinner.'

Henri sat down on Lily's other side and helped himself from the platter. 'Well, Rose is certainly old enough,' he said.

Rose ignored him and turned to Lily. 'What was that plan for the garden centre you mentioned? Do you want to talk about it now?' she asked.

Lily nodded and picked up her knife and fork. 'Yes, I was going to talk to Granny and Arnaud about it too, and now is a good opportunity.'

'Yes,' Sylvia said. 'Now that we're all together, and Rose has officially started in her role, we can discuss any kind of idea you have to draw visitors to the gardens. So go ahead, Lily.'

'It's something I've been thinking about for a while,' Lily started. 'I saw in the plans I found among the old drawings of the house that there was a walled garden here once. I think it was laid out in the early eighteen hundreds, just after the manor was built. I thought we might restore the walls that are still there, along with the little pavilion. There could be herbaceous borders and fruit trees and also a vegetable garden. It would be like a Regency garden, like something out of Jane Austen. Marlay Park in Dublin has one just like it and it's gorgeous.'

'And then there's Swiss Cottage in Cahir,' Rose cut in, suddenly excited. This would be a perfect link to what she was going to propose. But she'd hold on for a bit, until she could see where Lily's plan was going.

Lily shot Rose a warm smile. 'Oh yes, that's very popular and draws a lot of visitors.'

Sylvia stopped eating and looked thoughtfully at Lily. 'That sounds like a good plan.'

'But expensive,' Henri cut in. 'We would need a detailed financial report and quotes from several garden landscaping firms before we decide if we're going ahead.'

'I think it's a wonderful idea,' Sylvia said with a stern look at Henri. 'We will take it up at the next board meeting, of course.' She looked at Lily and Rose. 'Any other ideas you want to put forward?'

Rose nodded. 'Yes, but I'll wait until I have drawn up a cost sheet. Then I'll send it to all the board members for consideration.'

'Why don't you share it with us now?' Henri asked. 'I'd love to hear it.'

'I'm not ready to tell anyone,' Rose replied. 'But I might have a chat about it privately, Granny. Just to see what you think. You still own most of this property and this is about something to do with family history, you see.'

'Good idea,' Sylvia said, looking at Rose with approval. 'We don't want to be impulsive, and we have to throw out ideas that might be impractical. We'll discuss this later in private, Rose.' She sipped from her glass. 'Wonderful wine, Arnaud. Worth every penny.'

'I thought we'd celebrate being back and having all the family around the table,' Arnaud replied.

'That is something to celebrate,' Sylvia agreed.

They finished their meal chatting animatedly. As they all rose to have coffee on the terrace, Sylvia led Rose into her small office just off the new hall. 'Let's chat in here,' she said and closed the door behind them. 'I felt you had something to tell me that you didn't want the others to hear.'

'Lovely office,' Rose said, looking around at the small room with its sage green carpet and wallpaper with tiny pink rosebuds. The windows had light pink silk curtains. There was an antique desk and chair, which had a seat cushion the same colour as the curtains.

'A bit girly, but Arnaud did the design,' Sylvia said with a fond smile. 'He said I needed a soft and feminine space to kick ass in.'

Rose laughed. 'I know what he means. He knows that your soft and feminine shell hides a will of steel, and that you take no prisoners.'

'Well, what would I do with them?' Sylvia joked. 'Prisoners are such a nuisance. Better to cut off their heads at once. But sit down on that chair over there and tell me what's on your mind.'

Rose sat down on the chair by the window while Sylvia settled by the desk. 'I had this idea when I got an invitation to the opening of a vintage shop in Dingle... And also when I gave the topaz necklace to the jewellers in Killarney to be cleaned.' Rose paused. 'That we could go through all the items that are piled in the storeroom and see if we could sell them to the vintage shop. I could do some repairs to whatever is ripped or torn. I'm sure there's lots of stuff that they'd love.'

'That's not a bad idea,' Sylvia said, looking thoughtfully at Rose. 'You're very good at sewing and embroidery too, so I know you could mend and stich anything that needs to be repaired.'

'So you'll let me sort through those things?' Rose asked, feeling excited at the thought.

'I need to think about this,' Sylvia said. 'I'm not sure I could sell anything without asking Lily. And I have to check with Noel if it would be legal.'

'Yes, but I could at least start doing some sorting and research,' Rose suggested.

Sylvia nodded. 'So much to think about. It's overwhelming, actually. You and Lily have such energy in you. It's hard for me to keep up sometimes.' She patted Rose's arm. 'I will consider all this and talk to Arnaud about it. Let's leave it for now.'

'Oh, but...' Rose started. 'I'd love to start looking into all that stuff in the attic. In any case, they'll be starting the building work up there soon for the new apartments.'

'That's true,' Sylvia said. 'I don't actually have the key. I think it's in a bunch at the site office. I'll see if I can find them for you.'

'Thanks, Granny.' Rose kissed her grandmother's cheek before she got up. 'I'll be off soon. I'm a little tired after my first day here. And I'm sure you'll want to go to bed soon, too.'

Sylvia patted Rose's cheek. 'Yes, I do. Let's call it a night and think about all this. Tomorrow is another day. Now let's go out and look at the sunset before we go to bed.'

Rose followed her grandmother out and joined the others on the terrace. The baby had woken up and was all smiles and gurgles in her father's arms. She was indeed a beautiful baby, with dark curls and big green eyes fringed with long lashes. A dimple appeared in her cheek as she smiled at Rose, and she felt her heart melt as she smiled back at her little niece.

'Do you want to hold her?' Dominic asked.

Rose hesitated. 'If you show me how. I don't want to break her.'

'She's quite solid.' Dominic held the baby out to Rose. 'Just make sure you support her head.'

Rose took the baby in her arms, a little awkward at first, but then settled Naomi in the crook of her arm. 'Oh,' she said, putting her face against the downy head, breathing in the sweet smell of soap and milk and baby oil. The infant looked up at her with wonder and then smiled again, a smile only for her aunt. Rose felt a surge of love and the beginning of a bond that would last the rest of their lives. 'I love you,' she whispered into a tiny ear, and was rewarded with what sounded like a chuckle.

'Oh, she's laughing,' Lily exclaimed, rushing over to look at her baby daughter. 'Did you hear that, Dom?' She took the baby from Rose and held her tight. 'She loves you.'

'And I love her,' Rose said, overwhelmed by the emotions of connecting with the little girl. 'I never knew babies were so adorable.'

'When they're not screaming in the middle of the night,' Lily remarked. 'But then they smile and coo and you forgive them anything.'

'Of course you do.' Rose patted the little bundle on Lily's shoulder. 'I'll babysit any time you want. But maybe you could give me a crash course first?'

'I will,' Lily promised. 'Come over on Sunday and you can practise changing her nappy.'

'Brilliant.'

The baby started to whinge and Lily put her back in the pram. 'I think we'd better go. It's nearly bath time and, to be honest, I'm really tired.'

'Me too.' Dominic shot Rose an apologetic smile. 'We have to sleep when we can. We'll slip away, if you don't mind. Maybe you can explain to everyone?'

'Of course.' Rose kissed them both and watched while they carried the pram down the steps, then wheeled it around the corner to their car. She stood there and enjoyed the salt-laden breeze from the sea, looking up at the darkening sky where stars were beginning to appear one by one, breathing in the smell of woodsmoke from a fireplace somewhere nearby. She thought about the baby and how it felt to hold her, wondering if she'd ever have one of her own. But even if she didn't, she'd still have her niece, and could be the fun auntie who taught Naomi to walk in high heels and try makeup and do things that were slightly risqué... She smiled at herself and wondered what Lily, who had always been a little straightlaced, would think of that.

During the next few days, Rose familiarised herself with the building project and looked into all the files, deciding what to do first. The website needed to be finished and she had to contact the web designer and then work out a marketing plan. Then there were the furnishings to be ordered and the bathroom and kitchen equipment installed. She also wanted to run up a plan for selling to the vintage shop. So much to do in a very short time.

Rose was so busy she nearly forgot about the wedding, but was reminded of it when the jewellery shop in Killarney contacted her.

'Hi,' the woman said. 'Is this Rose Fleury?'

'Yes, it is,' Rose replied, sitting up straighter at her desk in the living room.

'This is O'Hara's Vintage Jewellery. I'm calling about your necklace you left with us for cleaning. The topaz and pearls set in white gold?'

'Oh, yes,' Rose said. 'Is it ready?'

'Yes,' the woman replied. 'But...' She paused. 'There's something else I have to tell you about it.'

'What's that?' Rose asked, suddenly worried by the tone in the woman's voice. 'It's not broken, I hope? I mean, it's very old and it's been in the family for generations, so it's quite precious.'

'Hmm, yes.'

'A beautiful piece don't you think?' Rose said. 'Very well made, I always thought.'

'Oh yes. Very well made,' the woman agreed. 'For a copy.'

Rose froze. 'A copy? What do you mean?'

'I mean it's fake,' the woman replied.

## 5

'Fake?' Rose stammered, feeling suddenly cold despite the warmth of the room. 'That's not possible. It's been in the family for over a hundred years. You must be mistaken.'

'We don't make mistakes like that,' the woman snapped. 'We're experts with a long experience in vintage jewellery. When I suspected the stones were not real topazes, I called in our gemmologist. He confirmed my suspicion. Those topazes are made of glass and the pearls... Also some kind of glass. We think it was done a long time ago. Maybe sixty or so years back, or even earlier. But I have to do some more research to put an exact date on it.'

'Oh,' Rose said, still so shocked she couldn't think of anything else to say. This felt like yet another disaster to hit her after everything else. But how could it be? That necklace had graced the necks of Fleury women since the 1870s, when it was first gifted to a newly married young bride. Her name was Maria Fleury, née Connolly, a renowned beauty with black hair and flashing green eyes. Her portrait had hung in what used to be the library, now the new office of the senior apartments complex. Then it had been gifted to the National Gallery in

Dublin, and Rose had gone there with Gavin to see it over a year ago. She had been so proud to own the necklace depicted in the portrait and told everyone about it.

'This is terrible. What am I going to do?' she whispered into the phone.

'I wouldn't do anything,' the woman said, her voice softer. 'It's so well made only an expert would know it isn't real. I'd wear it as you always have. It's a lovely piece, even though the stones aren't genuine topazes.'

'Maybe you're right,' Rose said, trying to get used to the thought that her beautiful necklace she had been so proud of was not the genuine article.

'You could perhaps try to find out what happened to the original necklace,' the woman suggested. 'This is part of the famous Fleury collection so it could have an interesting history.'

'Oh no,' Rose exclaimed, feeling cold sweat breaking out. 'Maybe they're all fake.'

'Oh don't worry. I know for a fact they're not,' the woman replied. 'Your sister Lily's pearl necklace with the diamond clasp is the real thing. And that emerald necklace, the one your grandmother is minding for your younger sister Violet, has just been left to be cleaned and the chain repaired, so we can assure you that's genuine too.'

'So I'm the lucky winner, then,' Rose said with a touch of bitterness.

'I'm really sorry to be the bearer of such bad news,' the woman said.

'It's not your fault.'

'Thank you. I didn't know if I should tell you, but it wouldn't have been right not to.'

'Of course not.' Rose thought for a moment. 'But I think you're right. I will wear it as if it was the real thing. I need it for a wedding I've been invited to. It goes so well with the dress I want to wear.'

'Good idea,' the woman said, sounding a lot more cheerful. 'As I said, it would be hard for anyone except an expert to spot that it's not real. And now that it's been cleaned, it really shines. I think it's an interesting piece as it's quite old. As I said, it would be fascinating to know what happened to the real necklace. Maybe you should try and find out? Do a little digging into the family history?'

'Maybe,' Rose muttered, not feeling very enthusiastic. 'Anyway, thank you for letting me know. I'll come and collect it in the next few days.' She said goodbye to the woman and hung up, the shock of what she had just learned making her feel quite weak. This was very upsetting. How could it be possible? And who had owned the necklace and then had a copy made while the real one was... where? She decided to do some research. She didn't want Sylvia to find out it was fake; it would devastate her. She had been through so much in the last few years. Although she knew her granny was happy to breathe new life into Magnolia Manor, it must have been hard for her to give up a piece of her heritage. She couldn't let another heirloom disappear.

Now that the house was being restored and a lot of old boxes, family albums and other memorabilia had been discovered in cupboards and drawers, perhaps it wouldn't so hard. It was all piled into one of the rooms in the attic. All she had to do was to go through it all. Quite an undertaking, but it would be worth it. She already had an excuse to go through the stuff in the attic room – the clothes she was going to sell through the vintage shop.

Later that evening, Rose walked up to the manor to see her grandmother. She didn't want to tell Sylvia the truth about the necklace, deciding to keep it to herself for the moment. But Rose thought she might get some information from Sylvia through a casual conversation about the vintage shop, and what could be sold from the family collection in the storeroom. That way she could get her grandmother to talk about the women who had worn all the lovely family pieces through the years and get some kind of lead.

Rose found her grandmother in her living room, sitting on the sofa. She looked up from her book as Rose entered. 'Hello, Rose. Have you been out for a walk? It's a lovely evening. Did you see Henri on your way here? I thought the two of you were getting to know each other better. That's what he said anyway.'

'He might have said that, but the truth is that we're not getting on at all. In any case, I haven't seen him.' She paused, not wanting to worry Sylvia, but she'd been thinking about Henri a lot. He really irritated her and she wasn't sure why. 'I'm sorry, Granny, but I'm not in the mood to make friends with Henri right now. He reminds me of Gavin, to be honest. Maybe I'm just too raw still.'

'Oh, darling, I know what you've been through,' Sylvia said with a sigh. 'Come and sit here with me.'

Rose sat down beside her grandmother and put her head on Sylvia's shoulder. 'I know I sound bitter, but I'm not really. And I don't feel that all men have to pay for what Gavin did. But Henri gets up my nose and I can't help that.'

'I know.' Sylvia tucked a strand of Rose's hair behind her ear. 'But I think you should try to be a little more understanding. I know Henri is a bit hard to take, but he's a little younger than you and he's been through a lot.'

'Like what?'

'He grew up without a mother for a start. She died when he was only six.'

'I grew up without a father,' Rose countered.

'Yes, but you had your mum,' Sylvia said softly. 'And me.'

'I know,' Rose said. 'But it doesn't excuse his behaviour towards you when he tried to claim ownership of Magnolia Manor, I have to say. That was quite horrible.'

'Yes, but I think they have both made amends,' Sylvia replied. 'It's in the past, and now we have to look to the future. Henri is really eager for the senior apartment project to succeed. He knows accommodation for older people is a big market, and he's working hard on it. I'm sure he'd like your ideas.'

'But you just said we shouldn't let on what I want to do,' Rose cut in. 'You seemed to be on my side.'

'I am, darling,' Sylvia soothed. 'I want to go ahead with both your and Lily's plans. But I know we have to be diplomatic and not show all our cards at once. Not because I think Henri is bad person, but because he wants to call all the shots. That's something we won't be able to change. So we just have to be clever about it and not let on what we want until we get support from the other board members. That's all.'

'And the key to the storeroom?' Rose asked.

'I'll get it for you,' Sylvia promised. 'And Henri shouldn't be allowed to behave so badly.'

'No he shouldn't,' Rose said with feeling. 'He gets away with a lot around here, it seems. And all that flirting gets on my nerves.'

'French men flirt all the time,' Sylvia said with an amused smile.

'Does Arnaud?'

'Arnaud would flirt with a rock, given the chance. I find it funny. My friends find him adorable because he kisses their hands and tells them they look wonderful. It's just his way.'

'I suppose that's kind of sweet at his age,' Rose agreed. 'But not with someone of my generation.' She got up. 'Now I'm going home. Let me know when you get the key to the storeroom. I'd love to have a little root around and see if I can find anything interesting.'

'Oh, there's lots to discover there,' Sylvia said. 'But I wouldn't want anything bad to come out. Some of the Fleurys weren't on their best behaviour at times.'

Rose laughed. 'Ah, but they are the more interesting ancestors. Like Maria Fleury, for instance.'

'She was very ordinary,' Sylvia said. 'The model of good behaviour. But her children were quite badly behaved at times.'

Rose stopped on her way to the door. 'Who were her children?'

'Your great-grandfather Cornelius,' Sylvia remarked. 'We all know what he got up to.'

'We certainly do,' Rose said.

'Then there was his sister, who was very beautiful. A debutante in London at around the turn of the last century, I believe.'

'Did she wear the topaz necklace?' Rose asked, intrigued.

'I'm sure she wore the Fleury pearls with the diamond clasp to the debutante ball. But you will find out about her and all the others when you dig into the family archives. Great material for the website, I'd say, if you have the time and energy to write it. I'll leave it all to you. I'm too busy to go through all that.'

'Fabulous,' Rose said. 'I can't wait.'

'It'll be hard work, but it'd be great to have it all sorted out and organised. I'll text you when I have the key. Goodnight, pet. Sweet dreams.'

Rose said goodnight to Sylvia, and with her head full of thoughts she walked back to the gatehouse as dusk turned into night. The name she had just heard echoed through her mind. *Cornelius*, she thought. *What a rascal he was. But who was his sister and what happened to her? A beautiful debutante at the beginning of the twentieth century? That has to be an interesting story, even if she had nothing to do with the topaz necklace...* She suddenly couldn't wait to get that key and get into the room with all the family memorabilia. It was as if she was getting access to an Aladdin's cave full of treasures.

# 6

---

Two days later, Rose drove to Killarney to collect her necklace from the jewellers. She was a little apprehensive and wondered how she would feel holding the necklace now that she knew it was a fake. Who had made the copy and where was the real one? She would probably never find it. The fake one had had her fooled; she had treasured it and worn it to all kinds of dressy events, proud of what she had thought was a Fleury heirloom. And now she would have to pretend it was true. The thought made her feel nearly dizzy as she walked into the jewellery shop, her mind conflicted.

The shop was charmingly old fashioned, with a red carpet and mahogany display cabinets full of beautiful pieces of antique jewellery, which glimmered in the light of the little lamps dotted around the room. A young woman with dark brown hair in a bun looked up as Rose entered.

'Hello, how can I help you?' she asked.

'My name is Rose Fleury and I'm here to collect my necklace. The one with the... topazes,' she said. 'I mean the one that looks like topazes but...'

'Oh yes,' the woman said. 'I know the one you mean. I'm

Angela, by the way, we spoke on the phone.' She smiled apologetically. 'I was the one who gave you the bad news. Sorry about that.'

'Not your fault,' Rose replied. 'You had to tell me the truth, of course.'

'I know, and I was really sorry. But you know what? It's a beautiful piece even if it's not real. Hang on, I'll get it for you.'

She disappeared into the back room and came back moments later with a familiar dark blue velvet box. She handed it to Rose.

Rose took the box and opened it, staring at the necklace and the stones she now knew were glass, the little pearls she had thought were real. 'It's so strange to look at it now that I know...' She looked at the woman. 'Have you any idea when this was made? I mean it looks old, so it can't have been made recently.'

'No, we think it's quite old,' Angela replied. 'Our antiques expert thought somewhere around the eighteen nineties to about nineteen-oh-five, judging by the clasp and the way the stones are set into what looks like white gold but is actually silver. Strangely, that must be the box the real necklace came in. It was from Weir & Sons in Dublin, as you can see written inside the lid. A very old jewellers that was established in eighteen sixty-nine.'

'Oh.' Rose studied the necklace that lay against the cream silk lining of the box, the false topazes glinting deceptively in the soft light of the little lamps. They looked so real and just as beautiful as when she had brought the necklace in to be cleaned. 'But the original was white gold and would have been very valuable, don't you think?' she asked.

Angela nodded. 'Oh yes. With the white gold and the topazes and pearls... Very expensive indeed.'

'I see.' Rose closed the box with a feeling of immense sadness. 'Such bad luck that it's fake.'

'But a very well-made fake,' Angela remarked. 'I think it's gorgeous. I wouldn't mind wearing it actually.'

'Oh, I'm going to,' Rose declared. 'And now that you've told me how old it is, I'm a little less upset. But I hope this will stay between us.'

'Of course,' Angela replied. 'I won't tell a soul, I promise. We wouldn't want it to come out that the famous Fleury topazes aren't real, of course. Wild horses wouldn't... Well whatever they do.'

'I know what you mean.' Rose heaved a sigh of relief. She was still worried about Sylvia finding out the truth. She wanted to get to the bottom of this mystery first. 'Thank you. How much do I owe you for the cleaning and repair of the clasp?'

Angela mentioned a sum that was quite reasonable and Rose paid the bill. Then she thanked Angela, and walked out of the shop with the velvet box in a paper carrier bag that displayed the logo of the jeweller. As she drove home through the beautiful countryside, she took a detour into Muckross Park, part of Killarney National Park, to have a bite to eat and sit in the garden before she returned to work.

At the counter of the café, Rose chose a sandwich with ham and cheese, a tall latte and a raisin bun. Then she went outside with her tray to sit at one of the tables in the garden. It was a warm day with a mild breeze and intermittent sunshine through the clouds. She looked out across the lawn that lay like a green velvet carpet, dotted with azalea and rhododendron bushes in full bloom. The blossoms were a vibrant red, pink and purple interspersed with white, a stunning backdrop to the glittering water of the big lake in front of the old mansion. Rose imagined ladies in long dresses carrying parasols, going for leisurely walks in the bygone days of Queen Victoria, who was said to have visited here once.

'Hi, Rose,' a voice said, pulling Rose out of her reverie.

'Yes?' Rose shaded her eyes against the bright sunlight and

discovered a pretty woman with chestnut curls and lively hazel eyes standing at her table.

'I'm Vicky,' she explained. 'We spoke on the phone when you rang Noel's office.'

'Oh, yes, of course,' Rose said, smiling at the woman. 'Hi, Vicky. Lovely to meet you. What are you doing here?'

'I had an errand nearby and then I took the day off,' Vicky replied.

'I see.' Rose pushed her lunch to the side. 'Why don't you sit down? Great opportunity to catch up and get to know each other.'

'Ah, brilliant.' Vicky put her tray on the table and sat down on the chair opposite Rose. 'As you can see the place is filling up, so I would either have to stand up or sit on the tiny wall over there, which doesn't look very comfy.'

'I know. It's a very popular place on a sunny day.' Rose picked up her sandwich and took a bite. 'I'm so happy to meet you here. I was going to call you and suggest we have coffee someday, but you beat me to it.'

'I was delighted when I spotted you just now,' Vicky replied. 'It's so crowded here today and I needed a place to sit down. I recognised you from a group photo Noel showed me, so I thought I'd say hello and see if you'd let me sit at your table.' She nibbled at her wrap, her eyes sparkling. 'I'm like that, I'm afraid. Too forward, my granny would say.'

'Ah, grannies,' Rose said with a sigh. 'Don't we love them though, even if they're like the dowager countess in *Downton Abbey* at times.'

'Yes that's true,' Vicky agreed. 'Mine makes me feel like a little girl even though I'm pushing forty.' She took a swig of her coffee. 'But I want to know all about you. I know you came here from Dublin, although you're kind of Dingle royalty, I've been told.'

Rose was highly amused. 'Dingle royalty? That's a laugh,

there's nothing royal about us. We only barely managed to save the old wreck that was our ancestral home, and now it's being turned into an apartment complex.'

Vicky nodded. 'Oh, yes, Noel told me all about it. We'll be handling all the legal stuff once the apartments are being let.' She paused, looking thoughtful. 'Just wondering, are all the flats for seniors only?'

'Yes, they are. Why do you ask?'

'I'm looking for a place. The cottage I'm renting is being renovated so I have to move out soon. I was looking for something to buy, that's why I looked up your website, you see.'

'Oh, well,' Rose started, 'there are a few houses for sale right now, I've seen. I used to be an estate agent, so I'm still interested. But as the high season is coming up, I'd wait until after the summer if I were you. Then prices will drop a bit and there will be a lot more choice. But of course, it all depends on what you're looking for. Are you living alone, or...'

'Yes I'm on my own,' Vicky said with a little sigh. 'Never found Mr Right, despite my desperate efforts. But I haven't given up hope, you know. I know he's out there somewhere, waiting for me. The trick is to find exactly where, though. That's why I came to Kerry. I thought I'd have better luck here in the wonderful Kingdom. Plus my dad was from Tralee, so I have a few little roots here.'

'Of course you do,' Rose agreed. 'I partly grew up in Dublin but I have always felt Dingle is my real home. My father grew up here of course and we spent all our holidays at Magnolia.'

'Must have been nice,' Vicky said. Then she put a hand on Rose's arm and looked at her with great sympathy. 'I know what happened to you. Your father and grandfather died in that freak accident at sea. And you and your sisters lost your dad and granddad all at once. You were all so young. Such a tragedy. I'm sure there is still a great sadness inside you.'

Rose nodded, touched by Vicky's empathy and understanding. 'Thank you. And you're right. There is still a feeling of loss with us all. That's why we're so close. We know how life can change so suddenly. So we value every moment we have together.'

'I'm sure you do,' Vicky said, her voice softer.

'But life goes on and you have to adjust and accept,' Rose continued. 'And yes, we were so young. I was only eight when it happened. It's a long time ago, but sometimes it feels like yesterday. Especially now that I'm back. And then there is the restoration of the house and sorting through the stuff. That bring back memories.'

'How do you feel about the Magnolia Manor rebuild?' Vicky asked. 'Must be strange to see the house being used for something else, rather than a family home.'

'Strange but also nice,' Rose replied. 'The house couldn't continue being the home for only one family. You'd have to be very rich to afford keeping that big place going. It feels right to turn it into flats for older people, who want to keep their independence but also need a little extra care and attention. The gardens will be restored to what they were before and the people in town will be able to enjoy them. This way, the house will live again in a different way. That's really what life is all about. Change and improvement and making places accessible to everyone.'

'I love that,' Vicky said. 'I'd love to come and live there when I get older. But in the meantime, I hope I'll have a bit of fun.'

'I'm sure you will.' Rose smiled at Vicky, feeling she had found a friend. 'And your Mr Right is out there, I'm sure.'

'I'd even settle for Mr Wrong,' Vicky said with a sigh. 'This dating game is getting very tired. Tinder has not delivered either, I have to admit.'

'I don't like dating apps,' Rose declared.

'You're still single too?' Vicky asked.

'Yeah, well...' Rose started. 'I was in a relationship but we broke up.'

'Oh, I'm sorry,' Vicky said with sympathy in her eyes. 'That must have been hard.'

'Thanks,' Rose said with a little shrug. 'It was tough, but I'm doing my best to get over it. So I suppose I have to get back into that tedious dating game. Not on a dating site though. Most of those profiles seem so fake.'

'Oh many of them are, of course. You might get a great match, but then you meet in person and they look a lot less attractive than their photos. And that sizzling personality?' Vicky rolled her eyes. 'More often than not they're beyond boring and so full of themselves you want to scream. Or looking for second wives!'

Rose couldn't help laughing. Vicky was a hoot. 'So what were you doing in Killarney today?'

'I had to go to a funeral. No relation or anything,' Vicky assured Rose. 'It was a client who's been with the firm a long time. Noel had to go to court in Tralee so he sent me to represent him. I went to the mass and signed the book but skipped lunch with the family. I thought I'd have lunch here instead, on my way home. How about you?'

'I had to collect my necklace from the jewellers. It's an old piece that had to be repaired,' Rose explained.

'I love antique jewellery,' Vicky exclaimed. 'Can I see it?'

'Yes, I have it here in my bag,' Rose said without thinking. Then she hesitated for a moment. Now that she knew it was fake, she didn't feel like showing it. But then she changed her mind. Why not put it to the test? If Vicky believed it was real, then everyone else would too... She took out the scuffed velvet box and opened it. 'Here it is.'

'Ooh,' Vicky said, looking at the necklace. 'So beautiful. Are they topazes?'

'That's right,' Rose replied.

'I love the setting and the pearls. But...' Vicky paused, still staring at the necklace. 'You know, I've seen it before. The exact same one.' She stared at Rose. 'Are there two of them?'

'What?' Rose asked, shocked, staring at Vicky. 'No, there's only this one. Where did you see it?'

'In *OK! Magazine* when I was at the hairdressers. It was in the society pages. A feature about a celebrity party in Cork.' Vicky studied the necklace. 'I could swear it's the same one. Do you lend it out to friends sometimes?'

'No, I never do.' Rose snapped the box shut. 'You must have been mistaken.'

'I'm sure I wasn't,' Vicky insisted. 'It was so unusual, I couldn't stop looking at it.'

Rose shook her head. 'It can't have been the same one. It must have been a similar necklace, but not identical, I'm sure. Who was wearing it? And where?'

'Well,' Vicky started, looking as if she was trying hard to conjure up an image, 'it said it was a fortieth birthday party for someone at a big hotel in Kinsale. You know, in West Cork.'

'Yes, I know where Kinsale is,' Rose said.

'Well this woman with black hair in a navy off-the-shoulder dress was wearing that necklace – or an identical one – in one of the photos. As I said, I'm interested in antique jewellery and that's why I remember it.'

'Do you know who this woman was?' Rose asked.

'No. It was one of those huge parties and I didn't recognise any of the other guests. It seemed like a fun evening though.'

'I'm sure it was.' Rose looked at Vicky thoughtfully. 'Are you sure it was the same necklace? I mean it could have been something similar.'

'I'm quite sure. It was something you couldn't help notice. And when you showed me yours, it rang a bell. I have a very good visual memory for things like that.'

'I don't know, I think you must have remembered wrong,' Rose declared.

'Maybe,' Vicky mumbled, not looking very convinced. 'I'm sorry if I upset you.'

'You didn't really,' Rose replied, touched by the contrition in Vicky's voice. She couldn't know what Rose had just found out about the necklace, or how shocked she had been to hear it was fake. Was the one Vicky had seen the real necklace? Rose felt dizzy. She suddenly got up and gathered her bag and jacket. 'I have to go,' she said. 'I'm expected somewhere in about half an hour.'

'Oh,' Vicky said. 'So nice to meet you. Maybe we can do lunch or something soon?'

Rose smiled. 'That'd be great. Let's exchange phone numbers and I'll give you a shout when I have some free time. And please don't feel bad about what you told me. No hard feelings at all. I'm sure it was a genuine mistake.'

'Yes, probably. But I could try to find out the name of that woman if you like,' Vicky offered. 'I'll go back to the hairdresser to see if I can find that issue of the magazine.'

Rose nodded. 'Yes, that'd be great. Not that I think it really was the same necklace, but it would be interesting to see it.'

'I'll try my best,' Vicky promised.

They exchanged phone numbers and agreed to meet up for lunch very soon.

After their goodbyes, Rose walked across the lawn, thinking about what Vicky had said. When she thought about it, she felt in her bones that Vicky had not been mistaken. There was another necklace out there. It had to be the real one, and it had to be found. But how? She had to dig deeper. It would be tricky, but it had to be done. *I'll catch up with Vicky after the wedding*, Rose thought. *I have to get through that ordeal first. Meeting everyone again and pretending to be fine, with a new life, a new job and, well, if not a new boyfriend, at least a man who is ready to stand by me, even for a few hours. The best revenge is to live well, they say. If that's true, I'll make sure it's a hell of a revenge...*

# 8

Rose had a few run-ins with Henri during the following week as they worked together on the marketing plan, but she found sparring with him oddly enjoyable. He didn't manage to get to her with his little digs, which seemed to annoy him. But her mind was on other things – the wedding, and then the possibility that she had found a clue as to where the real necklace was. She had tried to push that to the back of her mind, but it kept popping up, especially at night, when she found it hard to sleep.

When Sylvia gave Rose the key to the storeroom in the attic, she felt she could at least find some clues. As she made her way up the winding back staircase to take a look at what was there, she decided how she would conduct her search. The storeroom contained a mish-mash of old ledgers, photo albums, piles of letters and diaries, all stacked on shelves and packed in cardboard boxes, nothing labelled or organised in any order. She would start with the photo albums, then flick through the letters and go on to the diaries later, most of which seemed to have belonged to the men of the family. The albums were the most important items, she decided, and they would also be the most interesting.

On Saturday afternoon, after a long root around the storeroom, Rose ran into Henri on her way down from the attic. Covered in dust, she was carrying a stack of photo albums and trying not to drop any as she went down the stairs. Henri, on his way up, nearly bumped into her and stopped in his tracks, looking surprised.

'Hey, what are you doing?' he asked, catching one of the albums that had escaped from her grip. 'Clearing out the attic before the building work starts up there?'

'Well, yes. In a way,' Rose said, feeling flustered. 'I'm trying to sort the family archives and put them in order, starting with the photos.'

'Why?' he asked as he handed her the album. 'That must be hard work. I had a look in that room but it was all such a mess. Why not burn the lot and be rid of it?'

'Burn it?' Rose asked, horrified. 'Are you mad? Of course we don't want to get rid of all our family's memorabilia. I want to sort it all, and then—' Rose stopped, not wanting to give away her secret about the necklace, or let him know what she was planning before she could present it at the next board meeting.

'Then – what?' he asked, lifting an eyebrow.

'I'm going to write a section on the website about the history of the Fleury family,' Rose said, sticking out her chin. 'Anything wrong with that?'

'Nothing at all. If anyone would want to read it. The Fleurys seem so boringly well behaved. Except for your great-grandfather Cornelius, they all look like butter wouldn't melt in those portraits. But I'm sure you don't want to write much about old Cornelius, do you? He nearly caused the illustrious Fleurys to be without a roof over their heads, paying his gambling debts by giving the house away.'

'And you tried to use that against us,' Rose retorted. 'Bringing up old letters to prove my great-grandfather had gifted Magnolia Manor to your granddad Etienne. Don't think I've forgotten your part in all of that.'

'Why not? Everyone else has, we're all friends now.'

'I'll never be your friend,' Rose declared.

'But we work so well together,' he said, stepping closer. 'I think we're quite alike, actually. Like peas in a pod.'

'No, we're not,' Rose protested. 'I'm not in a pod with you.'

'Really? I could have sworn you liked me. You're very dusty,' he added, running a finger across her shoulder. 'And there are cobwebs in your hair.'

'I know.' She stepped back, still clutching the albums. 'Nobody has been in that room for ages. So it's not exactly the Ritz in there. I saw your draft for the main website,' she said in an attempt to change the subject. 'Quite good, I thought. But it needs some work before it goes live. I'll email you a few suggestions.'

'Maybe we can discuss it over dinner?' he suggested.

'I'm very busy right now,' Rose said. 'So emailing works better for me. See you around, Henri. Have a good weekend.' Then she walked around him and down the main staircase without waiting for an answer. She lugged the heavy albums through the front door, loaded them into her car and drove off, trying to clear her mind of any thoughts of Henri. But the look in his eyes, and the little smile on his lips, lingered in her mind all the way back to the gatehouse. Was he hiding something? She didn't trust him, even though she knew she was overdoing the hostility.

As it was Saturday, Rose was looking forward to getting stuck into the albums. She made herself a cup of tea and settled on the sofa. As there was no way to know what year any of the albums were from, she decided to start with the one that looked like the oldest and most worn. Wiping the dust off the cover, which was decorated with leaves and flowers etched into the leather, she opened it and studied the first photos. She had often looked at old family photos in their silver frames in the library, study and the old drawing room, but the albums had been put away a long time ago and never been accessible to her or her sisters. But now she could look into the bygone days of life at the manor from over a hundred years ago. She had been right. This album dated from the last decade of the nineteenth century, so it had to be one of the oldest.

Fascinated, Rose stared at photos of family groups, of rows of servants in full livery standing in front of the manor, portraits of men and women sitting stiffly in their best clothes looking solemnly at the camera, as if they were afraid to move. Which they probably were. In those old days, it took a long time for the exposure to take, and if the subject moved, the photo would fail, or at least be blurred.

It was the portraits that interested her most, especially the young women, some of them in ball gowns, wearing the family jewels, mostly the pearl necklace with the diamond clasp that was now owned by Lily, as was the right of the eldest daughter. Rose hadn't spotted her own necklace yet, but as she came to the last pages of the album, there it was – worn by a lovely young woman with blonde hair and huge eyes that gazed at Rose across a century of time. *Iseult on her 18th birthday, April 1904*, it said in beautiful handwriting under the photo.

Rose studied the face of the young woman, trying to see if there was any family likeness with either her or her sisters, but found none apart from the blonde hair and what she guessed were blue eyes. Iseult had a heart-shaped face, a long nose, a tiny pouty mouth and slim eyebrows, unlike Rose, who always had a struggle plucking her thick, dark brows. Rose's mouth was full and wide, and her nose quite small, so there was nothing she could recognise in Iseult's features. Except maybe the rebellious look in those eyes and the way she stuck her chin out, which made Rose smile, feeling she was looking at someone who could have been a kindred spirit. She turned the last page of the album and discovered more photos of Iseult. She was sitting on a horse, riding side saddle, and then, in another photo, standing on the jetty wearing a strange bathing costume, this time grinning as if she was about to jump into the water and looked forward to the thrill.

Rose closed the album, smiling to herself at the images she had seen. What a fun girl Iseult must have been. But was she the one who had had the necklace copied? Rose had never heard of Iseult, but she knew that Maria Fleury and her husband John had had a son – her great-grandfather Cornelius – and a daughter whose name she hadn't known. But here she was. This must be Cornelius's sister, the youngest in the family. The rest of the albums were of a later time, fun to look at as the photos were more alive; the stiff backs and unsmiling faces were no more. Here were the 1930s and 1940s, with ski trips to the alps and sailing and picnics on the beaches all around the Dingle Peninsula.

The photos of her father and grandfather as children and young men brought tears to her eyes, as did Sylvia and Liam's wedding pictures, and subsequent photos of them as newlyweds in their sailing boat, which was to be the vessel that many years later would bring Liam and his son Fred to their early deaths. How sad that their passion for the sea and sailing would end like that. Rose closed the last album on the table and wiped her eyes with a tissue. A trip down memory lane was not always a happy one. She felt she needed a break from her search and would start again a little later. Tomorrow was Sunday – she would go for a hike up the mountain and see if she could get Lily to come if she wasn't too tired. That idea cheered her up.

As an afterthought, Rose took the first album out of the pile and opened it, gazing at the photos of Iseult, wondering what kind of life she had had as an adult. That was the one thing Rose felt she had to find out. When she looked at Iseult it was as if she saw a tiny glimmer in those lovely eyes – a glimmer of hope, and a strange connection.

She suddenly felt dizzy thinking about it and she knew it would take a lot of searching before she found out the truth. In the meantime, she could ask her grandmother if she knew anything about Iseult. Deciding not to waste any time, Rose picked up her phone and called Sylvia's number.

'Hello, Rose,' Sylvia said. 'What's up?'

'Hi, Granny. Nothing really, just a question,' Rose replied. 'As you know, I'm going through all the stuff in the storeroom. I started with the photo albums, which were fun to look at, especially the old photos from over a hundred years ago.'

'Yes. I know the ones you mean,' Sylvia said. 'They all looked as if they had swallowed a poker. Must have been such torture to sit still for so long just for a photo. No wonder they looked so grim.'

Rose laughed. 'Yes, exactly what I thought. But they didn't all look so serious. There was one girl that seemed so alive in the photos. Her name was Iseult. Do you know anything about her?'

'Hmm.' Sylvia paused. 'I know who you mean, I remember those photos. I also thought she looked interesting. I don't know much about her, just that she was Maria Fleury's youngest daughter and Cornelius's sister. When I asked Liam, he said she had been quite wild.'

'In what way?' Rose asked, intrigued.

'She was involved in women's rights and I think she went to London to join the suffragettes there. You know how they fought for the right to vote.'

'Of course. I always thought they were so brave. What did Iseult do with them?'

'Well, it is said she came back here in nineteen sixteen and joined the women who fought in the Easter Rising. Countess Markievicz and the like.'

'Oh, wow,' Rose exclaimed. 'She is now officially my hero. Imagine, we had a real heroine in the family.'

'Exactly. Quite amazing. But then...'

'Then?' Rose asked, feeling quite breathless.

'She disappeared. Nobody seems to know what happened to her after that. Cornelius never talked about her. It was as if she never existed.'

'Maybe she was killed,' Rose suggested.

'No, I don't think so. I have a feeling she ran away with someone and didn't tell anyone where she was going. She might have left the country.'

'That's possible, of course.' Rose felt a pang of disappointment. 'I would love to find out more. She's wearing some amazing garments, and I want to see if we can find them and do some repairs. The vintage shop might be interested in them.'

'Good idea,' Sylvia agreed. 'You should keep looking through the stuff in the storeroom. Some of it hasn't been looked at since it was put there years and years ago. Hard work of course, but you have all the time in the world now that you're here permanently.'

'That's true.'

'Don't get obsessed with it though,' Sylvia warned. 'Just have fun with it. There were some really quirky characters in the Fleury family, so that should give you a few laughs. But give yourself plenty of time, and have some free time too.'

'I will,' Rose promised.

But despite her promise not to take it all too seriously, Rose opened the album again as soon as she'd hung up.

*Who were you, Iseult?* Rose gazed at the photo with the lovely young girl wearing the necklace. *Where did you go? Did you sell the real necklace and have a copy made? If so... why?*

# 9

During the two weeks before the wedding, Rose found little time to do any family research. She was too busy working on the website and the marketing plan, as well as getting as polished and perfect as possible before she was away for the weekend. Not having the funds to go to an exclusive spa hotel, getting top-to-toe treatments, she borrowed her grandmother's brand new bathroom in the manor, giving herself a facial with homemade ingredients and spending a blissful hour in a bubble bath. Then she splurged on a haircut at a very expensive salon in Killarney called the Mane Event, which resulted in a shorter style that suited her better than the shoulder-length hair she had worn for the past year. She also tried her best to relax, doing yoga and meditation on the terrace as the weather turned warm, enjoying the balmy breezes in the early morning sunshine. She tried not to think too much about the wedding and the party afterwards, knowing she had to appear cool without showing the heartache that was still there – even though two months had passed since the breakup with Gavin. All this helped a lot, but the butterflies in her stomach still whirled around that morning. Noel was picking her up and they would drive there together, then she would stay at the hotel while Noel had booked a room at a B&B within walking distance. That way he wouldn't have to worry about drinking and could indulge in 'a glass or two' as well, as he put it.

Lily came over early that morning to help Rose get ready and provide a little moral support. They had a fun brunch together before they went upstairs, Lily lounging on the bed while Rose had a shower, her hair in curlers. Lily was glad of the small break from rocking a baby to sleep, with Dom taking over for a few hours.

'Love the new haircut,' Lily said when Rose appeared, taking the curlers out. 'That short bob is so cute on you. Are you pleased with it?'

Rose nodded, looking at herself in the mirror. 'I am, now that I'm used to it,' she said, liking the way the hair had been cut that gave it a lovely bounce, framing her face. The pale blonde highlights gave her a fresh, new look and brought out her blue eyes. 'It cost an arm and a leg, but it was worth it. I was getting tired of the long hair.'

'Out with the old, in with the new,' Lily quipped. 'You needed a boost.'

'That's for sure.' Rose held up her blue silk dress, the thin straps ending in a little bow on each shoulder. 'I also splurged on a new dress. What do you think?' she asked when she had put it on.

'Fabulous,' Lily said, getting up to help zip up the back. 'Where is the necklace? I'll put it on for you.'

'In the case on the bedside table,' Rose said, and suddenly shivered. 'Maybe I should wear something else though.'

'Why?' Lily asked, taking the necklace out of the case. 'It's fabulous now that you've had it cleaned.' She held it up against the sunlight that streamed in through the window. 'Just look at how the topazes shine.'

'Yeah, but,' Rose started. Then she stopped.

'But what?' Lily asked, stepping behind Rose and putting the necklace around her sister's neck. 'It's perfect with the dress.' She stepped back when she had snapped the clasp shut, her head cocked. 'Wow. They really bring out your eyes. You must wear it. Why did you think you shouldn't?'

'Oh, no reason,' Rose mumbled. 'Just a silly idea. I saw it worn by this young woman in an old photo when I was looking through the family albums. It made feel a little weird.'

'What young woman?' Lily asked.

'Her name was Iseult. She was the youngest daughter of Maria Fleury. Cornelius's sister.'

'Maria Fleury? The woman who got this as a wedding present?' Lily asked, looking excited.

'Yes, that's her,' Rose replied. 'Iseult got the necklace after her.'

'Did she get it when she was married?' Lily asked.

'No, she didn't,' Rose said. 'Nobody knows what happened to her, or if she was married. But she seems to have worn it from time to time.'

'Strange. Iseult...' Lily muttered. 'I think I saw her name somewhere... In an old letter, or maybe...' She shook her head. 'Can't remember.'

'When was it?' Rose asked, her heart beating faster. 'When did you see that name?'

Lily sat down on the bed again. 'I think it was written in a book in the library. We were sorting everything before the builders came, and went through the books trying to decide which to keep.' Lily nodded. 'Yes. That's where I saw it. The name stuck somehow because I had just read a book about Maud Gonne. She had a daughter called Iseult.'

'I see. Not that they would have anything to do with each other,' Rose remarked.

'No, but that name stood out to me just then. It was written in some old book I found in the library when Dominic and I went through the stuff in the bookcases. I think it was quite wrecked so we threw it out. That's all I can tell you about it.'

'A name in a book,' Rose said, as if to herself, feeling disappointed. 'You can look at the photos in the album I left on the coffee table. Then you'll see how pretty she was. And she wore the necklace in one of them.'

'But she wasn't the only Fleury girl to wear it,' Lily argued. 'So maybe we can find the rest of them in other photos. Wouldn't it be fun to put together an album with all the girls who wore the necklaces Granny gave us?'

'That's a great idea,' Rose said, excited at the thought. That way they might be able to trace the necklace to whoever had had the copy made. She would have to tell Lily about it eventually. But not yet. 'You could help me go through the albums.'

'Yes, I'd love to do that when I have the time.'

'Great.' Rose pulled a brush through her hair, then sprayed it with a little hairspray. 'We can divide them up next week.' She applied lipstick and stepped back from the mirror. 'How do I look?'

'Absolutely amazing,' Lily said, looking impressed. 'What time is the wedding?'

'Three o'clock.' Rose checked her watch. 'Noel is picking me up in a few minutes and then we'll go straight to the church. After that, we'll go to the hotel and I'll check in while they take the photographs, then the party will start with a champagne reception at five, followed by dinner and dancing.'

'Are you wearing a hat?' Lily asked.

'Yes. It's in the hall. A light blue little fascinator with small white flowers. Granny gave it to me. Just for the church. Then I'll take it off for the dinner.'

'Perfect. Should be a fabulous evening,' Lily said. 'I'm so glad Noel is going with you. He'll help you feel less nervous.'

They were interrupted by a car horn tooting.

'Noel is here,' Rose said, picking up her evening bag from the bed. 'My overnight case is downstairs.'

'Great.' Lily held the door open. 'Off you go. I'll say hi to Noel while you get your hat and jacket.' Lily clattered down the stairs while Rose took a last look at herself in the mirror. The dress was perfect, and the fake topazes glimmered in the sunlight that streamed in through the windows. There was no way anyone would guess they weren't real. Feeling a lot better than before, Rose made her way downstairs and carefully attached the little fascinator in her hair. Then she put on the light blue jacket that went with her dress, picked up her overnight bag and went outside, where she found Noel, looking handsome in black tie, standing by his old Ford Focus chatting to Lily.

He looked around and let out a whistle as Rose went down the front steps. 'Wow. You look wonderful, Rose.'

'Thank you,' Rose said, cheered by the admiration in his eyes. 'You don't look too bad yourself,' she said as she handed him her bag.

'Oh thanks. Pity about the car,' he said. 'Should be something expensive and sporty, but that's all I have, I'm afraid.'

'I don't care what car you drive, as long as it gets us there,' Rose said, smiling at him. He looked better than 'not too bad', Rose thought as she took in his wide shoulders, slim body, the shock of light blonde hair and twinkly blue eyes. The tuxedo fitted his tall frame perfectly, and she was surprised at how polished he looked. He was normally very professional looking, but nerdy and quiet, and he seemed more confident somehow. 'You look great,' she said.

Noel blushed and laughed as he put Rose's bag on the back seat. 'Ah sure, I do my best to scrub up well.'

'You certainly do,' Lily cut in. 'And the two of you make a fabulous couple. Everyone will be impressed.'

Rose and Noel looked at each other and laughed. Then Noel checked his watch and told Rose to get in or they'd be late for the wedding. 'You don't want to walk into the church when the priest says that thing about speaking up if you know any reason for them not to be married.'

'I think that would be the best moment to arrive,' Rose quipped, getting into the passenger seat. 'I can imagine the fright it would give them. But come on, let's go.'

Noel hopped into the car and started the engine. 'Bye, Lily, nice to see you,' he called out of the window. 'I wish you'd reconsider and come back to my office.'

'No chance,' Lily called back. 'But I'll give you a hand if you ever need some extra help. Have fun, you two.'

'We will,' Rose shouted back before they drove through the gates and onto the main road. She glanced at Noel, happy to have such a good-looking man to escort her to an event that she could never have faced alone.

As if feeling her gaze on him, Noel took his eyes off the road for a moment and shot her a glance. 'What?'

'Oh, I was just thinking that it's so kind of you to come with me.'

'Lily rang me and told me you needed support. I wasn't exactly going to call you and tell you I'd changed my mind. And anyway, who says no to an evening at Aghadoe?'

Rose smiled. 'That's true. I hope you'll have fun.'

'I will, and so will you,' Noel stated. 'We'll dance the night away and drink all the champagne we can manage. Don't worry about a thing.'

'I'll try not to,' Rose promised, suddenly looking forward to the evening. 'I'm glad I'm not an object of pity to you. It'll be a great break from working with Henri Bernard. I don't know why he annoys me so much, but he makes my teeth grate.'

'I think I can understand that,' Noel remarked. 'I've dealt with him briefly about some legal details in your contracts. He's a bit arrogant all right, which could get up your nose if you let it.'

'But you don't?'

'Not any more. He's behaved correctly after a little guidance from me.'

Rose smiled. 'You mean you told him off?'

'Not exactly. I just changed my tone and demeanour slightly. Made him feel a little uncomfortable perhaps.' Noel paused, changing gears. 'You know, of course, the best thing to do with people who are... well, annoying, is not to react at all if they try to upset you.'

'I know, and I do try,' Rose said. 'But I think my face reveals what I really feel.'

'You have to practise the poker face,' Noel suggested. 'Not easy, I know. But of course that's par for the course in my profession.'

'I bet you're as cool as a cucumber in court.'

'I'm known as the ice man,' Noel said, looking just a tiny bit smug.

'I can imagine,' Rose said. 'I'd say you're the king of cool.'

'Well that's a little over the top, but thanks,' Noel said, smiling.

They fell silent while the drive took them along the coastal road, with lovely views of the ocean and the mountains on the other side of the bay. Then they chatted about this and that, Noel concentrating on driving – there was a lot of traffic on the winding road, most of them heading for Inch Beach, which was famous as a great surfing spot. The waves were, as always, huge, and the large expanse of sand was dotted with surfers in wetsuits heading out into the foaming water to ride their surfboards. Rose opened the window just to smell the salt-laden air, closing her eyes as the wind caressed her face. Then she wound up the window again, not wanting the breeze to ruffle her hair too much.

She leaned back and tried to relax, wanting to be rested and calm before she had to face all her old friends from Dublin. It would be her first public appearance after the breakup, and she wanted to look as cool and untroubled as possible. And if any of Gavin's friends were there, she would be as poker-faced as a seasoned lawyer facing a courtroom.

But she couldn't stop the butterflies fluttering wildly in her stomach as they drove through the church gates. A lot of glamorous-looking people were already filing into the church, some of the women in large hats and wearing a lot of jewellery.

'What a fancy-looking bunch,' Noel exclaimed as he drove slowly along the path. 'You'd think it's a royal wedding the way some of the women are dressed.'

'I know. There is always some kind of competition going on with them.' Rose closed her eyes tight, thinking, *I will be cool and composed and not show how horribly scared I am right now.*

Noel found a parking space behind the church. As the car came to a stop, he put his hand on Rose's. 'You'll be fine,' he assured her. 'Conjure up that Fleury spirit and smile.' His gaze drifted to the necklace. 'The Fleury topazes will give you strength as well. They look magical, they suit you so well. You're the real deal, Rose. Don't forget that.'

Those words resonated with Rose and she felt suddenly stronger and better able to face her old circle of friends. They might look at her sideways, but so what? She had nothing to be ashamed of – she should be proud of the way she'd handled herself since the breakup. 'You're right,' she said, getting out of the car as Noel held the door open for her. 'What am I afraid of anyway?'

'That's what I was wondering,' Noel said, offering Rose his arm.

Rose laughed, took his arm and they walked across the gravel to the church doors together, just as the limousine with the bride and her father pulled up to the front steps.

'Hurry up,' Noel urged, taking Rose's hand. They ran up the steps and into the church while the organ struck up the bridal

march. Noel pulled Rose into one of the pews only seconds
before the bridal party walked up the aisle.

It was a beautiful procession. Four little flower girls in frilly
pink dresses, with wreaths of tiny white roses in their hair,
carried little posies. They were followed by four bridesmaids in
pale lilac full-length gowns. And then Louise, the bride, on her
father's arm in a white silk and lace dress, a white gold and pearl
tiara on her dark hair and the long veil trailing behind her. Rose
felt tears well up as she watched them proceed up the aisle to
where the groom was waiting, looking as if he couldn't believe
his luck. *How romantic*, she thought, feeling a pang of envy,
remembering how she had imagined she would one day walk up
to the altar just like this.

Then she froze in shock as she saw the best man beside the
groom. Oh no. It couldn't be. But yes. It was him. Gavin.

# 10

Noel threw Rose a worried glance. 'What's the matter? You look so pale. Are you not feeling well?'

'It's...' Rose whispered. 'The best man...'

'What's up with him?'

'He's my ex,' Rose hissed. 'I didn't know he'd be here. I thought he was in New York. What am I going to do?'

Noel squeezed her hand. 'Nothing at all. Try to calm down. Then, when he sees you, just say hello and smile. Okay?'

Rose nodded as the music stopped and the wedding ceremony began. As if in a dream, she watched as Louise and Aiden said 'I do' in turn, and Gavin handed the groom the ring. He looked so handsome in his tuxedo. He had a slight tan and his brown hair was a little longer than she remembered. He smiled at the couple and whispered something to the groom, before they went down the aisle and out the door to the forecourt, where everyone gathered to congratulate them. Rose hung back for a while, but then had to go and kiss both Louise and Aiden.

Louise grabbed Rose's hand. 'I know it must have been a shock to see Gavin,' she said softly in Rose's ear. 'I was going to tell you, but there was so much going on with the wedding and everything that I forgot.'

'Don't worry about it,' Rose whispered back. 'I was a bit shaken up to see him, but I'll be fine. Lovely ceremony and you look so beautiful.'

'Thank you.' Louise's eyes sparkled as she smiled at Rose. 'I really appreciate that you came. It means a lot to me. We were always good friends.'

'Yes, we were,' Rose agreed, and glanced at the long queue behind her. 'But now I'd better let everyone else congratulate you. See you at the hotel later.' She smiled at Louise and turned away, coming face to face with Gavin.

They stared at each other for a split second. Then Gavin smiled. 'Rose. Hi. How strange to see you, I mean...'

The wind blew a lock of hair into his eyes and she wanted to push it away, like she'd always done, but stopped herself in time. 'Hi, Gavin,' she heard herself say in a strong, confident voice that surprised her. 'Why are you surprised to see me? Aiden and Louise were part of our gang in Dublin. And Louise worked at the firm for over two years. Of course I'd be here.'

'Yes, of course. I should have known.'

'I should be the one to be surprised,' Rose said. 'I didn't expect you to come over from New York for the wedding. To be best man and all.'

'Aiden's brother was supposed to be best man,' Gavin explained. 'But he got sick and Aiden asked me to step in. I was planning to go home for a visit anyway.'

'Oh,' Rose said. 'I see. Nice of you to help out.'

'I was happy to do it.' Gavin took a step back and looked her up and down. 'You look great. Are you here on your own?'

'No, she's with me,' Noel said, stepping up beside Rose. He held out his hand. 'I'm Noel Quinn, a friend of Rose's.'

Gavin smiled and shook Noel's hand. 'Hi, Noel. I'm Gavin Lynch. Rose and I are old friends.'

'More than friends once, I believe,' Noel remarked.

Gavin nodded, looking awkward. 'Yes, we were in a relationship for a while. Still friends though. Our breakup was very amicable. Right, Rose?'

Rose shot him a thin smile, trying to hide her anger. 'If that's what you want to call it,' she mumbled. *Amicable?* she thought angrily. *Is that what he calls leaving me without a word of warning?* She looked at him and suddenly didn't feel anything at all. No attraction, lingering love or even a hint of fondness. She wondered briefly how she could have been so insanely in love with him and not seen how false and in love with himself he really was. 'No hard feelings at all,' she added, feeling oddly relieved. She was over him at last, even if not over the way he had behaved. That would never go away.

'Great. So,' Gavin said after a moment's pause, 'you moved to Kerry, I believe. How is it going?'

'Grand,' Rose replied, comforted by Noel standing beside her – a solid wall to lean on if she needed to. 'I'm handling the family property that's being turned into apartments.'

'So you're busy?' Gavin asked.

'Very. How about you?' Rose enquired.

'Getting into the New York real estate scene,' Gavin replied. 'Tricky, but exciting.'

'I can imagine.' Rose hovered on the spot for a minute, glancing at Noel. 'But now I think we'll head for the hotel. What do you think, Noel?'

'Yes,' he said. 'I think that would be good. We'll have a drink in the bar and watch them take the photos against that amazing view up there. Such a lovely evening, isn't it?'

'Beautiful,' Gavin agreed. He started to move away. 'Well, see you up there then, lads. We could have a dance or two later, Rose.'

'Maybe,' Rose said, taking Noel's hand. 'If I'm free. See you later, Gavin.'

'You did well,' Noel said when they were in the car. 'Nobody would know you ever had any feelings for him.'

'I was shaking like a leaf,' Rose said. 'But you standing beside me helped a lot.' She let out a deep sigh. 'Oh why did I go to this stupid wedding? Why didn't I say I was going away or my granny was sick or something?'

'Because it wouldn't be true.' Noel started the engine. 'And you're not a chicken. In any case, your friend Louise would have been upset if you hadn't been at her wedding.'

'Yes, that's true. She thanked me for coming and apologised about not having warned me about Gavin being the best man. But she would have had more important things on her mind, of course.'

They drove the short distance to the hotel while enjoying the beautiful views of the lakes and the mountains beyond. The late afternoon sun cast a golden light on the landscape. They took a moment to stand in front of the hotel to enjoy the views. The air felt so clean, with a faint smell of newly mown grass mingling with the scent of wild roses just coming into bloom.

'Such a heavenly spot,' Rose said, taking deep breaths. 'The air is like wine here. The perfect venue for a wedding.'

'Oh, I'm not sure about that,' Noel said. 'I think the gardens of Magnolia Manor are even better. There is such peace there, and the view over the ocean is fantastic. And the house... So beautiful, with such a fascinating history. All those people who lived there through the years, especially the women, were all so interesting.'

Rose nodded, her eyes on the view. 'Yes they were actually. I'm doing some research right now, going through the family archives. Well,' she added with a derogatory little laugh, 'I'm actually ploughing through a jumble of papers, letters, photos and other junk that were shoved into one of the attic rooms during the renovation downstairs. "Family archives" sounds as if there is some kind of order. But that's far from the truth.'

'So you have a lot of work ahead of you?' Noel asked. 'Sounds daunting. Except if you're interested in history.'

Rose looked at Noel and smiled. 'Sure it's a lot of work. But I adore history. Always have. Because history is about people, and I want to find out how my ancestors lived, about their passions and interests and everything else. Looking at their stiff figures in paintings and photos doesn't tell you much other than what they looked like.'

'And that they wore tight corsets,' Noel quipped. 'I love history too. If you need help, I'd be happy to come and assist with the ploughing.'

'Really?' Surprised, Rose smiled at Noel. 'That would be great.'

'Your grandmother asked me to do some cataloguing of her assets anyway, so I can look out for anything of value that we might find.'

'Then it'll be part of your work for her,' Rose remarked. 'You'll be doing something useful at the same time.'

'Exactly. I'm not very tidy though, as Lily might have told you,' he warned her. 'But it could be good to have a fresh pair of eyes that might see things from a different angle.'

'I know what you mean. And that is very useful during research, so yes, I'll give you a shout if I get desperate.' She turned to look at the hotel entrance where she saw guests beginning to arrive. 'I think we'd better go inside. The bride and groom will want this very spot for the photos. And to be honest, I'm dying for a drink after the fright of seeing Gavin again.'

'Yes, that must have shaken you up a bit,' Noel remarked.

'It was a huge shock,' Rose said. 'I didn't expect to see him there. But then...' She paused, then suddenly laughed. 'When he started talking to me in that condescending way, I realised that I didn't feel anything at all for him. It was a bit like looking at a pizza when you're not hungry. And that was a huge relief.' She started to walk towards the hotel. 'I'd better take my overnight bag and check into my room before dinner.'

Noel followed Rose. 'I like your metaphor. Not that I think your ex looked like a pizza, but I get what you mean. And I'm glad he didn't upset you.'

'Let's forget about him,' Rose said as they walked up the steps with her bag. 'Well, he's here and he'll probably make some kind of soppy speech, but then we can ignore him and dance the night away. If you like dancing that is.' She suddenly realised how little she knew about Noel, even though they had met on many occasions – family dinners and meetings about the new apartments. But she didn't know who he really was or anything about his personal life, apart from the fact that he lived in an old house in Anascaul with his elderly father.

'I like dancing,' Noel said. 'Not good at it really though.'

Rose laughed. 'Me neither, so we're a perfect match. I'll step on your toes and you'll step on mine.'

'I'll try not to,' he promised.

'I'll hold you to that. But now, while I go check in and put my bag in the room, you go on to the bar and get yourself a drink.' Rose took her bag and started to walk to the reception desk.

'I'll wait for you,' Noel called after her. 'And we'll get that drink when you come back.'

'You're such a gentleman,' Rose said, smiling.

'I do my best.'

Rose felt so happy she had asked Noel to be her plus one. He was such a kind man.

She was still smiling when she went into the lift, her keycard in her hand. She was on the second floor and the room was easy to find. Rose quickly put the bag on the bed, took off her jacket and hat and looked at herself in the mirror. The topazes gleamed in the light of the bedside lamp, looking nearly real. Rose touched them and wondered if anyone would guess the truth. Probably not, just as she had been convinced they were real until she had been told otherwise. Oh well, there was nothing much she could do until she found out what had happened to the real necklace. If she ever did.

## 11
_____

The evening turned out to be more enjoyable than Rose had expected. Mostly because of Noel. To her surprise, he proved to be more fun than she would have believed at first. Yes, he was a little awkward and shy with the Dublin crowd but, as the evening wore on, he seemed to find his feet. He was simply himself, a country lad at heart with a love of nature, hillwalking and birdwatching, and the female guests seemed to warm to him.

'He's so unusual,' Kate said as they touched up their makeup in the ladies'. She was one of the girls from the office in Dublin. 'He told me all about the birdlife on the coasts around here at this time of year. Did you know that many of the migratory birds stop here to feed on their way to the Arctic, where they nest in the summer? And that the ringed plover has been spotted in this area?'

'Eh, yes,' Rose said as she applied blusher. 'I spent most of my childhood here, so that's something we learned at an early age.'

'How lucky you were,' Kate said. 'Must have been fun to be

here when you were a kid. Not that I'd like to live here now, but the odd visit is great.'

'I live here permanently now,' Rose cut in. 'And I love it.'

'Do you?' Kate looked at her in astonishment for a moment. 'Wasn't it hard to adjust after all those years in Dublin? And being with Gavin and everything...' Her voice trailed away as she glanced at Rose in the mirror. 'Sorry, didn't mean to be tactless. I'm sure it was devastating, him going off with another woman like that.'

Rose stiffened, her hand with the blusher frozen in mid-air. 'What woman?'

'The one he went to New York with.' Kate stared at Rose. 'I thought you knew.'

Rose shot her a fake smile, even though she was seething inside. 'Oh yes, her. Of course I knew. But the whole thing between us was over for a while before that, you know,' she lied. 'But what does it matter now? It's in the past and I'm moving on. Noel is great company.'

Kate nodded. 'Oh yes, and very nice he is too. Very different from Gavin.'

Rose nodded. 'He's a darling. I wasn't interested in dating, but Noel changed my mind,' she said with what she hoped was a happy smile. 'He's been such a sweetie. Things are looking up, I feel. I've just become an aunt, too,' she added proudly.

'That's lovely. Congratulations,' Kate said, looking disappointed. 'I was going to ask if you and the tall guy you're with were... together.'

'Eh, yes, we are,' Rose lied. 'Why do you ask?'

Kate looked a little awkward. 'I was hoping you wouldn't mind me flirting with him. But I see now I was wrong. Sorry.'

'Oh please don't apologise. I can understand that you'd like him. Who wouldn't?'

'He's really nice,' Kate agreed, and applied another layer of mascara. 'He's such a break from the guys I usually meet. But you never know, there might be someone like him out there.' She put the mascara away in her bag and paused on her way to the door. 'I love your necklace, by the way. Absolutely stunning. Is it an old family piece?'

Rose touched the topazes that seemed suddenly to burn her skin. 'Thanks. Yes, it's something I inherited from my grandmother.'

'What are those stones? Aquamarines?'

'No, topazes,' Rose replied, feeling guilty about lying. But what else could she do?

'Must be worth a fortune,' Kate said, her eyes still on the necklace.

'Probably.' Rose smiled. 'But that's not why I love it.'

'I'm sure,' Kate said, looking impressed. 'It's about family and the history of it, isn't it?'

'Exactly.'

'Lovely.' Kate's eyes twinkled. 'Well I'm off to flirt with... Someone who's single. You're lucky to have – what's his name again?'

'Noel. He was born on Christmas Eve.'

The girl giggled. 'How cute. Well, see ya out there on the dance floor.' She swished out of the ladies', leaving Rose standing there, still shocked at what she had heard.

So Gavin did leave her for someone else after all, despite his protestations that there was no other woman and that it was all about his fear of commitment. He was never going to come back to her, and it hadn't been about anything except some other woman. Well, Rose hadn't really believed they would ever get back together, but the lies he had told her now felt like a betrayal.

Rose shook herself, straightened her back and put her lipstick away. She wasn't going to let this ruin her life, or even the evening. It could just be idle gossip anyway and not true at all. Then she marched out into the ballroom, where the party was still in full swing. She saw Noel dancing a little awkwardly with Kate, who was bopping away to the music, smiling and batting her eyelashes at him, despite what she had just said. He seemed to take it in good stride, even if his dancing was not what anyone would call smooth.

Someone grabbed Rose by the arm and pulled her out on the dance floor. 'Hi there,' Gavin mumbled in her ear. 'How about a dance for old times' sake?'

Without replying, Rose let him twirl her around for a few beats but then stopped and pulled him away. 'I'll dance with you, but I want to ask you something first.'

His smile stiffened slightly. 'Yes?'

'Did you leave me for someone else?'

Gavin looked suddenly guilty. 'Why do you ask?'

'Because that's what someone told me just now,' she said, her voice cold. 'And I suppose everyone knew except me. If what I was told is true, I mean.'

Gavin didn't reply for a while. Then he shrugged. 'Yeah, okay, that's true. I didn't tell you because I thought it would upset you.'

'More than the fact that you were leaving and never coming back, you mean? The moment you walked out of the flat, I knew that was it. You could have been honest about why you left.'

'I suppose so.' Gavin shrugged. 'But whatever. It would never have worked with us anyway.'

'You're right. It wouldn't. I know that now. But then... I had such hopes and dreams,' Rose said, tears welling up as she remembered that awful day. 'And you stepped all over them.'

Gavin's eyes softened. He touched her cheek. 'Oh Rose, I'm sorry. I really am. Is there anything I can do to make it up to you?'

'No, nothing.' She looked at him for a moment. 'All I can say is that I think it was lucky in a way. You leaving me like that pushed me to come here. And that is the best thing I've done for a long time. Dublin was not really me at all. Nor were you and all these fancy people. Some of them are really nice, but I don't really fit in with them. I was always a Kerry girl at heart. Maybe that's what you didn't like.'

'No,' he protested. 'There was nothing I didn't like about you. It was just… Well, I met this woman who…' He shook his head. 'I won't go into all that. I didn't behave very well, I know that.' He smiled his brilliant smile she had once thought was so alluring. 'You have changed, you know. You look even prettier and a lot stronger than before. That dress, your new hairdo, that necklace that make your eyes sparkle like sapphires… wow.'

'Thank you,' Rose said, finally able to smile at him. 'You look well too.' She was surprised that she was over Gavin, much quicker than she'd expected. Was it her new job, the Kerry air or possibly even Noel?

'Do you forgive me? For everything that happened?' he asked, his face brightening. 'Can we be friends?'

'I suppose I forgive you,' she said, after a moment's reflection. 'But I won't forget. And I don't think we can be friends. Yet.'

'No, I suppose not.' He took her hand. 'Thank you for forgiving me. I'll never forget you, Rose. How about that dance now?'

She stepped away, looked across the dance floor and saw Noel waving at her. 'Sorry, Gavin, but I want to dance with Noel. I promised I would.'

He nodded. 'Of course. He's a lucky fella.'

'I'm the lucky one. I do like him a lot,' she said, realising to her surprise that it was true. Her feelings for Gavin were fading fast, and Noel's support and kindness had been such a comfort. 'Bye for now, Gavin.'

'Bye, Rose. I'm glad we had that talk.'

'Me too,' she said, before she gave him a sad little smile and walked away, her step light and her mind at peace. She had finally closed that chapter.

'Hey, Rose,' Noel said when she reached their table. 'I've had a word with the bride and the band and they agreed to play some Irish dance music. How about a jig or two? That's a dance I know I can handle.'

'Brilliant,' Rose exclaimed. 'I used to take Irish dance classes when I was a teenager. I thought you did too?'

'I was ten when I had to give it up,' he said, laughing. 'I was too tall for the lineup at the dance school competitions. But I still remember the steps.' He held out his hand as the band started to play a lively Irish tune. 'Come on, girl, let's have a go.'

Delighted at the chance to shake herself up and turn her mind away from Gavin, Rose kicked off her high heels, took his hand and they bounced onto the dance floor in time with the music. They were soon joined by other guests, and the floor was suddenly thronged with people dancing and whooping and laughing until the music stopped. Still laughing, everyone returned to their places declaring the idea 'pure genius'. Some people came up to Noel and clapped him on the back, offering to buy him drinks. Rose looked on as the bride and groom, Louise and Aiden, started to dance again as the band played another tune.

'Oh, gosh,' Rose said as she collapsed on her chair. 'That was exhausting but such fun. Thank you, Noel.'

He grinned and wiped his forehead with a napkin. 'Don't know what got into me. I didn't murder your toes, I hope?'

'You didn't step on them once.' Rose grabbed a jug of water and filled her glass, then held the jug out to Noel. 'Here. Have a drink. You'll need it.'

A phone suddenly pinged.

'Was that your phone?' Rose asked Noel.

He pulled it out of his inside pocket and looked at it. 'No, not mine,' he said.

'Oh, must be mine, then.' Rose took her evening bag that was hanging on the back of her chair. She pulled the phone out and saw a text message. 'It's from Vicky.'

*I remember now. The woman wearing a necklace similar to yours was called Melanie Blennerhassett. Such an unusual name that it stuck in my memory. Hope you're having fun at the wedding and Noel isn't boring you silly. Talk soon Vx*

'What did she want?' Noel asked.

'Nothing important.' Rose turned off her phone and put it back in her bag. 'Just asking if I was enjoying the wedding.'

'And you are,' Noel stated. 'I can see that. And I could also see you talking to your ex. How did that go?'

'Oh, fine,' Rose replied, her mind on the text message. *Melanie Blennerhassett*, she thought. *That name sounds familiar... Where have I heard it before? I'll google it later...*

'Are you okay?' Noel asked, sounding concerned. 'He wasn't rude to you, was he?'

Rose looked up, pulled from her thoughts. 'No, not at all. It was all very civilised. We'll never be friends but there are no hard feelings any more. All done and forgotten.'

'That's good. I was wondering why you looked so worried just now.'

'It's not about that,' Rose tried to explain. 'It's about something else. But I can't go into it right now. Or ever, really.'

'I'm sorry,' Noel said, looking embarrassed. 'I didn't mean to pry.'

'I know you didn't,' Rose soothed. 'You're always so considerate. I really appreciate that.'

'The bride and groom are about to leave,' someone suddenly shouted. 'And the bride will be throwing the bouquet, so all you girls out there, gather in the lobby and we'll see who will be walking down the aisle next.'

'Oh no,' Rose muttered, panic rising in her chest. 'I don't want to do this. She'll throw the bouquet straight at me and everyone will be applauding and it will be so totally embarrassing that I'll die.'

'You won't die, but I get it,' Noel mumbled back into her ear, grabbing her hand. 'Let's slip away now while everyone's moving off. Then we can reappear when the bouquet throwing is over.'

Rose nodded. They managed to sneak through the door and into a corridor that led to the restrooms, and waited there while the noise of many voices died down. They stood squashed together for a moment and, as their eyes met, Rose felt a strange little tug at her heart. The way he looked at her was so endearing that she was tempted to reach up and kiss him. He had been such a support to her all through the evening, but that wasn't what made her feel a sudden attraction to him. It was something else, something she hadn't expected.

But then she heard cheering and guessed someone had caught the bouquet. Noel slowly pulled away and opened the door to the lobby. What she saw made her laugh out loud. Kate, the woman she had been talking to earlier, stood in the middle of the crowd holding the bouquet, her face red. Then she laughed and waved the flowers in the air while the bride and groom went down the stairs, through the throng and into a sportscar, which was festooned with a 'just married' sign and cans on strings clattering loudly as they drove off.

Kate handed the bouquet to one of the bridesmaids and joined Rose, who was hanging back a little. 'You're the next one to get married, then?' Rose said, still laughing.

'So it appears,' she replied with a grin. 'I hope it's true.'

'I'm sure it is,' Noel said, still holding Rose by the waist.

'What about you two?' Kate asked. 'I can tell you're getting close.'

'Oh we're taking it nice and slow,' Noel said, letting go of Rose.

'Not too slow,' Kate said with a wink. 'Life's short. Get married while you're still in love. See you later, lads.' She moved away and disappeared into the throng of guests who were heading back into the dining room.

'Wise words,' Noel said, smiling at Rose.

'Oh, I don't think I want to get married just yet,' Rose protested, still feeling odd after that moment in the corridor. 'How about you? Anyone on the horizon?' she asked.

He shook his head. 'No, more's the pity. It's getting a little sad to still be single at my age, but there you are. Not many takers for a lanky impoverished country solicitor with size thirteen feet.'

'You have so many good qualities, though. But how old are you?' Rose asked without thinking.

'I'm thirty-eight. Many years older than you.'

'Not at all,' Rose protested. 'I'm thirty-five. Getting a little long in the tooth as well.'

'You still look like a girl,' Noel remarked. 'I'm sure it won't be long before someone snaps you up.' He paused for a moment. 'Forgive me for asking, but Lily hinted that there might be some chemistry between you and Henri Bernard.'

Rose felt her cheeks flush. 'No, she is totally barking up the wrong tree. Nothing going on there except mutual dislike.'

'But you're attracted to him?'

Rose sighed. 'Not really. That type of man is what I'm trying to get away from. In any case, as his father and my grandmother are together, he feels like family, even if we're not related in any way. But any woman with a pulse would be attracted to Henri Bernard. He's incredibly good looking.'

'He might feel the same about you,' Noel suggested.

'I don't think so. He just enjoys ribbing me. We're always arguing. A kind of one-upmanship that we are both trying to win. It's going nowhere and I don't want to talk about it tonight. It's been such a nice evening thanks to you, Noel. You're the best friend a girl could wish for.'

Noel's face brightened. 'Ah, that's lovely. So happy to have helped you through what must have been a difficult evening.'

'It wasn't too bad at all,' Rose said, smiling. 'I saw Gavin clearly for the first time today, and realised what a lucky escape I had. And the wedding turned out to be good craic all around, I have to say. All thanks to you.' Rose stifled a yawn. 'I think I'll go to bed now though. But you stay on. I hear the band has been replaced by disco music. I'm sure everyone will be partying until breakfast.'

Noel smiled and shook his head. 'No, I think I'll turn in too. It's only a few minutes' walk to the B&B and the fresh air will clear my head after all the champagne.'

'What's the B&B called?' Rose asked.

'Graceland. The owners are huge Elvis fans, there are photos and memorabilia all over the place. I'll be going to sleep with a portrait of the king himself over my bed. And they pipe his music into the rooms in the morning to wake you up.'

'Sounds like fun. But waking up to "Jailhouse Rock" after a night of heavy drinking might be a little hard to take,' Rose suggested.

'And if they play "Are you Lonesome Tonight" at bedtime I'll cry myself to sleep,' Noel quipped. 'But I don't think they'll be so cruel.'

'That wouldn't be good for business,' Rose remarked. 'Thanks for coming and for being such a great support.' She stood on tiptoe and kissed Noel on the cheek. 'Sweet dreams.'

'Oh, eh, thanks. My dreams will be very sweet,' Noel said, having nearly fallen over with shock at her kiss. 'Goodnight, Rose. See you tomorrow.'

'Yes. No later than ten. I want to get home and start the research.'

'I'll be there. I'm sure I'll be sick of Elvis by then.'

'I'd say you will. Goodnight.' She waved and walked away, her thoughts on what had happened that evening, and the look in Noel's eyes as they stood together in the corridor. How strange it had felt. But it was probably just deep gratitude for the way he had supported her.

Rose turned her mind to the day ahead and that name Vicky had sent her. Was it a red herring, or a clue that would lead her to the real necklace? She had to find out more.

## 12
———

At what felt like the crack of dawn, Rose's phone rang. She groaned, groping at the bedside table, and put the phone to her ear. 'Hello? Who is waking me up this early on a Sunday morning?'

'Your grandmother,' Sylvia's voice said. 'Good morning, darling. It's nine-thirty. I thought you'd be up by now.'

'Oh no, is it?' Rose sat up in bed. 'I'd better get dressed. I was at this wedding yesterday and I'm at the hotel and I said to Noel to be here at ten and now...' She stopped. 'Sorry, Granny. Why did you call me?'

'Oh I forgot about the wedding,' Sylvia said apologetically. 'Was it fun?'

'Yes, lovely. But what's going on with you?' Rose got out of bed, the phone to her ear. 'Nothing wrong, I hope?'

'Absolutely not. I'm calling to tell you that we're having a meeting today about the estate and what to do in the grounds,' Sylvia explained. 'I know it's a little unusual to do it on a Sunday, but everyone's free so we thought it a good idea all the same.'

'Oh. Okay,' Rose said, trying to gather her thoughts. 'What time?'

'Four o'clock. In the new office downstairs.'

'Will Henri be there?'

'Of course. Everyone will. All the board members, meaning you and Lily too, of course.'

'All right, Granny. I'll be there.'

'Good. And make sure you're prepared for battle about Lily's walled garden and whatever you want to suggest.'

'I'll do my best. See you then, Granny.'

Rose hung up with a feeling of dread. A meeting with the board – and Henri – today. The other board members were Mrs Moore, who owned a chain of pharmacies, Linda Moriarty, a prominent business woman, and Diana McMillan, the owner of a big hotel in Killarney. Tough women who all wanted to see a return on their investment. Not what she needed on a Sunday after a late night. And she wasn't prepared. She would have to put something together in a hurry and make sure she had a strong case. Lily needed her support if the garden centre and café was to provide an income for her. Rose wasn't worried about Sylvia or Arnaud, but Henri might have wooed some of the female members to side with him, and then they would have a battle on their hands. She'd have to take care not to annoy him and also make sure she looked her best. That was possibly a minor detail, but a little power dressing always gave her the confidence she needed in difficult situations.

Her thoughts were on the meeting during the drive home. Noel seemed to gauge her mood and didn't try to involve her in any conversation, except for remarking on the beautiful views of the mountains when they stopped for coffee at a little café near Farranfore. They sat at a round table outside and Rose felt the warm breeze, the smell of coffee and newly baked buns soothing her troubled mind.

'You're very quiet,' Noel remarked. 'Anything wrong?'

'No. It's just that I have this meeting with the board this afternoon that Granny sprang on me, so I'm trying to prepare the ground in my head. Henri will be there, so it's going to be tricky.'

Noel nodded. 'I see. Prepare the ground for what exactly?'

'It's for Lily's garden centre and café, and also the walled garden she wants to restore. We think we could repair the old orangery and have the café there. It would be such a charming place to have coffee, surrounded by this lovely Regency garden that used to be there,' Rose explained. 'But it will add cost to the budget so the board might vote it down. Lily wants it to be like the Regency garden at Marley Park in Dublin. So we're both trying to add that plan into what's already in the budget.'

'Maybe you should try to raise some money?' Noel suggested. 'By doing an event that people would come to.'

'An event?' Rose looked thoughtfully at Noel. 'Like a fair or...'

'Or a concert?' Noel said. 'You could get Dominic's band and a few other local talents to perform and do a raffle as well and—'

'That's a great idea,' Rose exclaimed, feeling suddenly excited. 'I'll work on that and put it forward this afternoon. It would be a fantastic way of raising money, and have a bit of fun as well. We could have it in the garden beside the greenhouses, I'm sure Dominic could help us build a stage and...'

'Well, you need a plan B too, of course,' Noel warned. 'In case of rain, I mean.'

'Yeah, sure. Then we can hold it in what used to be the ballroom.'

'What is it now?' Noel asked.

'It's going to be a communal dining room and also a place to hold parties and events. And this will be the first one. You are so clever, Noel. Oh I can't wait to present this to the board.' Rose shot out of her seat. 'Let's get going. I have so much to do before this afternoon.'

She chatted all the way home about the idea while Noel nodded and smiled and threw in his own suggestions. When they drove in through the gates and pulled up outside the gatehouse, Rose felt she had a lot of things to say at the board meeting, which made her feel more confident that she would win her case. She smiled at Noel as he opened the door for her, then jumped out of the car, grabbed her bag and ran up the stairs. 'Thanks a million, Noel,' she called to him as he got back in. 'You've been a true star.'

'I was very glad to help,' he replied. 'Oh and... I was wondering... Why did Vicky text you last night? You didn't tell me all of it and I was curious. You looked a little startled.'

'Oh, nothing serious. We bumped into each other recently and exchanged phone numbers. As I said, she was asking if I was having fun at the wedding. And another thing...' Rose paused as a thought struck her. 'Just in case... Have you ever heard the name Melanie Blennerhassett?'

Noel looked at Rose for a moment. 'Melanie... Yes, that name rings a bell, I have to say.'

Rose felt a surge of excitement. 'Really? Who is she?'

'Hmm.' Noel frowned while he looked as if he was trying to remember. Then he shook his head. 'She must have been involved in some case or other. I'll look through my files and see if I can find the name.'

'Would you? Oh please let me know if you find anything,' Rose begged.

'Of course. Why is it so important?'

'I can't tell you yet. But please don't tell anyone about this.'

'Of course,' Noel promised. 'I won't tell a soul.'

'Thanks, Noel. I have to go now. So much to prepare. See you soon, I hope.' Then she ran inside without waiting for him to reply – so much was going through her head. She simply had to solve the mystery before Sylvia found out about the fake necklace. Ever since she'd learned that her necklace was a copy of the real thing, Rose had felt an urge to find out more. There had to be a fascinating story waiting to be told. And now there was this woman Vicky had told her about, who Noel thought he might know. She didn't quite know why, but she felt that if she found out what happened to the necklace, it would lead to other revelations that might be even more startling.

Rose spent the rest of the morning preparing for the meeting. She typed up a document on the computer with all the points she needed to raise – and the idea for raising funds. But as she worked, she suddenly had another idea, like a flash of lightning through her mind. *Oh yes!* she thought, feeling a dart of excitement, *why didn't I think of this before?* It was truly ingenious – something far better than a concert and easier to organise. And totally irresistible to any of the female board members. Henri wouldn't have a chance.

She smiled and nodded to herself, mentally clapping herself on the back. *This will be impossible for the board members to resist. Even the preparations alone will be so much fun. And what a hoot it would be...* She couldn't wait to announce this at the meeting.

**13**

---

Most of the board members were already sitting around the big table in what had been the formal dining room, back in the glory days of Magnolia Manor, when there had been a butler and maids to serve dinner to the family every evening. But, as Sylvia often said, they had to move with the times, using every room in a way that served the purpose of the new era that had just begun.

Rose found to her dismay that the only empty chair was beside Henri, who was looking annoyingly handsome in jeans and a pale pink shirt, his hair falling into his eyes. He had pulled out all the stops to look attractive to the female board members, Rose thought. Trying to appear cool, despite being slightly irritated as the scent of his aftershave wafted in the air, Rose settled in her chair. She smiled as she looked around the table. 'Hello,' she said. 'How nice to see everyone here. Sorry if I'm a little late.'

The board members – Arnaud, Sylvia, Lily, Henri and the three main investors – all murmured a greeting in unison. 'Lovely to see you, Rose,' Mrs Moore said, while the other two ladies simply smiled and nodded.

Henri cleared his throat. 'So,' he said. 'I would like to know why you have called this extra meeting on a Sunday, Sylvia.'

'Well,' Sylvia started, 'I thought it was a good idea as everyone was free. We want to put forward a few ideas that were not in the original plans.'

Henri nodded. 'Fine. Can we hear those ideas, then?'

'Of course,' Sylvia said. 'Lily, why don't you tell everyone what you told me about that walled garden and the café and the rest?'

Lily nodded. 'Right, well, this is what I thought we could do,' she said, unfolding a large sheet of paper with the outline of a garden. 'As you know, Dominic, my husband, is a structural engineer, and he drew up this plan for you all to see.' She went on to explain how she thought the Regency garden could look. 'And here,' she said, pointing at the plan, 'I thought we could put the café in the old orangery... It's already there so it won't involve a huge amount of construction. This was Rose's idea and I think it's brilliant.'

'The orangery is a complete wreck,' Henri interrupted. 'It would be very expensive to restore. And that garden... Even more money to start planting.'

'We can do a lot of the work ourselves,' Lily cut in. 'Dominic said he'd be willing to do some of the work for free, and Rose and I are going to do a lot of the planting.'

'We are?' Rose blurted out. 'Oh, of course. That's what we'll do,' she added after exchanging a look with Lily.

'I'd like to see that,' Henri said with a sarcastic twist to his mouth. 'Rose digging and planting and getting her hands dirty? Hmm.'

Rose glared at him. 'I'm able and willing to work hard for this. So I'd be grateful if you didn't jump to conclusions, Henri.'

'But I do think he's right about the money aspect,' Mrs Moore piped up, looking at Henri with a conspiratorial little smile. In her early sixties, with curly grey hair and a round face, she had obviously taken a shine to Henri. She was all smiles and dimples as she looked at him.

'I agree,' Linda Moriarty said as she flicked back her auburn hair. 'It seems too expensive, and our funds are already dwindling as it is.'

'I'd hardly call nearly a quarter of a million euros "dwindling",' Sylvia interrupted. 'But we could try to raise more money, all the same.'

'Exactly.' Rose jumped up and waved her piece of paper in the air. 'I have here a proposal for a fantastic event that would raise a lot of money for the Regency garden.'

'What kind of event?' Mrs Moore asked. 'Not a fair, I hope.'

'No,' Rose said. 'A fashion show.'

'What?' Henri exclaimed. 'I don't think—'

'If you could listen for a few minutes, I'll explain it all to you,' Rose interrupted, feeling she wanted to tell Henri to just shut up. But that would not be quite correct at a board meeting.

He leaned back and looked at her with an insolent air. 'Okay. Let's hear this brilliant idea.'

Rose stood there for a minute, gathering her thoughts. 'So,' she started. 'As I just said, I had this idea to do a fashion show here in the gardens if the weather is nice. If not, we could do it in the ballroom, which is nearly finished. The clothes would be from local shops and boutiques, which will be great exposure for all their brands. But not only that, we would also do a vintage event with clothes, both from our own collection and the new vintage shop in town that's just about to open. We would build a catwalk, which is not hard to do, and also put up long benches, or hire chairs. Then we could sell tickets at around twenty euros each and have raffles with prizes donated by the boutiques in the area and—'

'What about the models?' Linda Moriarty asked. 'Won't they charge an arm and a leg to model the clothes? Those girls don't get out of bed for less than ten thousand, I read somewhere.'

'Ah but they will,' Rose said, smiling at Linda. 'Because the models will be – *you*.' She made a sweeping gesture around the table. 'All of you could model the clothes if you want. Wouldn't it be nice to see normal women of all ages and sizes model clothes for everyone?' Rose drew breath and looked around the table for a reaction to her announcement.

'Oh,' Linda said, looking stunned. 'That makes a difference.'

'You bet it does,' Rose said. 'You'll all be amazing models.' She sat down, glancing at Henri, trying to gauge his reaction. 'What do you say to that, Henri?'

He smiled and shook his head. 'I'm not sure what I think at the moment. A different idea, I'll give you that. And not a bad one if you manage to do it. But I don't think you'll be able to pull it off.'

'Of course we will,' Rose said. 'I think the women all around Dingle will be happy to take part. Just for the craic and the dolling up and a chance to strut their stuff.'

'Will the clothes shop agree to this kind of marketing?' Henri asked. 'You can't be sure they will.'

'I think they'll jump at the chance of showcasing their collections,' Rose countered. 'There are so many small local businesses and handmade clothes shops, like the little boutique at the top of Green Street that sells printed silk scarves and dresses, and the shop with the crocheted hats and cardigans. Then we have Paquita, where they have those gorgeous T-shirts and skirts imported from Spain. I'd say the owners would love a chance for some extra exposure. It won't cost them anything.'

'But it will take a long time to put it all into practice,' Sylvia argued. 'I mean, to get the shops to agree, and get the clothes together, the models and the makeup and the sponsors—'

'Not at all,' Lily piped up. 'It's only early May, we can organise everything and have the show in six weeks, I'd say.'

'Really?' Henri looked doubtfully at Lily.

'Absolutely,' Rose said, feeling slightly wobbly about the

short time span. 'No problem at all. I've done this before in college,' she added. 'I did a course in dress-making and fashion, thinking I'd get into that field, but then went into real estate instead.' She sounded very sure of herself, despite feeling doubtful deep down. Would they really have everything ready in six weeks? There was so much to organise, and then there were all the other things she was managing to do with the renovation. One thing she did know was that it was the perfect excuse to get her close to uncovering the mystery of the necklace and Iseult Fleury. She could continue to go through the attic to find pieces for the show.

But how was she going to fit all that in? Maybe she had been too hasty in agreeing that the fashion show could be done in six weeks. But they had to, she realised. Otherwise the whole summer would be lost, and they wouldn't be able to start working on the garden and the orangery before the winter storms. She would have to try and remember how she organised that charity fashion show in college. It was more than a few years ago, but it had been a very successful event. She looked at Henri with what she hoped was confidence but, deep down, she didn't feel very positive at all.

'That'll be interesting to see,' was all Henri said. He looked around the table. 'I take it that it's useless to fight the inevitable. You all agree to this mad scheme, no doubt.'

'I think so,' Sylvia replied. 'But let's see a show of hands. All of you who agree, hold up your hand.'

Everyone except Henri raised their hands. 'It's a little bit of a *folie*,' Arnaud said, smiling as he raised his hand. 'But I like the idea.'

'Me too,' Sylvia said, and waved her hand in the air.

'What's mad about it?' Linda asked with a defiant look at Henri as she raised her hand. 'That we're going to model clothes for normal women?'

'No, of course not,' Henri mumbled. 'I was just thinking of

the short time to get it off the ground, that's all. But if you all say it'll work, I'm not going to stop you. But if you don't get the money together for the walled garden and the café in the orangery, I'm afraid I will not contribute from the accounts of Magnolia Senior Apartments.'

'You won't have to,' Rose said, sticking out her chin. 'Because it will all work fabulously and then you'll look more than a little foolish.'

'I'll hold you to that,' Henri said and picked up his phone. 'So... six weeks from now... That will bring us to the middle of June, is that right?'

'Let's say the twentieth,' Lily cut in. 'It's a Saturday and a lot of people will be on holiday in the area then. That should help to get a good crowd together.'

'Okay,' Henri said. 'Let's put the twentieth of June in the diary for this event. And I don't mind helping out in any way I can.'

'You don't?' Rose asked incredulously. 'After having poured cold water on the whole thing, you now want to help out?'

Henri shot her a wide grin. 'Yes, why not? If you can't beat 'em, join 'em is my motto.'

'Really?' Rose raised an eyebrow. 'In that case, I suppose you wouldn't mind modelling some of the menswear?'

'Er...' Henri's smile died. 'That sounds like a challenge. But why not?'

'My firm will provide the makeup,' Mrs Moore announced. 'We stock all the big brands. We could even try to get some of them to sponsor the event.'

'Oh brilliant,' Lily exclaimed. 'And Nora, Granny's former housekeeper, has a daughter who is a beautician. I'll ask if she could do the makeup for the women who'll be modelling.'

'It's all coming together amazingly well,' Rose said, feeling a lot more hopeful. 'Does anyone else have any other ideas?'

They all shook their heads.

'That's all settled then,' Sylvia said after a moment's silence. 'If there is nothing else, maybe we can end the meeting? Did anyone take notes?'

'Yes,' Mrs Moore said. 'I did. I'll type them up and email everyone later.'

'Thank you.' Sylvia rose from her chair. 'Arnaud, how about a walk before dinner? It's a nice evening.'

Arnaud got to his feet. 'Absolutely, dear Sylvia. But before we go, I just want to say to Lily and Rose, your ideas are wonderful. It will add a lot of interest to the gardens. I'm looking forward to a stroll through the Regency garden one day.'

They both thanked Arnaud and then everyone filed out of the dining room. As Lily had to rush home to feed Naomi, she kissed Rose on the cheek and promised to call her later.

Henri caught up with Rose as she walked through the door. 'Hold on,' he said. 'I want to ask you something.'

Rose stopped. 'Yes?'

'As you challenged me to be a male model for a day, how about you doing something for me?'

'Like what?' Rose asked suspiciously.

'Like having dinner somewhere nice on Tuesday night. Just to talk through our marketing plan and all the other stuff we need to get through. A business dinner, if you like. What do you say?'

Rose met his gaze levelly, although she was doubtful about his motives. She wasn't sure if she really wanted to go out with him, but she was too intrigued to refuse. 'Is this a dare?'

'If that's what you want to call it.'

She nodded. 'Okay. I'll go out to dinner with you. You're right, we do need to go through the business plan. Tuesday night is fine. Where are we going?'

'Cloghane,' he replied. 'It's a little village on the other side of Dingle.'

'I know where Cloghane is,' Rose said impatiently.

'I suppose you do,' Henri replied. 'The Harbour Pub there has great food. I'll pick you up at seven.'

'I don't want to be picked up. I'd prefer to meet you there.'

'But it involves driving over the Conor Pass,' he remarked. 'Maybe it would be better if I drove?'

'Why? she asked. 'Because I'm a little woman who doesn't know how to drive across a mountain pass?'

'No, but I thought... It's quite a challenging road, especially from the top. Hairpin bends and no barrier at the side. I don't like it myself.' He stopped and smiled. 'Oh okay, Miss Independent. In that case I can do a bit of surfing on Fermoyle beach beforehand. We'll meet at the pub at seven-thirty, if that suits you?'

'I'll be there.'

'Good. Don't dress up.'

'I'll wear my best wetsuit,' Rose said. 'But now I have to leave you. I'm going up to the storeroom. I need to put together material for the vintage part of the fashion show.'

'Sounds like hard work.'

'But very interesting. Bye, Henri. See you Tuesday.'

'Looking forward to it,' he said, before walking down the corridor to the main entrance.

Rose shook her head and went up the two flights of stairs to the attic and the storeroom. Whatever that was about, she would find out on Tuesday. She had no idea why Henri suddenly wanted to have dinner with her, but she had to admit that it would be interesting. *Who is he really?* she wondered as she continued up the stairs. *And when I find out, will I like him better – or maybe dislike him even more?*

## 14

Rose forgot all about Henri and the dinner as she delved into the attic. She found huge piles of papers, albums and boxes with knick-knacks, as well as leather suitcases with scarves, gloves and bits of fabrics from clothes that had been discarded long ago. They could be made into quilts, Rose thought as she put the nicest ones in little piles to be looked at later. Portraits in gold frames were stacked against the wall, and she studied each one, thinking they might be hung in the café – it would be a pity to hide them away. Some of them were a little eerie to look at, as she met the gaze of her ancestors who had lived at Magnolia Manor many years ago.

She smiled as she pulled out Cornelius's portrait. He looked so charming and mischievous, but what a calamity he had caused, she thought, remembering the near disaster his gambling had brought on the family. It had resulted in the present connection with the Bernard family.

Two of the portraits brought tears to her eyes – her grandfather Liam and her father, Fred, both of whom had been painted when they were young men. Rose remembered that they had hung in Sylvia's old study before the renovations. The oil paintings had been replaced by photographs, and no more Fleurys had adorned the walls of the manor after the tragedy.

Rose looked for any portrait of Iseult but found none. She must have been of less importance being the younger daughter. The painting of Maria Fleury, however, was leaning against the wall beside the bookcase. Rose studied it for a while, remembering how it had always fascinated her when she was a little girl. That black hair and the flashing dark eyes spoke to her in a strange way. Maria looked like a woman to be reckoned with. Had Iseult had her mother's personality, or had she been more demure? Rose remembered the steely look in Iseult's eyes in the later photos and felt that she must have been both adventurous and determined. What had happened to her? And was she the person who had had the copy of the necklace made? That question kept nagging at Rose, and she knew she had to find out soon.

As Rose was sorting the more interesting mementoes into piles, something fell out of a folder onto the floor. She picked it up and found that it was a photo of a family group against the backdrop of a big villa. She tried to figure out who they were, but the faces were so faded it was hard to see any features. All she could see was that the clothes they wore were from the early 1920s, with shorter skirts and bucket hats. As she kept looking at their faces, she could see that the woman in the middle, holding a baby, had a square chin and fair hair, just like Iseult.

Rose was so absorbed by the photo that she gave a start as the door suddenly opened and a voice called her name.

'Rose?' Sylvia peered in, looking concerned. 'You've been in here for hours. It's past dinnertime. What have you been doing here for so long?'

'Oh.' Rose was pulled out of her thoughts. 'I didn't realise it was so late. I got carried away by all the stuff, trying to decide what to include in the vintage part of the fashion show. And then I thought that there could be a display cabinet in the café with some of the more interesting items. But I stacked all the portraits over there, because I think they should all go on the walls of the orangery with little plaques explaining who they were and when they lived here.'

'That's a good idea,' Sylvia agreed. 'They will make a wonderful display. They should all certainly be hung in the orangery. It could be a whole wall of portraits through the years.'

Rose nodded. 'Exactly. And then we could have a few glassed-in display cabinets for the more interesting things, like old snuff boxes and candlesticks and brass bedwarmers and fun stuff like that, to show what life was like in the old days.' Rose paused. 'Maybe some of the less valuable jewellery could be in the fashion show?'

'Oh like costume jewellery from the nineteen twenties and thirties?' Sylvia asked. 'And old hats and fur boas, maybe? I put them away in boxes, but we can go through them and see what would be suitable.'

'Yes. That would be great.' Rose looked at her grandmother as a thought struck her. 'Talking about jewellery... Those lovely necklaces you gave us as gifts to keep... That wasn't what usually happened, was it?'

'No,' Sylvia said. 'They had to be returned on the death of the recipient. The pearls then went to the next eldest daughter and so on. Just so the pieces stayed within the Fleury family and weren't dispersed all over the place.'

'But you gave me and Lily and Vi the necklaces to keep.'

Sylvia nodded. 'I did. But that was because the manor had to come to the end of its present existence. Now there will be no more Fleurys in Magnolia Manor, so I thought you should keep those pieces and pass them on to your daughters or nieces as you wish. The house will still stand but be reborn in a whole new form. Sad, but at least the house will not be lost.'

'Or the gardens,' Rose filled in. 'The Fleurys will live on in the memories of all who knew them. But the next generations will want to know about the family who built the manor. That's why it would be good to have a display.'

'And the walled garden is going to be wonderful,' Sylvia remarked. 'What you and Lily are doing is truly wonderful, and I'm so grateful to you both.'

Rose smiled tenderly at her grandmother. 'That makes me so happy. I felt so strongly that we had to do it. Just so the family is not lost. I know you will live in Magnolia until the end, and maybe one of us will take over your part of the manor, but it will never be the same again. So this is a new beginning with a connection with the past.'

'Lovely,' Sylvia said. 'But now, my darling, you have to rest. Come and have something to eat in our kitchen, a glass of wine and a chat. Arnaud made a wonderful beef stew and I can heat up what's left.'

'Oh that sounds perfect. I'm actually starving.' Rose looked at the photo she was still holding and handed it to Sylvia. 'I just found this. Do you know who these people are? One of them looks like Cornelius's sister Iseult. But where was it taken? And when?'

Sylvia took her reading glasses from the top of her head and studied the photo. 'I have no idea. I've never seen it before. But it could be Iseult. I never met her though, so I can't say for sure.'

'Yes, but I saw those photos of her when she was young, and that woman looks so like her. The chin and the hair and the way she holds herself.'

Sylvia gave the photo back to Rose. 'Yes, she does look a little like Iseult, now that I think about it. Interesting. I can see that you're hooked on it all. But you have to give this a rest for now and come and have some supper.'

Rose wiped her hands on a rag. 'I will. Must clean up first though. I'm covered in dust.'

'You can use my bathroom. I'll go and heat up the stew for you.'

When Sylvia had left, Rose tidied up the stacks of photos and bits of paper as best she could, trying to get some kind of order in the storeroom. As she did, what she'd found out from her grandmother went through her mind. *So the necklace had to be returned when the recipient died*, Rose thought. *Maybe that's when the copy was made? So... All I have to do is to find out who died around the time it was made. I have to find the hallmark and look it up online. That will tell me when it was made and I can go from there...*

Rose ate a hurried supper in Sylvia's kitchen, itching to go home and look at her necklace. She had a glass of wine, declined the offer of dessert, kissed Sylvia – promising to let her know how the fashion show planning went – and ran out the door. Once at home in the gatehouse, she took out the necklace from its hiding place behind the bookcase in the living room. She peered at the tiny hallmark on the back of the clasp. After a little searching she saw that it was an 'e'. She went to her laptop to look it up online. She found that the 'e' on sterling silver meant the necklace was made in 1920. Strange that the jewellers didn't remark on that. But perhaps they just noticed that the necklace was fake and didn't bother to look. So 1920... was that when Iseult had died? It seemed unlikely, as she would only have been around forty years old then. But you never knew. She had to find out more about Iseult, and who had been given the necklace after her possible death... This search was becoming harder as time went on. Every clue seemed to lead to an impasse instead of a road ahead. It was so frustrating.

Rose put the necklace away, feeling disappointed, and went to bed, knowing she needed a good night's sleep to prepare for the week ahead. Mondays were always busy, as the builders and workmen would be looking at the plans and asking all kinds of questions. She also had to talk to all the shops that would be providing clothes for the fashion show, and have a chat with the owner of the vintage shop so they could decide how to combine the items from Magnolia Manor and their own stock. Then there was the dinner with Henri that she was looking forward to, with a feeling of both dread and anticipation. What would happen between them during their evening together? She had decided to be on her best behaviour. But would he?

## 15

Rose thoroughly enjoyed the drive to Cloghane, the little village on the north side of the Dingle Peninsula. The road up to the Conor Pass had recently been widened and was now an easy drive, if a little steep. But she knew the road down on the other side was still narrow and full of hairpin bends with no barrier in parts. A real challenge for any driver. But her little Volkswagen Polo was small enough to cope with the size of the road, even if she met cars coming the other way, and she felt confident she'd arrive safely.

Once at the top of the pass, Rose pulled up at the little carpark and got out of the car to admire the view before she carried on her journey. Up here, the wind was chilly, as usual, but the views of both sides of the peninsula so spectacular. To the south, she could see across Dingle Bay to the Iveragh Peninsula with the Ring of Kerry, and out to sea the Skelligs. To the north, she recognised Castlegregory, a lovely old village at the beginning of the Maharees, a peninsula of sand edged with long golden beaches, pushed flat and green into the deep blue water of Tralee Bay. She could also see in the distance the mountains, the long spine of the Slieve Mish mountains inland, the hills around Mount Brandon away in the west across Brandon Bay, outlined in dove grey and pink against the ever-changing sky. And the Atlantic spread out below, the intense blue meeting the sky at the horizon, waves crashing onto the rocks. It was dramatic and beautiful and Rose never tired of it, despite having looked at this view since she was a little girl. As she stood there, she wanted to spread out her arms like that famous *Titanic* scene, close her eyes and feel like she could sail away on the wind, far out to sea. But then she laughed at the idea, worried someone would see her, so she gave up the notion.

The cold wind bit into Rose's shoulders through her white linen shirt. She reluctantly got back into the car and shrugged on her blue fleece. It was time to drive down to Cloghane and meet Henri for their dinner date. On the way down, a low cloud shrouded the road momentarily in a mist, only to lift again. Rose found the mountainside empty. She drove down the narrow winding road with only a few sheep for company, through an ancient landscape, past the waterfall, as if lost in the mists of time. It was an eerie feeling and she could imagine donkeys loaded with supplies walking up the steep hill years before.

Then she was in the valley and turned down the narrow road that led to the charming village of Cloghane, with its old houses painted in vibrant colours, and hostels for hikers who'd climbed the steep slopes of Mount Brandon. She made her way down the slipway to the quays and parked in front of the Harbour Pub, where she could see Henri's car with his surfboard on the roof. This made her feel apprehensive, but here she was and there was no going back. At least she had come in her own car and could leave whenever she wanted if he was obnoxious.

'*Bonsoir*,' Henri said, standing just inside the door as she entered. He was dressed in a black polo shirt and jeans, with a white sweater across his shoulders. 'Nice evening, but the wind is cold.'

'Not as cold as on the Conor Pass,' Rose said as she shrugged off her fleece. 'I always stop there to look at the view when I come this way. It was freezing up there.'

'So do I,' he said. 'The view from there is so amazing.' He looked across the old pub with its timber floor and rough white walls. 'Not many people here yet. Let's get a table while we can.'

'Okay,' Rose said. 'Why don't we sit over there?' she suggested, pointing at a round table in an alcove. From there she could see the little harbour and the boats moored by the quay-side through the window.

'Good idea.' Henri led the way to the table and pulled out a chair for Rose. '*Voilá, mademoiselle.* Please sit down while I go and get some menus. There doesn't seem to be a waiter anywhere.'

'Thank you.' Rose sat down and peered out the window while she waited, enjoying the view. Lobster pots were piled up beside the boats, and there was a pile of nets and floaters by the little shed. Seagulls hovered in the air, though some of them were waddling across the paving, picking at bits of crab shells.

'Got some menus,' Henri said as he arrived back with two big cards, handing Rose one of them. 'Not much of a selection, but what they have is good, I've been told.'

'Mostly fish and seafood,' Rose said, scanning the list of dishes. 'Which I love. I see they have crab claws, one of my favourites, so I'll start with that. Then the grilled tuna.'

'And some white wine?' Henri asked.

'No. I'm driving.'

'Well I'm not, so I can indulge,' Henri said.

'You're not driving?' Rose asked, surprised.

'No. I'm staying at the hostel tonight. The surf will be great tomorrow, they said. So I decided to stay as I don't have to drive you home.' He grinned. 'Independent women are very handy sometimes.'

'Especially if the surf's up,' she quipped. 'You must be happy to have such a great choice of beaches around here. Fermoyle and the Maharees on this side of Dingle are great right now, after the spring storms.'

'Yes, they are,' he agreed. 'I sometimes go up the coast to Sligo as well. Fabulous surfing up there.' He looked around. 'Where is that waiter?'

'Right here,' a voice said beside them, as a tall young man arrived at their table. 'Sorry you had to wait, but it's early and we're getting things ready in the kitchen. What can I get you, lads?'

'"Lads"?' Henri asked haughtily, glaring at the young man. 'Is that a nice way to address customers?'

'Sorry, your lordship,' the waiter said, winking at Rose. 'I forgot my manners there. Didn't know you were royalty.'

Rose giggled. 'Hey, Henri, you have to get used to the way we speak around here.' She looked at the waiter smiling at him. 'It's not his fault. He's French and a little bad tempered at times.'

'Aren't we all?' the waiter quipped. 'Maybe it's the hunger getting to him. But we'll soon fix that. So,' he continued, 'what would you like to eat?'

'I'll have the crab claws and the grilled tuna to follow, please,' Rose replied. 'And just water for me as I'm driving.'

'And for monsieur?' the waiter asked, his lips quivering.

Henri didn't reply as he was still staring at the menu.

'Henri?' Rose met his angry gaze. 'What do you want? Come on, you have to order something.'

'Okay, I'll have the chowder and the fish and chips,' Henri muttered. 'Could I see the wine list?'

'We don't have one,' the waiter said. 'But we do have a very nice Pinot Grigio that most people seem to like. Or a nice Pinot Noir, of course, if you prefer red. That's our choice of wines.'

'Red? With fish?' Henri rolled his eyes. 'Oh, okay,' he continued when Rose glared at him. 'I'll have the white. Pinot Grigio.'

'Brilliant. Coming right up.' The waiter smiled and walked away.

'Did you have to be so rude?' Rose asked, still glaring at Henri.

He shrugged. 'I suppose not. It's just that I'm not used to the casual way people in restaurants treat you here. There's a politeness in France among service staff. It makes you feel taken care of in a way.'

'Taken care of?' Rose stared at him. 'You mean like an honoured guest or something? I find waiters in posh places quite snooty, to be honest. I prefer the friendly, casual way we have here. And it makes you feel you're on an equal footing. We're not better than that nice waiter in any way. I thought he was funny and he took your rudeness on the chin. Very professional, I have to say.'

'I'll apologise,' Henri said, looking only slightly contrite.

Rose nodded. 'Good.'

'So can we forget about it now?' Henri asked, smiling sweetly. 'You look very nice today. *Très chic*.'

Rose smiled, mollified by the compliment. 'Thank you. It's just an old shirt and a fleece.'

'Which you carry so well.'

Rose's eyes narrowed. 'What are you up to?'

'Why do you think I'm up to anything?'

'You're being nice and that makes me suspicious,' Rose replied. 'And asking me out on a date. What's that about?'

'I just wanted to get to know you better,' Henri said with an innocent air. 'And perhaps try to bury the hatchet.'

Rose opened her mouth to reply but was interrupted by the waiter bringing them their first course. 'Crab claws for the lady,' he said, putting a platter in front of her. 'And chowder for his lordship,' he continued, putting a steaming bowl in front of Henri. 'Drinks coming up.'

Henri looked at the waiter and cleared his throat. 'Hey, wait a minute. I just want to say sorry for being rude earlier. Didn't mean to upset you. I was just—' Henri shot a look at Rose '—being a bit snooty.'

'So you were,' the waiter said. 'But as you apologised so well, I'll forget all about it. No hard feelings at all.'

Henri nodded. 'Great. Thanks.'

'No problem. I'll go and get your drinks,' the waiter said with a little wink at Rose before he left.

'I'm so glad you did that,' Rose remarked. 'I couldn't have stayed here with you if you hadn't.'

'I know,' Henri said with a rueful smile. He picked up his spoon. 'So let's enjoy our dinner and talk, okay?'

'Oh yes.' Rose picked up a crab claw and dipped it into the little bowl with mayonnaise. 'Don't look. This could be messy. I don't think anyone could eat these in any other way.'

'I'll slurp my soup just to make you feel better,' Henri offered.

Rose had to laugh and suddenly she felt the ice had broken between them. Maybe Henri wasn't so bad. She felt like she could finally enjoy the evening. They started to talk while they finished their first course, about trivial things, and then about themselves. The wine seemed to cheer Henri up and, as the evening wore on, and the main course was eaten, he was relaxed, funny and much nicer than ever before. He told Rose about his childhood, how his mother had died when he was a small child, and how his father had been doing his best but seemed to bury himself in work to dull the pain of having lost his wife.

'My mother was much younger than him,' Henri explained. 'My father was in his forties when I was born, my mother only twenty-eight. He adored her and then, when she became ill with cancer and died soon after, he was devastated. Couldn't get over his grief, and really struggled to look after me. I think he found work more comforting than being with a child, so I had a number of childminders and nannies until I was old enough for boarding school.'

Rose put her hand on Henri's. 'How terrible to lose your mother when you were so young. I'm so sorry.'

He shrugged. 'Well, I don't actually remember much about it. I was only six years old and the memories of my mother faded with time. I didn't really miss *her*, I was only sad not to have a mother like everyone else. It made me feel different and inferior, somehow.'

'Yes,' Rose said. 'Exactly. I do know what you mean. I used to say that my father was away at sea when I was in school. Then I was told off for lying when my mother found out. But I was ashamed of not having a father like the other kids. Of course I understood later that some of my friends' parents were divorced, and their dads didn't spend much time with them. Must have been worse to not be loved than to have lost a father who really cared.' Rose sighed and sipped her water. 'Nobody escapes sorrows in life, do they?'

'I suppose not.' Henri looked at Rose with sympathy. 'But you lost both your father and grandfather at the same time. That must have been terrible.'

'Yes it was.' Rose paused. 'But I had my mother and grand-mother, who took great care of us and helped us through it all. My mother was so brave and Granny was amazing. Mum married again a few years later and now she lives in Donegal with my stepfather, who we like a lot. And you know how close to Granny we all are. So we're very lucky, really.'

'I think you're all so brave.'

'We have a lot in common, I think,' Rose remarked.

'Yes, we do.' Henri took a swig of wine and finished his fish and chips, then looked at Rose. 'But I know you are angry with me for some reason. I'd like to know why. It can't be because of that old story.'

'Why couldn't it?' Rose bristled, all her pent-up resentment towards him bubbling up to the surface. 'I'd like to know how you could do what you did to my grandmother.'

'You love her very much, I take it,' Henri said in a matter-of-fact voice.

'I adore her,' Rose replied. 'She was there for us after the accident. She was our rock then, and still is.'

Henri nodded. 'Yes, so you said. But I want to explain what happened at our end. We found out about your great-grandfather's gambling debt, and that he paid it by gifting Magnolia Manor to my grandfather by sheer accident. Our accountant was going through all the old papers and records when we were merging with another company. He was the one who suggested we take possession. We had no idea who you were or what Magnolia Manor was at all. The letter that was sent to your grandmother was drafted by him, and then I just read through it and signed it and it was posted. My father didn't know anything about it at all.'

'And you didn't stop to think how the recipient would feel when they got the letter?' Rose asked, her tone scathing. 'How very considerate of you.'

Henri looked a little guilty. 'Not very nice, I agree now that I know the details – and the people. Sylvia is a remarkable woman who has given my father a new lease of life. He told me how upset she was when she thought she was going to lose Magnolia Manor.'

'And that is why I'm so very angry with you.' Rose met Henri's gaze, her eyes blazing.

'How about forgiving me?' he asked.

'How about apologising first?' Rose retorted. 'If you do, I'll think about forgiveness.'

'I have apologised,' he said quietly. 'To her.'

'You did? Really?' Rose asked incredulously. 'She never said anything about it to me.'

'It was between her and me. We were on our own and we had a long talk. She was very nice about it.'

'When did this happen?' Rose couldn't believe her grandmother hadn't told her about it.

'When she came back from France.' Henri made an impatient gesture. 'Why is this so hard to believe?'

Rose shook her head. 'I do believe you, but I can't understand why she didn't tell me, when she knew how angry I've been with you.'

'And now?' he asked. 'Are you still angry?'

'I don't know,' Rose said, feeling confused. 'I have to think about it.'

He leaned forward and put his hand on hers, fixing her with his eyes. 'I hope you can come to terms with it. And I hope you can accept my apology to you, too. Rose, I'm sorry I caused all this sorrow and stress. It was the wrong thing to do. I know that now.' He took his hand away and leaned back. 'There. I said it. I meant it. But it wasn't easy, you know.'

'I'm sure it wasn't,' she said, still affected by the touch of his hand and the look in his eyes. It told her he truly wanted them to be friends.

'So we're good?' he asked, looking a little unsure. 'You forgive me?'

She smiled. 'Yes. Thank you. I accept your apology. And I forgive you.'

'Great.' He returned her smile, looking relieved. 'So then we can be friends and continue teasing each other?'

'Why not?' Rose suddenly felt a surge of warmth towards Henri. He had been honest with her, she felt, and had meant his apology. The story of his childhood was sad, and she realised he must have grown up with very little love from a father who had escaped his sorrow by burying himself in work. He'd built a business that had been very successful while ignoring his little boy who needed him. 'How do you get on with your father now?' she asked.

'My father? We get on well now after all these years. He's told me he regretted neglecting me and we've become closer, which is good. But he didn't approve of me writing that letter to your grandmother, and he was very angry when he found out about it. But it was all resolved in the end. Everyone's happy now, all thanks to Sylvia and her project, really. It's going to be very successful. We're planning to create more senior apartments in other areas of Ireland, actually. But that's all in the future.'

'I didn't know that,' Rose said, amazed at what he had just said. 'Does this mean you also approve of Lily's and my plans? For the walled garden and the café in the orangery, I mean.'

'Approve, yes,' he said. 'But I still think you should fund it yourselves. Most of it anyway. We'll see how much cash you can raise with the little fashion show.'

Rose was going to say something scathing but then realised he was goading her. 'Okay.' She smiled sweetly at him. 'It's going to be a huge success and we'll have to turn people away.'

'Can't wait to see it,' he said, meeting her smile with one of his own.

'And you'll take part?' Rose asked.

'As a model?' He shook his head. 'No thanks. I have this gammy knee, you see. Twisted it while surfing in Biarritz last year. Intermittent limp. Could play up on the catwalk and then it would make you look bad.'

Rose lifted an eyebrow. 'Really? Never seen you limp.'

'I've been lucky lately.'

Rose let out a snort. 'Yeah, right. But never mind. I don't think you're model material anyway. You're too short.'

'And you're too transparent,' he retorted. 'I'm over six foot. How tall do you have to be?'

Rose laughed. 'Oh, okay. I think you won that one.'

He raised his glass. 'Who cares? We're having fun and we've buried the hatchet. Cheers to that.'

Rose lifted her glass of water and clinked it against Henri's wineglass. 'Cheers, Henri, This date has been great fun. Thank you for being so brave and saying sorry. That felt really good.'

'So we can be friends?' he said in a tone that hinted at something else.

'Friends sounds great,' Rose replied.

He nodded. 'I agree. That's a good start anyway.'

There was a calm between them after that. Henri talked about his love of surfing and Rose told him about her former career, how she had loved finding the right houses for her clients. As the evening wore on and the sun dipped behind Mount Brandon, they walked barefoot on the beach for a while, just enjoying the fresh wind from the sea, the warm air and the sand between their toes. Then Rose told Henri she had to go home, as she wanted to see the sunset from the top of Conor Pass and then drive home before it became too dark.

'That's a good plan,' he said. 'And I'll go and meet my surfing buddies in the pub later before I go to bed. We'll get up early to catch the waves as the tide comes in.'

'I'm sure you'll enjoy that,' Rose said. 'Both the pub and the waves.'

'Yes, I think both will be great.'

He walked with her to the car and opened the door for her.

'Thanks for dinner,' Rose said. 'Next time it's on me.'

'I'm glad you want to do this again. But we forgot all about work, didn't we? The website and all that, I mean.'

'We can do those things online. The website is nearly done anyway,' Rose replied. 'We need to adjust it a bit and add a few links and then it can go live. I'll get onto the firm's web designer and ask him to help. We're handling the rentals after all.'

'Sounds good. Are you sure you should be driving across

Conor Pass so late?' he asked. 'The road through Anascaul is safer.'

'And miss the sunset? I'll be fine. I've driven up that road hundreds of times.' Rose started the engine. 'I'll be in touch. Have fun tomorrow.' He waved as she drove up the slipway, and she waved back as she turned onto the road.

Rose felt a huge sense of relief as she went through their conversation. The apology she had wanted for over a year had been made and she had forgiven him, simply because he seemed genuinely sorry. Now she could leave all that in the past and move on, have a real friend in Henri. She had a good feeling after their long talk. It was as if she had found, if not a brother, a kind of family member she would come to like and trust.

# 16

Rose put all thoughts of Henri away as she drove along the narrow winding road up the mountainside to Conor Pass. She had wanted to see the sunset, but now black clouds were rolling in above her. She suddenly found herself enveloped in a thick fog. She could see the grassy verge and felt relatively safe as it guided her along, but if she met another car coming the other way, she'd be in trouble.

Rose held the steering wheel so tight her nails dug into her palms. Cold sweat began to break out on her forehead. Then, suddenly, there was a clap of thunder and rain started to smatter against the windscreen. 'Oh, great,' Rose muttered, staring ahead, trying to figure out how far she was from the top. Once there, she would feel safer as she began the descent on the other side, where the road was wider. But when she was nearly at the top, the car suddenly started to wobble and she knew the worst had happened. A flat tyre. Just her luck. She made it to the top and managed to pull up. Then she got out, into the downpour, to take a look – she was soaked in seconds. But her suspicions were confirmed and she could see the tyre was completely flat. Shivering, she got back inside. While the wind shook the little car and the sound of the rain was nearly deafening, Rose took her mobile out of her bag and saw the battery was nearly at zero. She'd have to act fast if she was to call for help. She was about to dial Lily's number, hoping Dominic could come and rescue her, when the phone rang.

'Hello,' Rose croaked. 'Whoever it is, please help me. I have to talk fast because my phone is dying.'

'What's wrong?' a voice asked. 'Rose, this is Noel, what's the matter?'

'Oh Noel,' Rose said, and burst into tears. 'I'm at the top of Conor Pass,' she sobbed. 'It's raining and I just got a flat tyre and I don't know what to do.'

'What are you doing there in this weather?' Noel asked.

'I had dinner with Henri in Cloghane,' Rose explained.

'You were on a date with him? And he let you drive home alone?' Noel asked, sounding angry.

'No, not really. It wasn't a date and I wanted to...' Rose stopped. 'I'll explain later.'

'Oh never mind,' Noel said. 'Sit tight, I'm on my way.' He hung up.

Rose sat there, shivering, wondering how long it would take Noel to come and rescue her, mentally kicking herself for being so stupid. She should have checked the weather report and taken the longer way through Camp and Anascaul as Henri had suggested. It would have taken another half hour, but at least she wouldn't have ended up with a puncture in the pouring rain. And she should have made sure her phone was charged. 'I'm so stupid,' she said out loud. 'Why did I drive up here thinking I'd see the sunset?' She said a prayer that Noel would get here soon, before the weather got even worse. The loud claps of thunder were terrifying, but at the same time she was fascinated by the forked lightning over Dingle Bay, illuminating the water and the mountains again and again. Eventually the thunder died away, but the rain kept beating and the wind shook the little car.

Rose knew Noel lived in Anascaul, so she assumed it would take him a while to get to her. But then, only minutes later, she saw the headlight of a car coming nearer and nearer until it was right beside her. She saw a dark figure getting out, then her door opened and she heard Noel shouting against the wind.

'Get into my car,' he ordered. 'We have to leave yours here for the night. There is no way I could change a tyre in this weather.'

'Okay.' Rose gathered up her handbag and got out, bracing herself against the wind that threatened to sweep her off the mountain. Noel held the door open for her and, shivering, she got in and sat in the passenger seat.

Noel closed the door to Rose's car and got in beside her. 'There's a fleece on the back seat. Take off your wet things and put it on. It's too dark for me to see you,' he added as he started to drive off.

Rose took off her wet sweater and shirt and put on the dry fleece, which instantly warmed her. 'Thank you so much for coming, Noel. You're a star. How did you get here so fast?'

'I was still at the office. Working late on a brief. I called you just to see how you were getting on with your research, and thought I'd tell you about that woman you asked me about. What were *you* doing up the Conor Pass so late?' His voice was barely audible over the noise of the rain and the swishing of the windscreen wipers.

'I told you. I had dinner in Cloghane. With Henri.'

Noel whipped his head around and stared at her for a moment. 'On a date with Henri? I thought you hated him.'

'It wasn't a date,' Rose exclaimed. 'I told you before. We just had dinner and a chat. And I don't hate him now. I kind of did before. But he wanted to make amends by taking me out to dinner. Bury the hatchet, he said.' Rose thought about what had occurred during the dinner. 'He apologised for what he did to us and I think he meant it. I said I forgave him, which seemed to make him happy. He wants the Magnolia project to be successful and that won't happen if we don't get on.'

'That's true. Arguing is very bad news if you're working with someone,' Noel said, sounding calmer. He glanced at Rose. 'So you had a good time, then?'

'Oh yes,' Rose said, smiling. 'I discovered that he's very nice really, and funny too. Such a relief that we can be friends now. And maybe go to the pub or go to the beach together and everything.'

'Not very nice of him to let you drive across the Conor Pass on your own, though,' Noel muttered.

'That was my decision. He stayed the night in Cloghane because he wants to do some surfing today. We had a lovely walk on the beach before I left.'

'Did you hear the curlew when you were there?' Noel asked. 'I've heard they nest there in the spring.'

'Eh, no,' Rose said, smiling at his passion for birds at all times. 'I mean, I might have if I was looking out for it.'

'I see. But why did you drive home that way instead of taking the road to Anascaul? Didn't you hear the weather report?' Noel sounded suddenly cross again.

'No, I forgot to turn on the radio,' Rose said, feeling a little foolish. 'I wanted to see the sunset on the way home.'

'But you got a thunderstorm instead. Must have been spectacular.'

'It was, actually. I'd have enjoyed it if I hadn't been so scared. I thought I'd have to spend the night up there. My phone was nearly dead too, so I wouldn't have been able to call for help. Lucky you called before it died.'

'Very lucky. Sorry I couldn't fix the tyre tonight.'

'Of course not,' Rose agreed. 'I'll get on to the garage in the morning and get someone to go up there with me.' She paused for a moment, remembering what Noel had just said. 'What was that about the woman? What woman?'

'The one you asked me about. Melanie Blennerhassett. You asked if I'd heard the name before. I thought maybe, but then something popped into my head. There was a court case in Cork recently. A woman by that name was suing someone for something a few months ago. I read about it in *The Examiner*. One of my lawyer friends was representing her. I'll look it up for you and let you know the details.'

'That would be great,' Rose said.

'Why are you so interested in her?'

'It's a bit complicated,' Rose started. 'But I believe she had something to do with a member of my family. Iseult Fleury, my great-grandfather's sister. It's a long story.'

'Oh?' Noel looked suddenly intrigued. 'Iseult Fleury? The famous Cornelius's sister? What do you know about her?'

'Not much,' Rose replied. 'I'm trying to trace her life story. She seems to have had quite a fascinating life.'

'You must tell me about it sometime. Have you started the research yet?' Noel asked as they reached the outskirts of Dingle town. The rain had eased, the wind had dropped and the moon had come out of the clouds, the light reflected in the wet pavement.

'Yes,' Rose replied. 'It's going to be a part of that plan I have for the manor. I'm planning a fashion show, and I want to put a lot of the manor's history into the event. I think I'll take you up on the offer of help, actually. I could do with another pair of hands and someone with good eyesight.'

'I'd be delighted,' Noel said, smiling broadly. 'I love history and looking at old photos.'

'Me too.' Rose felt a surge of affection for this tall, considerate man. With his square jaw and strong features, he wasn't conventionally handsome, but there was such a sweet expression in his face as if he expected everyone to be nice. With him, she could be herself without trying to impress. He seemed to like her as she was, even now, with her wet hair and all her makeup washed away by the rain. She knew he'd be a great help with her research and that they would work well together.

They drove across the bridge, up the road and then turned into the lane leading to Magnolia Manor. Noel pulled up outside the gatehouse. 'Here we are,' he said, opening the door on his side.

Rose put her hand on his arm. 'Don't get out. I can manage. I'll just take my wet clothes and my bag. Is it okay if I give you back the fleece tomorrow?'

'Of course.'

'Great. Thank you so much for rescuing me, Noel.' Rose leaned over and gave him a hug. 'You're the best.'

'Oh, shucks,' Noel stammered, his face red. 'It was nothing. Very happy to help.'

'And I'm so happy you did. I'll be in touch.' Rose got out of the car and slammed the door shut. 'Safe home,' she shouted before he drove off.

She stood there for a moment, as the rear lights of his car disappeared through the gates. *What was that?* she thought, remembering the feel of his strong chest through the rough wool of his sweater, which smelled faintly of turf smoke and soap. *Why am I suddenly feeling like this? Why did I want to stay in that old Ford and talk to him for another while? Good old dependable Noel, a friend in need... But also a charming, attractive man with no notions or feelings of self-importance. A man who's ready to drive through a storm to rescue a girl stuck on the top of a mountain...*

She laughed at herself and ran up the steps to the front door, happy to be home safely. Of course she would have warm feelings towards Noel. Such a dear, sweet man who had been there when she needed help. But not someone she could fall in love with. Or could she? She shook her head as she opened the door and went inside. No, not her type at all. She was just tired and emotional. It was time to go to bed and forget all about romance and men. The only thing she should concentrate on was the new project and finding out about that woman. Noel had said he'd get all the details of the court case. Maybe that would throw some light on the mystery of the fake necklace...

# 17

After getting Dominic to help with the car, Rose spent the next few days working through the accounts and marketing campaign for the senior apartments, the first of which would soon be ready for rent. Then there was the fashion show, and asking clothing shops to make their summer collections available, which they readily agreed to. The manager of the new vintage shop was delighted to help out with the clothes for that part of the show. She'd gone through the clothes with Rose, who was happy to spend a little time rummaging through everything, from Victorian and Edwardian clothes to the 1920s and '30s. Recruiting models was about to start as well through a Facebook page Rose had set up. Then the continuing work on the manor, which now included putting a laundry in the basement area that used to be the kitchen in the old days. The tenants of the flats would be able to do their washing there instead of having their own washing machines in their flats, which would take up too much space. This was Sylvia's idea that she had picked up from a Scandinavian property magazine. The cost of the laundry would be added to the rent of the apartments. Nobody objected to this addition, and it was voted through by the board at another meeting.

Rose was hoping to hear from Noel about the Blennerhassett woman, but he hadn't been in touch. Vicky, who was helping out with the fashion show, had said he was very busy at the moment. So Rose decided not to bother him and to keep going with her research on her own.

Lily was also trying to get the walled garden project started, and had brought in a landscape architect who had laid out plans using old drawings they had found in the storeroom. Rose agreed that it would be wonderful to recreate the original walled gardens that had been laid out around the time Magnolia Manor was built.

'All settled, then,' Lily said when the landscape architect had left and they were walking back to the manor. 'How are the preparations for the fashion show going?'

'All right I think. I hope we get together a good group of models,' Rose said, pulling her phone from the pocket of her jeans. 'I'll take a look at the Facebook page. Vicky said she'd manage it.' The phone pinged. 'That could be her. Oh no, it's from Noel,' Rose exclaimed and read the message.

*Found the woman. Call me when you have a moment and I'll tell you all about her.*

'What woman?' Lily asked, looking at Rose's phone over her shoulder.

'A woman called Melanie Blennerhassett,' Rose explained. 'I'm doing some research about the Fleury women for the fashion show, and this woman seems to have been connected to our family in some way.'

'What way?' Lily asked.

'It's to do with Cornelius's sister Iseult,' Rose replied. 'But I don't have all the details yet, so I can't tell you much.' She knew she should tell Lily the truth, but she couldn't bear to do it just yet. Not until she had the full story.

Lily kept staring at Rose. 'What's going on?' she asked, looking suspicious. 'You're hiding something. I can tell. You have that guilty look.'

'I can't say anything about it right now,' Rose said. 'I have to get to the bottom of this first. It's something a bit complicated.'

Lily sighed. 'Oh okay. I can tell it's useless to ask anything else. In any case I have to go. I left Naomi with Granny. She was asleep in her pram so hopefully she stayed that way. The baby, not Granny,' she added.

Rose laughed. 'I figured that. I have to call Noel. I'll see you later.'

'Okay,' Lily said and walked away.

Rose sat down on a tree stump and dialled Noel's number. 'Hi, it's Rose,' she said when he answered. 'Tell me about the woman or I'll explode. Who is she? Where is she? How can I get in touch with her?'

'Hold on.' Noel laughed. 'Calm down. I'll tell you what I've found out.'

'Okay.' Rose took a deep breath and tried to steady her nerves. 'Go on.'

'Melanie Blennerhassett lives in Cork city. She recently slipped on some spilled oil at a garage and sustained a fractured ankle. She sued the garage and got thirty thousand in damages. If you want to get in touch with her, I'll give you the address. Can't give you the phone number but, if she has a landline, it would be easy to look it up. A mobile number would be more difficult to find.'

'I know. So let's hope she's the old fashioned type with a landline,' Rose said. 'Wow, thirty thousand,' she added. 'Must have made her feel a lot better.'

'I'd say it did,' Noel agreed. 'May I ask what this is about?'

'You may ask, but...' Rose stopped. She was about to say it was a secret, but then felt she needed to tell someone she could trust. Noel was her best bet. 'I'll tell you next time we meet. If you're free tomorrow, I'd love some help with sorting out stuff in the family archives. It's going to rain, so a good time to be indoors.'

'I'm glad to see you're checking the weather report,' Noel remarked.

'Yes. It's my new hobby,' Rose quipped. 'I've learned from my mistake. I check it every day now, just in case there is another storm on the horizon.'

'Good idea.' Noel paused. 'I'm free tomorrow afternoon, if that suits you. Whatever the weather.'

'Yes, brilliant. Could you be here after lunch? So much to get through.'

'Looking forward to it,' Noel said. 'Can't wait to hear what the secret is all about. I'll text you that address. See you then, Rose.'

'Oh,' Rose said, as a thought struck her. 'I'd like to ask Vicky if she knows anyone who might have a phonebook for Cork. She has family there. Just to see if I can find that woman.'

'Look it up online,' Noel suggested. 'If there is a landline at that address, you'll find it in the yellow pages. I'll look it up and text it to you straight away.'

'Okay. That's terrific. Thanks. See you tomorrow.' Rose hung up.

The text came a few minutes later and Rose left the walled garden to go home and look it up on her laptop. A message from Vicky told her that there were a lot of responses to the modelling search, and they had to pick the best ones the following morning. *We'd better close the page soon or we'll be in trouble*, Vicky said in her text message, which made Rose laugh. They needed around ten models, but over fifty women had volunteered, so it would take a lot of diplomacy to pick the right ones and turn the rest away. But that was something Vicky could easily deal with, Rose decided. She was good at dealing with people.

It didn't take long to find a phone number that went with the name and address Noel had given Rose. Her heart beating like a hammer, she dialled the number.

A woman's pleasant voice answered after a few minutes. 'Hello?'

'Is this Melanie Blennerhassett?' Rose asked.

'Yes, that's me,' the woman replied. 'Who is this?'

'Oh, eh... My name is Rose Fleury and I'm an antiques expert,' Rose lied. 'I specialise in vintage jewellery.'

'Really?' Melanie Blennerhassett said, sounding mystified. 'What does that have to do with me?'

'Well, the thing is, I saw a photo of you in *OK! Magazine*. You were at birthday party for...'

'Ben McWilliams, the golf champion?' Melanie filled in. 'That was a while back. So...'

'You were wearing a necklace that looked very old. Topazes and pearls, I think...'

'Oh yes, of course I was.' Melanie laughed. 'It looked lovely in the photo, I thought. The light made the stones shine, don't you think?'

'Oh yes,' Rose agreed. 'The necklace really suited you.'

'Thank you. That's nice to hear.'

'So I was wondering,' Rose continued. 'If you could tell me where you got this beautiful necklace? Is it a family piece or...'

'Not at all,' Melanie said, laughing. 'My family has nothing like that. Or anything at all, really. I borrowed it from a friend. Had to give it back the next day, more's the pity. She inherited it from a great-aunt or something. Been in the family for generations.'

'Oh.' Rose frowned, feeling awkward. This was harder than she had thought. 'And who is this friend, if you don't mind my asking?' she finally managed. 'Sorry if I seem nosey, but that necklace caught my interest.'

'Of course it would, if you're into vintage stuff,' Melanie said. 'Her name is Penny Lincoln. I'm sure she wouldn't mind showing you the necklace or sending you a photo or something. I don't want to give out her number without permission, but I'll get her to call you if you like.'

'That would be great,' Rose said, her spirits rising. 'Please do.'

'Okay, then,' Melanie said, sounding as if she wanted to hang up. 'I'll ask Penny to call you as soon as she can. Your number is displayed on my phone.'

'Oh great. Thank you so much,' Rose said.

'You're very welcome. But I'm afraid I have to go now.'

'Of course. Thanks for helping out,' Rose said. 'Bye, Melanie.'

'Bye,' Melanie said and hung up.

Rose sat on the tree stump thinking about what she had just learned. Someone called Penny Lincoln owned the real necklace. But who was she and, more importantly, from whom had she inherited the necklace? It was making her dizzy to think about it. Rose got up, deciding to get back to her many tasks, the fashion show, the website and the sorting of memorabilia to include in the visitors' centre. She had finally agreed on the website design – it would be up and running the following week – so at least that was not on her agenda. It meant she could spend the weekend going through the family archives. As if pulled by an invisible force, Rose walked to the big house, through the entrance door and up the two flights of stairs to the attic room that held so much history. And so many secrets.

# 18

By Saturday afternoon, Rose, sitting on a rickety chair, had managed to go through a huge number of old photos, postcards, railway tickets, theatre programmes, political pamphlets, address books and other paraphernalia in the attic. A lot of what she found didn't help with her search for the truth about the necklace. But she knew the photos needed to be put in chronological order, if she had any chance of figuring out which ones might tell her more about Iseult. And help her choose what would go in the fashion show.

'It's a nightmare,' she complained to Noel, who had turned up after lunch. 'Just look at all the photos all the way from the eighteen eighties. How on earth can I date everything?'

Noel took a box full of photos from a shelf and sat down on a stool beside her. 'I know it's hard, but why not look at the clothes and the cars and the horses and the background? You don't have to be precise, just make a stab at it.' Noel took a photo of a family group from the stack in the box. 'Look at this one, for example. It was taken at the front of the house. There is no ivy on the walls, and the magnolia tree is quite small. Also, look at the ladies.

They are wearing dresses with bustles at the back. So it has to have been taken in the early eighteen eighties.'

Rose took the photo from Noel and studied it in the light from the window. 'You're right. And I know the magnolia tree was replanted sometime then, so it has to be that period.'

'Of course,' Noel agreed. 'Do we have folders to put the photos in?'

'Yes.' Rose pointed at a pile of folders on the small table by the bookcase. 'I bought those to do just that. Didn't know how to mark them though.'

'Why don't you put eighteen eighty to nineteen hundred,' Noel suggested. 'Then sort the rest into twenty-year periods or something, unless you're sure of the date.'

'Good idea,' Rose said, cheering up. 'In any case, we're only going to include the most interesting photos in the display. We also have a number of portraits that are really lovely, and then the items like snuff boxes, ladies' hats, gloves and shoes and evening bags that are like works of art, with embroidery and sequins and pearls. Some of them could be used in the vintage section of the fashion show.'

'Good,' Noel said absentmindedly while he studied the photos. 'I do love these. Look at the men and their huge moustaches. And those tall top hats that look like chimneys.'

Rose glanced at the photo and laughed. 'I know. They look so funny. It was all so formal then.'

'White tie and tails every evening, and all the ladies in pretty gowns and all their jewellery. Ladies' maids and valets and the whole shebang just to eat their dinner.' Noel handed her another photo. 'This one is interesting. It's a family group that seems to have been taken around nineteen twenty or so. The woman holding the baby is beautiful. Reminds me a bit of you. But it seems to have been taken outside some other big country house. It's a nice house, but not as big as Magnolia Manor. I wonder who they are?'

Rose took the photo and studied it for a moment. It was of a man, a woman, a little boy and a baby, and it was similar to the other one she had found, where the faces had been difficult to make out. This one was clearer and she immediately recognised the young woman. 'It's Iseult, my great-grandfather's sister,' she said excitedly. It was the first time she'd spotted Iseult that day. 'Nobody really knows what happened to her. She seems to have disappeared from the family archives around the beginning of the twentieth century. But here she is, with a family. But who are they? Her own children or someone else's?' Rose turned the photo to look at the back. 'Oh,' she said. 'Something is written here, but I can't quite make it out.'

Noel took the photo and went to the window, peering at the back of the photo. 'It says... "Willowbrook House, summer of nineteen twenty-one. The... something family." Can't see the name clearly. Starts with a "L" and ends with an "n".'

'Oh!' Rose suddenly exclaimed as something popped into her mind. A memory of a name she had heard recently... 'Could it be... Lincoln?' she asked.

Noel kept looking at the faint name with a strange expression. 'Yes, I think it is now that I look at it again... You're right. Definitely Lincoln. And Willowbrook House...'

'Gosh,' Rose whispered, feeling suddenly faint. 'That name... Lincoln. What does that mean?'

Noel looked at her with concern. 'Rose? Are you okay? You're very pale. Does that name mean something to you?'

'Yes... It's just that...' Rose started. 'I think I'd better tell you what's going on.'

Noel sat down on the stool again. 'Only if you want to. Will I get you some water first?'

'No thanks, I'm fine.' Rose took a deep breath. 'There's something I should tell you. I haven't told anyone about this, but I feel I have to now. I haven't said anything to Granny or Lily, so...'

'It'll be between you and me,' Noel assured her. 'I see that you're very troubled by whatever it is.'

'Yes,' Rose said. 'I am.' She paused, wondering for a brief moment if she should go on. But she had to share it with someone, and she trusted Noel. 'You see, just before the wedding, I found out that my necklace is a fake. A copy made sometime in nineteen twenty.'

Noel stared at her, looking shocked. 'Fake?' he said. 'Are you sure?'

Rose nodded. 'Yes. It was the woman in the vintage jewellery shop who told me. They are experts, so there's no doubt. I also found the hallmark stamp, which says it's silver not white gold, and the topazes are glass as are the pearls.' Rose drew breath, tears welling up in her eyes. 'It was such a shock.'

'I can imagine.' Noel put a hand on Rose's shoulder. 'I'm so sorry. But go on.'

'Then a weird thing happened,' Rose continued, recovering her composure. 'I showed the necklace to Vicky, pretending it was real, and she told me she had seen a woman wearing the same necklace in a magazine. And that was Melanie Blenner-hassett.'

'Oh,' Noel said. 'So that's why you were looking for her.'

'Yes,' Rose replied. She looked at Noel for a moment, feeling relieved to have finally shared what had been weighing on her mind. He was still looking as if he was trying to take it all in.

He shook his head. 'What a strange thing to happen,' he mumbled as if to himself.

'Really weird,' Rose agreed. 'Oh, it's such a relief to share this with someone. I don't want to tell Granny until I find the real necklace, she would be so upset.'

'She'd be devastated,' Noel agreed. 'But go on. What happened next?'

'Thanks to you, I found Melanie and talked to her. She said she'd borrowed the necklace from a friend called Penny Lincoln, and that she'd give this woman my number, but she hasn't called yet. Maybe she never will,' she concluded miserably.

'Maybe not,' Noel said. 'And you can't demand that she does. If the necklace she has looks similar, it might not be the same one at all. It can be hard to tell from a photo. Have you thought of that?'

'Yes.' Rose paused for a moment. 'But Vicky said she had seen it in an issue of *OK! Magazine* when she was at the hairdressers. She swore that necklace she saw in the photo was identical to mine. That's all I know.'

'And that yours is a fake.' Noel thought for a moment. 'Maybe we could try to find that magazine. Which hairdresser was it? They might still have it.'

'Vicky said she'd go back and look for the magazine, but she must have forgotten. I'll call her and ask her which one it is. And then we'll go there and see if we can find it.'

'Good idea.' Noel rose and put the photo on top of the others in the box. 'I'll take a look through these while you talk to her.'

'Okay.' Rose took her phone from her handbag and quickly called Vicky. 'Hi,' she said. 'I was wondering if I could ask you something?'

'Yes?' Vicky said. 'What?'

'Remember how you said that you'd seen the identical necklace to mine in a magazine you read at the hairdressers?'

'Of course I remember. Oh no, I was supposed to go and look for the magazine,' Vicky said. 'But there was so much going on that I forgot.'

'I thought you might have,' Rose said. 'So then I was thinking I'd see if I could find it and take a look myself.'

'You want to know which hairdresser?' Vicky filled in. 'Yeah, great idea. I went to that one near the post office. It's called the Witches' Hut for some reason. Not that I saw any witches.' Vicky laughed. 'But that's the name of it. Small place but they're good. Could recommend it, actually.'

'Great, thanks,' Rose said. 'You don't happen to know which issue it was?'

'I think it was the March issue. Yes, now that I remember, it was all about St Patrick's Day and the parades and stuff. Has a photo of Mary Kennedy on the cover. She looked lovely.'

'Okay.' Rose checked her watch. 'It's nearly four o'clock. I hope they're still open on a Saturday.'

'They close at five on Saturdays,' Vicky said. 'I hope you find the picture. Let me know if that necklace is the same as yours.'

'I will,' Rose promised. 'Thanks again, Vicky. Let's catch up soon.'

'Looking forward to it,' Vicky said. 'Bye, Rose.'

'The Witches' Hut,' Rose said to Noel when she had hung up. 'Next door to the post office.'

'Let's go,' Noel said. 'I'll drive.'

Rose didn't argue. As his car was parked outside the manor, they jumped in and drove off quickly. 'We have to get there before five,' Rose said. 'I hope we'll find a place to park. The town is always packed on a Saturday.'

'I'll pull up outside and wait while you go in,' Noel said. 'I don't think a ladies' hairdresser is my kind of place. I mean, they might want to give me a makeover or something. I'm sure I need it, but this is not the time for that.'

Rose laughed and glanced at him. 'You're fine as you are,' she said, thinking he looked very nice today, in his jeans and white sweater, which made his golden tan and bright blue eyes really stand out. His hair hadn't been cut for a while, but the slightly longer length suited him and softened his features. 'You're looking a lot more relaxed today,' she remarked.

He laughed. 'Relaxed? I suppose it's because I haven't had time to go to the barber for a while. Must see to that soon.'

'I wouldn't bother,' Rose said. 'I like this slightly scruffy look on you.'

'You might, but my clients won't. I have to look correct at all times.'

'Not with me, you don't,' Rose said, smiling. 'You're great to help me with sorting all the family stuff.'

'I find it fascinating. Like stepping into a time machine. Oh here we are,' he said as they neared the post office and the salon next door. Noel pulled up outside. 'I'll wait here.'

'Thanks.' Rose opened the door to get out. 'Pray for me,' she said.

'I'll say a whole novena,' Noel promised.

Rose went into the small cosy salon, where two older women were sitting under hairdryers chatting to each other. A stylist was blow-drying the hair of a client by the window. They all looked up as Rose slammed the door shut.

'That's Sylvia Fleury's granddaughter,' she heard one of the women say from under a hairdryer, to her neighbour under the other one. 'The one who used to be an estate agent.'

'Can I help you?' the stylist shouted over the noise of the hairdryer.

'Hello,' Rose said loudly. 'I haven't come to have my hair done today. I'm here for something else.'

'What would that be?' The stylist switched off the hairdryer and looked curiously at Rose.

Rose suddenly realised how strange her request was going to seem. 'Well... I... eh. I was looking for a photo in an old issue of *OK! Magazine*, you see. I heard you have those here for your clients,' Rose explained.

'We do,' the stylist said. 'But I'm not sure we'd still have the one you're looking for. Which one was it?'

'The Paddy's Day one in March,' Rose replied. 'Mary Kennedy is on the cover.'

'I remember that one,' the client who was having a blow-dry said.

'Me too,' the stylist said. 'But I think we threw it into the recycling bin yesterday. You can have a look if you like. It's around the back. The green bin.'

'Oh,' Rose said. 'I'll go and see if I can find it, if that's OK?'

'Yes. Through that door,' the stylist said, nodding at a door behind her. 'Should be at the top of the bin with some cardboard and a few other magazines.'

'Brilliant.' Rose went out the door into a small courtyard where the bins were lined up against the far wall. There were two green bins and Rose opened the first one, only to find envelopes, packaging and a paper sack. Must be the bin belonging to the post office, she assumed, and opened the other green bin. It was also full of packaging from various hair products. Rose pushed those aside and found stacks of magazines. She had to dive right in head first to retrieve them, but then found that she couldn't get out. She was stuck head first in the deep bin. She tried to wriggle out but she was too far down. 'Oh no,' she exclaimed, trying to get her hips back over the edge to no avail. 'Help!' she shouted as she sank deeper into the bin.

'It's okay, I got you,' a voice said, as a pair of strong hands grabbed her, pulled her out and put her back on her feet. 'There. Are you okay?'

Still hugging the stack of magazines, Rose discovered Noel standing beside her. 'I'm fine. Thank you for pulling me out,' she panted, shoving the magazines at him. 'Here, take a look. See if you can find the one with Mary Kennedy.'

Noel laughed and took the stack, quickly flicking through them. 'Whatever next?' he muttered. Then he pulled one of the issues out with a flourish. 'Here you are. Mary Kennedy. A little scrunched and torn, but she seems to be in one piece.'

'Oh fantastic.' Rose started to look through the magazine. 'It has to be at the back with all the society pages...'

'Come and sit in the car while you do it,' Noel suggested, tossing the other magazines back into the green bin.

'Yes, yes,' Rose replied absentmindedly as she riffled through the pages, her heart racing. She hardly noticed Noel leading her by the arm through the salon and out to the street where his car was parked. She got into the passenger seat, flicking to the society pages, and there it was, finally. 'Ben McWilliams's fortieth birthday party,' she exclaimed, peering at each photo in turn. 'A whole page of photos.' She held her breath while she searched and, after an agonising minute, there it was. A photo of a pretty dark-haired woman in a navy dress – wearing a necklace with topazes and pearls. It was identical to the one Rose owned. 'Oh holy mother,' Rose mumbled staring at the photo. 'That must be Melanie Blennerhassett.'

'Very attractive,' Noel remarked.

'Yeah, maybe. But it's my necklace, isn't it?'

'Looks very similar all right,' Noel agreed.

'Take a closer look,' Rose said, holding the page up for Noel to see. 'It's the same one, right?'

'Yes,' Noel said as he studied the photo. 'Vicky was right. It looks identical to yours.'

'Yes, it does,' Rose said, near tears. 'Only this one must be the real one. It must have been stolen a long time ago. How do I get it back?' she asked, staring at Noel, her eyes full of tears.

'I don't know,' he said.

'But you're a lawyer,' Rose insisted. 'You must have some idea what to do about this.'

'I'm a lawyer, yes. But not a miracle worker,' Noel remarked. 'If, as you say, the copy that you have was made around a hundred years ago, there is no way you can force the owner of the real one to give it to you. It legally belongs to her, I'm afraid.'

'Oh,' Rose said, staring blankly ahead. 'But... Oh, okay,' she said with a deep sigh. 'I understand what you're saying. All I have to do is go back in time and find out why this was done. Then maybe...' She shook her head. 'No. There's no way I can get the woman who owns it give it back.'

'There's no giving back of anything,' Noel stated. 'She must have inherited it or bought it or something. I think—' he took Rose's hand '—you have to accept it and move on. Your necklace is every bit as beautiful as the one in that photo. And that is because of how you wear it. Maybe you could learn to love the one you have and forget about the real one? I mean, how many people know about it?'

'Only you,' Rose said. 'I didn't tell Lily or Granny. I didn't want to upset them, especially Granny.'

'Of course not.' Noel started the car. 'I'd better drive off. I've parked on a double yellow line, and I see Sergeant Murphy coming down the street.'

Rose nodded. 'Yes, you'd better leave. No need for the best solicitor in town to get arrested.'

'He wouldn't go that far, but he'd give me a ticket,' Noel said with a laugh as he drove up the street.

'So what do I do now?' Rose asked as they drove along the seafront. 'Should I just give up? Learn to love my fake necklace?'

'Give up?' Noel said incredulously. 'Never. Aren't you a Fleury girl with the Fleury spirit? We'll go back into a time machine and search for the Lincoln family, and find out what the connection is. What were you thinking?'

'I wasn't,' Rose said, her spirits rising. 'You're right. Thank you for giving me that kick. I'm back in the saddle, I'm going to find out who had the copy made and who replaced it for the real one. Could be impossible, but I'll have to try.'

'Well, you know how that old saying goes,' Noel quipped. 'The difficult we do immediately, the impossible takes a little longer.'

'I'm ready,' Rose declared. 'Even if it takes all summer.'

# 19

---

They didn't get very far in their research that afternoon – or the following Saturday when Noel came back to help out. Penny Lincoln, the owner of the original necklace, had not been in touch either. Rose had called Melanie Blennerhassett to ask if she had passed on the request, but all Melanie said was that Penny had promised to be in touch when she had the time. Then she had said goodbye very curtly and hung up. Disappointed and frustrated, Rose felt yet again as if she was up against a brick wall.

'We have to find out who this Lincoln woman is,' she said to Noel as they were tidying up after another session in the attic room. 'There is nothing in the archives about them.'

'We just haven't found it yet,' Noel soothed. 'You have to be patient.' He gestured at the shelves on the far wall. 'There is all this to search through yet. But I also think you should ask your grandmother if she knows anything. Didn't you say your great-grandfather was still alive when Sylvia came here as a newlywed?'

'That's true. But she said she didn't ever meet Iseult, and that

Cornelius never talked about her. They didn't get on, apparently.'

Noel looked doubtful. 'I wonder if there was some kind of rift or argument between them. Iseult might have done something Cornelius didn't like. I mean, she's in some of the early photos and then, after that, there's no trace of her until that family group at this country house, whatever it was called.'

'Willowbrook House,' Rose cut in. 'But where is it?'

'It's not around here, as far as I know. I've heard of a house by that name, but I don't remember in what context. Where could it be?'

'Could be in Cork,' Rose suggested. 'After all, that's where Melanie Blennerhassett lives.'

'Ask your grandmother,' Noel urged.

Rose nodded. 'Okay. I think you're right. I'll ask her. I think she's downstairs with Henri right now. They're going through the plans for the communal dining room and the gym. It has to be right for older people who want to keep fit. There will be a yoga room where they can also do Pilates and other fitness classes.'

'Terrific idea. I'm sure it will be a busy place.'

'Or a place nobody will go to,' Rose filled in. 'Following an exercise programme demands a lot of self-discipline.'

'I'm sure some of them will turn up for a class or two. You might invite non-residents to join if there aren't enough people.'

'Great idea,' Rose said. 'But that's for the future. I'll go down now and see if I can catch Granny.'

Noel walked to the door and held it open. 'I have to go too. I have a date a little later so I have to go home and change.'

'A date?' Rose asked as she passed him. 'That's exciting.'

Noel shrugged and closed the door behind them. 'Not really. I met a woman I was at uni with earlier in the week. She's here on a bit of a break. Works in Cork city now. We'll just catch up and gossip about legal cases and such. She's a nice girl though. I always liked her.'

'And pretty?' Rose started down the stairs.

'Yes, she is actually. I had a bit of a crush on her in the old days. Feels like a hundred years ago now,' Noel added with a sad expression in his eyes. 'She married someone else so I had to get over her.'

'Ah,' Rose said with great sympathy. 'She broke your heart, did she? I feel quite cross with her now.'

Noel laughed as they arrived at the bottom of the stairs. 'You do? That's very nice of you.'

'I'm not saying that to be nice,' she replied. 'I've become very fond of you during the past few weeks. You've been so kind and helpful. You don't deserve having your heart broken.'

'Neither do you, Rose,' he replied softly. 'And I'm fond of you, too.' Then he backed away. 'But now I'd better get going,' he said, looking as if he was trying to regain his composure. 'Let me know how you get on with your granny.'

'I will,' Rose said with an odd feeling something was going on between them. But she couldn't quite decide what it was. Just a mutual fondness between two people who were becoming close friends, she decided. And that was a true gift.

Feeling happier than she had been for a long time, Rose went outside into the sunlit garden, looking for her grandmother. It was a beautiful late spring day – a warm breeze carried the scent of roses and newly cut grass, mixed with a hint of seaweed from the nearby shore. She continued down the garden path into the woods, where tall oaks stood beside small palm trees and other exotic shrubs, making this part of the garden an enchanting, lush space. The path wound through it all and down to the jetty where boats used to be moored. Rose kept looking around for Sylvia, but there was no sign of her, or Henri, so she retraced her steps. She went back to the house and around the corner to the greenhouse. Still no Sylvia, but she spotted Henri talking to a man on the edge of the lawn, where they were pointing at long lines of markings in the grass.

'Henri,' Rose called. 'What's going on?'

Henri looked around and smiled. 'Hi, Rose. This is Frank McPhee, the engineer in charge of the new heating system.'

'Hello, there,' Rose said. 'So it's all going ahead as planned?'

Frank nodded. 'Yes. We're laying out the plans for the geothermal heating. It's going to be a horizontal closed-loop system.'

'That sounds like Chinese to me,' Rose said, laughing. 'But I'm sure it will work beautifully.'

'Yes it will,' Frank said. 'And it's the most efficient system that's also environmentally friendly. They're going to start digging tomorrow. The whole system should be operational by September. Right in time for the inauguration and the first tenants.'

'Brilliant,' Rose said. 'It's wonderful that we're using a heating system that won't affect the climate.'

'It's the best option for this kind of building.' Frank folded the drawing he had been looking at. 'Well, I'll be off now. I think we've gone through everything. But give me a call if there's anything you want to ask.' He nodded at Rose. 'Nice to meet you, Miss Fleury.'

'Very nice,' Rose said. She turned to Henri when the engineer had left. 'That sounded expensive though.'

'Expensive to install, but it will pay for itself in the end. The most effective and climate friendly way to heat a house, as you just heard.'

'Great choice,' Rose said. 'I'm very impressed. But where is Granny? I wanted to talk to her about something.'

'She told me she was driving to Ventry to see Lily,' Henri replied. 'If you hurry you might catch her before she leaves.'

'I'll just give her a quick call.' Rose took out her phone.

'Granny,' she said when Sylvia replied. 'I heard you're going to Ventry. Mind if I come with you?'

'Not at all,' Sylvia said. 'I'd love to have some company on the drive. And we can visit Lily together. She'll be delighted to see you. I'll wait for you in the courtyard.'

'I'll be there in a minute,' Rose promised.

'All okay?' Henri asked when Rose had hung up.

'Yes. We're going to Ventry together to see Lily,' Rose said.

'Great. But wait a minute.'

Rose stopped. 'Yes?'

'I just wanted to say I enjoyed dinner with you the other night.'

'Me too,' Rose said. 'Except the bit where I got stuck up Conor Pass with a flat tyre.'

'I heard the gallant Noel came to your rescue though,' Henri said, smiling.

'He did. I couldn't ask you as you'd had quite a lot of wine. In any case, I didn't call him either. He happened to call me just before my phone died.'

'A happy accident, then,' Henri said. 'So are you two getting closer?'

'He's helping with my research,' Rose replied. 'But that's all.'

'I think he likes you more than he lets on,' Henri said with a wink. 'And maybe it's mutual?'

'What?' Rose stared at him. Then she shook her head. 'No, it's not. In any case, he's going on a date with some old flame, so...'

'That doesn't mean he's not interested in you.' Henri paused. 'But he might just be too shy to show it. Anyway, enough about that. I meant to ask you if you've ever been to the Blaskets?'

'I've been to the Great Blasket,' Rose replied. 'But that was a long time ago. Why do you ask?'

'I'm planning a trip there next Friday. I'm borrowing a rib

and thought I'd go out there and take a look. Do you want to come?'

'Next Friday?' Rose asked, considering the offer. 'But there is so much to do now, the marketing and the website and all that.'

'We can talk about it during the trip,' Henri suggested. 'The forecast is good and I want to take a look at this island. It's supposed to be amazing.'

'Oh, okay,' Rose said. 'I could do with a break. I'd love to come.'

'Great,' Henri said, looking pleased. 'Nice to have your company. I'll text you the details later.'

'Okay. I'm looking forward to it,' Rose said. Then a car horn tooted somewhere near the house. 'That's Granny. I have to go. See you next week,' she said before she moved away, breaking into a run as she rounded the corner. Despite agonising about the necklace and the frustration over difficult research, she felt happy about her budding friendship with Henri. It felt good to have him on her side and the outing was sure to be very enjoyable. And maybe... she might mention this trip to Noel, just in case he might get a tad jealous...


Sylvia was in high spirits during the drive to Ventry. She even sang a few bars of her favourite song, 'Wild Mountain Thyme', at the top of her voice. The windows were open to the warm breeze that brought with it the scent of wild flowers blooming in the hedgerows. Rose sat back and relaxed, enjoying her grandmother's slightly shrill but still melodious voice, joining in the chorus of 'will you go, lassie, go?' They laughed as they drew breath and agreed that neither of them would win any prizes for singing.

'So,' Sylvia said when they had been quiet for a while, 'what was it you wanted to ask me?'

'Oh it was about my research,' Rose replied. 'I'm looking at photos and trying to figure out who these people are and their place in the family history. It's all such a mish-mash.'

'I know,' Sylvia said with a sigh. 'I tried to sort it out for a while but then I gave up. It's a monumental task. Are you sure you want to do it?'

'Yes, I do. It's fascinating. Noel is helping me and he's been amazing. So I think we'll manage to sort it if we work hard. It's just that I want to draw up a family tree and sort out who's who through the ages.'

'You could set up a history page on the website,' Sylvia suggested. 'I'm sure a lot of people would love to read about the history of Magnolia Manor and the family who built it.'

'That's a brilliant idea,' Rose said. 'Noel will love that too. He's very interested in history.'

'He's a very nice young man,' Sylvia said. 'I'm glad he's helping you. It would be difficult to do it all on your own. So,' she continued, 'are you a bit stuck right now?'

'Yes. A little bit,' Rose admitted. 'I've come across a family I never knew about before. And a house I've never heard of. It seems to be connected to Iseult, Cornelius's sister.'

'What's the name of the house?' Sylvia asked as she drove up a hill.

'Willowbrook House. And the family is called Lincoln.'

'Willowbrook House,' Sylvia repeated. 'Lincoln... That does ring a very distant bell. Let me think...'

'Maybe Iseult married someone called Lincoln?' Rose suggested.

'Could be.' Sylvia frowned. 'Cornelius never spoke of her. But he was very old when I first came to Magnolia Manor. His memory had faded a lot, he said. But I have a vague memory of hearing that name. The name of the house, I mean.'

'Really? Granny, please try to remember,' Rose exclaimed. 'It's very important. It will give a clue to what happened to Iseult and where she went after she left Magnolia. After all, she wore my necklace once. And I was thinking we'd have all three of the necklaces on display at the fashion show. I'd love to be able to tell Iseult's story then.'

'Yes, yes,' Sylvia interrupted, putting a calming hand on Rose's arm. 'I understand that you want to know. But calm down and let me think. It'll come to me in time. Give me a minute or two, or more. My memory bank is so full of things at my age, it's hard to sort it all out at times, you see. But it falls into place with a little patience.'

'Oh, okay,' Rose said apologetically. 'Sorry, Granny. Didn't mean to rush you.'

'You're impatient like all young people,' Sylvia said with a smile. 'I remember how that felt. Everything has to happen yesterday.'

'Yes, that's true,' Rose admitted. 'But now we'll just take it easy and go and see Lily and Naomi. And maybe walk on the beach. Ventry is so lovely right now in early summer. No tourists yet, so we'll be all alone.'

'We're nearly there,' Sylvia announced, slowing down. 'I'll park above the house. The lane is so narrow, I hate driving down there in case I meet any cars.'

'Good idea.' Rose tried to control her impatience. She felt in her bones that Sylvia knew something about the Lincolns and Iseult's connection with them. But she had to wait for Sylvia to remember what it was, which might take some time.

'Don't let me forget the cupcakes I bought for tea,' Sylvia said. 'I got them in that nice little bakery on Green Street. The box is on the back seat.'

'I won't,' Rose said. 'I love their cakes.' She got out as soon as Sylvia had parked. They gathered up their things, including the cupcakes, and locked the car.

'Don't worry,' Sylvia said as they walked down the lane. 'It'll come to me. You know how you sometimes wake up in the middle of the night, as if a bolt of lightning has hit you?

And it all comes to you all of a sudden. That's what will happen.'

'You'll let me know the moment you remember, won't you?' Rose pleaded. 'Even if it does hit you in the middle of the night. I've become fascinated by Iseult, but what happened to her is still a mystery.'

'I will try to remember,' Sylvia promised. 'But let's not worry about it now. I can't wait to see little Naomi. She grows so fast I find it hard to keep track.'

'Four months already,' Rose said as they arrived at the front door. 'And she's smiling and nearly sitting up. She's grown out of her first baby clothes too.'

'I think she's going to be tall,' Sylvia said, pressing the doorbell that resulted in chimes inside the house.

Then there was barking and Lily flung the door open, the baby on her hip, a big woolly white dog with a black patch over one eye at her side. 'There you are! And you brought Rose. Brilliant. Don't you dare jump up on them, Larry,' she snapped at the dog, who seemed to get the message and simply wagged his tail furiously. Lily held the baby out to Sylvia. 'Here. I know you love holding her. But be careful, she's getting very heavy.'

'So she is,' Sylvia said, nearly toppling over as she caught the baby. But then she found her balance and managed to carry both Naomi, her handbag and the box with cupcakes into the house, Rose following behind, Larry at their heels.

'Great balance,' Lily said, laughing. 'Sorry, Granny, I'll take her off you.'

'I can manage,' Sylvia said as she sailed into the bright airy living room with her burdens. 'I've carried more awkward things in my life.' She held out the box. 'But you might take these and put them on a plate, then go and make tea.'

'Yes, Granny,' Lily murmured demurely while she shot Rose an amused look. 'Come and give me a hand, Rose.'

When Sylvia had settled on the sofa with the baby, Larry

keeping an eagle eye on them at Sylvia's side, Rose followed Lily into the open-plan kitchen that had all of the most modern appliances.

'How are you?' Lily asked as they busied themselves putting cups, saucers, a milk jug and a plate with the cupcakes on a tray. 'Haven't seen you for ages. So what's new?'

'Oh nothing much,' Rose said airily. 'Just work. And then the fashion show, but Vicky is looking after casting the models, which seems to be going well.'

'That's great. But I was just thinking that you never told me how you got on at the wedding? With Noel?'

'We had great fun,' Rose said, smiling at the memory. 'Noel was such a sweetheart. I discovered what a nice guy he is. And fun and...' Rose paused, smiling. 'He's actually very cute. We're becoming close friends.'

'Friends?' Lily stopped pouring hot water into the teapot and looked at Rose with a dubious expression. 'Is that all? I have a feeling there are serious vibes between you two.'

Rose felt her cheeks flush. 'I'm not sure about that. He's going on a date with someone else tonight, and he seemed quite excited about it. So maybe he just wants to be friends and that's okay for now.'

'That doesn't mean anything.' Lily resumed making tea. 'Anyway, let's not stress about it. I'm so glad all our plans are going ahead, despite Henri's efforts. He nearly had the whole board eating out of his hand. You had to lure them with modelling and free dresses to get them to agree.'

'But it worked,' Rose said, smiling. 'And now it's all going ahead.'

'And you're friends with Henri at last. Never thought I'd see that happening.'

'Neither did I,' Rose said. 'But it was when I heard about what he went through as a small child that I began to understand him. He lost his mother when he was only six years old, and then his father was unable to look after him because of his own grief. He had a very lonely, sad childhood. He told me about all that when we were having dinner. And then we realised that we have a lot in common. It was a lovely moment and I began to see another side of him.'

'Oh,' Lily said. 'That's good to hear. I didn't like the way you were bickering.'

'I know. A lot of the aggro between us was my fault. All is well and we get on fine.'

'Peace at last,' Lily said, putting the lid on the teapot. 'I'm so glad you seem to be over Gavin. He was never right for you. Too afraid to commit.'

'He's forty-two,' Rose said. 'Mature enough to want something that lasts, I would think.'

'Men like that never grow up,' Lily said drily. 'He's rich and good looking. He can have anything he wants. Why would he want to grow up and settle down? Men don't have to worry about a biological clock.'

'He's a good businessman,' Rose said.

'What does that have to do with anything?' Lily asked.

'Nothing at all,' Rose said with a deep sigh. 'I'm so over him. You know, Noel reminded me of Gavin when we first met,' she continued. 'It was the suit and tie and the hard work at the office and all that. But then I realised he's much nicer and more considerate than Gavin. And not self-centred or full of himself. He's not that comfortable in his office clothes either. He always pulls down his tie and takes off his blazer when we meet for coffee on a working day.'

Lily laughed. 'And you're just friends with him? Pull the other one.'

'Maybe a bit more,' Rose agreed. 'Can we forget that now? I feel a little stressed about it to be honest.'

'Okay. I won't say anything else.' Lily lifted the tray. 'Come on. Let's forget about this and have tea with Granny. Naomi seems to be falling asleep in her arms after all the shenanigans.'

Rose grabbed the teapot and followed Lily into the living room, her mind full of what Lily had just said. It made sense, of course, but she hadn't wanted to hear it. *Okay,* she thought, *Lily might be right. I do feel more than friendship for Noel. But what if he doesn't feel anything for me?*

Then she forgot everything as Sylvia suddenly stood up, a sleeping baby in her arms.

'It suddenly came to me,' she hissed, staring at Rose. 'The Lincolns and that house and the connection with our family. How could I have forgotten that strange story?'

## 20

'What, who?' Lily asked, looking from Rose to Sylvia. Then she put the tray on the coffee table and held out her arms. 'Here, I'll take Naomi and put her in her cot. Then you two had better explain what's going on.'

'We will,' Sylvia said as Lily took the sleeping baby and carried her away.

Rose, still holding the teapot, looked at her grandmother. 'So? What do you suddenly remember?'

Sylvia sat down on the sofa again, looking pale and shaken. 'I'll tell you when I've had some tea and Lily's back. She deserves to hear it after the fright I gave her.'

Rose poured tea into a cup, added some milk and handed it to Sylvia. 'There. Drink that, it might help calm you down. You look as if you've woken up from a bad dream.'

'That's how I feel.' Sylvia sipped some tea and the colour slowly came back into her cheeks. 'I mean, how could I have forgotten something so important?'

'What was it?' Lily asked, walking back into the room. 'What shook you up like that?'

Sylvia drained her cup and put it back on the table. Then she sat up and folded her hands in her lap. 'Lily, Rose asked me about Iseult, your great-grandfather's sister.'

'I didn't even know he had one,' Lily said.

'Well he did,' Sylvia said.

'I found photos of her in an old album in the attic,' Rose filled in. 'I thought she looked interesting, so I asked Granny about her.'

Sylvia nodded. 'That's right. I told Rose I didn't know what happened to her and that Cornelius never talked about her. But I was wrong. I mean, not about Cornelius, but about Iseult. I do know what happened to her. But it wasn't Cornelius who told me. It was an old cousin of his who stayed at the manor during my first summer there. I had just arrived and was trying to adjust to living in that old house, trying to run it and cope with the gardens and all that. We had practically no staff so we did a lot of the work ourselves. Lots of people came to visit during that first summer and it was hard work. I had Nora's mother, Mary, and later on Nora, who was very young then, and a maid, and that was all. We had one gardener for that huge garden. Poor Liam tried his best to cope and run the estate with the farm.' Sylvia drew breath. 'So it's not so strange that some of the things that happened slipped my mind, is it?'

'Not very strange at all,' Lily said. 'It must have been hard being so young and having to cope with everything.'

'Yes, but I loved the house and the whole place from the start,' Sylvia said, her eyes sparkling at the memories. 'It felt so amazing to live there and be part of it all.' She reached out and took one of the cupcakes. 'Goodness. We forgot about these.'

Rose squirmed in her seat, anxious to hear about Iseult and the Lincolns. 'So what about this memory that just came back to you?' she asked.

'I'll come to that,' Sylvia replied. 'So,' she said, after a brief pause while she nibbled on a cupcake, 'Cornelius's cousin came to stay that first summer. A nice, very tall woman called Josephine, who everyone knew as Cousin Jo. She was a little younger than Cornelius, in her sixties at that time, I think. She knew all the gossip about the family and mentioned Cornelius's sister to me and Liam during dinner, when Cornelius was out. His wife, Caroline, had died two years earlier and he was still very sad and lonely. But that's beside the point. You asked me about Iseult and the Lincolns. This is what I remember. Cousin Jo told us that Iseult had married a man against her father's wishes. He was twenty-five years older than her and a widower. His name, as far as I remember, was Patrick Lincoln, and he lived in West Cork.' Sylvia looked at Rose. 'What was the name of that house again? The house in the photo?'

'Willowbrook House,' Rose said. 'The woman I think is Iseult was holding a baby. It was hard to make out if it looked like her.'

Sylvia looked doubtful. 'Iseult had no children according to Cousin Jo. So that baby must have been someone else's child, or the cousin was mistaken. Iseult's husband had children by his first wife, a daughter and a son, I believe, nearly the same age as Iseult. He died only a few years after he and Iseult married. His children must have inherited that house. Maybe their children, or grandchildren, still live there?'

'What happened to Iseult?' Rose asked.

Sylvia shrugged. 'I don't know. There was some kind of rift between Iseult and her father, and I think Cornelius took their father's side. This to me, at the time, was just family stuff that happened a long time before I came to Magnolia. It didn't really register. I was so young, only twenty-two, and my new life seemed so challenging and exciting. Old people's lives seemed unimportant. I only listened with half an ear to their stories. It didn't seem to be relevant to me.'

*But the topaz necklace must have been handed back to our family when Iseult died*, Rose thought, not wanting to mention it in case it would alert Sylvia that there was something else going on.

*Or Iseult or someone else had a copy made and kept the real one,* Rose mused while she stared at Sylvia, trying to take it all in. *I need to talk to this Penny Lincoln as soon as possible. She must know something about it.*

'Such a sad story,' Lily said, looking emotional. 'That poor young woman having no children of her own.'

'Yes, that must have been awful for the poor girl,' Sylvia agreed. 'But it was such a long time ago. Let's not dwell on it.'

'I'd like to see that photo,' Lily said. 'I suddenly feel I want to know more about that woman. What year was it taken, do you think, Rose?'

'Judging by the clothes, around nineteen twenty or so,' Rose said after a moment's reflection.

'Iseult would have been around thirty years old then,' Sylvia suggested. 'She was ten years younger than Cornelius, that's all I know about her. He died in nineteen seventy at the age of ninety. The funeral was a huge celebration of his life. Everyone in town came and we had a wake in the ballroom that lasted all night. There was singing and music and speeches and a lot of laughter. A wonderful send-off for a very charming man.'

'Who caused us a lot of trouble,' Rose filled in.

'Oh I know. But it ended well in the end, and here we are, making it work.' Sylvia sighed and stared through the window at the stunning view of the ocean. 'How time flies,' she mumbled. 'It seems like yesterday sometimes, and then it's as if it happened in another life, another world...'

'The sixties must have been great craic, though,' Lily said.

Sylvia brightened. 'Oh yes, such fun. The beginning of a whole new era. The music, the fashion, the whole youth revolution. Liam and I went to London to see if it was really as swinging as they said. And it was. I wore the short skirts and the boots and we heard the Beatles and the Rolling Stones in tiny little clubs and danced the night away.'

'I bet the skirts looked great with your fabulous legs,' Lily said. 'Rose, you must include those fun photos of Granny and Granddad in the display at the café.'

'Good idea,' Rose said, her mind still on what Sylvia had told them about Iseult. She was getting closer to finding out the truth – she felt it – but not close enough. There were still many pieces missing in the jigsaw. She had no idea what she'd do next, but she was dying to tell Noel what she had just heard. He had been a huge help finding Melanie Blennerhassett, so maybe he would have some idea how to find the Lincolns and Willowbrook House, if any of them still lived there. Noel would know what to do next.

Noel was nowhere to be found that weekend, however. Rose tried to phone him several times but all she got was his voice-mail. He didn't reply to any of her texts, so she assumed his date had been of the 'hot' variety, and that the old friend he was meeting was single again. This gave her an odd feeling of loss. He had been so available to her, always there to help and to join her in her quests. He had also been nearly as eager as she to delve into the family memorabilia. Now it seemed as if he had disappeared. Had he suddenly lost interest? Was that date the start of a romance between him and a girl he had been in love with when he was in college? Rose felt as if she had lost her security net – someone in her life who'd always come to her aid whenever she needed it, be it stuck on a mountain in a thunder-storm, or finding the answer to a riddle she had been trying to solve ever since she found out about the necklace. She had never experienced a friendship like that before, not with a man anyway. She'd thought there was something else brewing between them, sweet and nearly romantic. But now she felt she had lost it, and that made her sad.

Rose tried her best to overcome her disappointment. She

decided to carry on alone and not involve anyone else again. She'd find Penny Lincoln and that house eventually, even if she had to bother Melanie Blennerhassett again. She hadn't sounded very friendly the last time Rose spoke to her, but there was no other way than to have another go. After all, it was her only link to the owner of the necklace, which, she suspected, was the real one.

On Sunday afternoon, Rose, sitting on the sofa in her living room, called the number again, her stomach churning, trying to think of a way to convince the Blennerhassett woman to help her contact Panny Lincoln.

'Hello?' Melanie said.

'Hi, Melanie,' Rose said, her mouth dry. 'This is Rose Fleury again. I'm really sorry to bother you, but it's important that I get in touch with Penny Lincoln.'

'Is this about the necklace?' Melanie asked.

'Yes, that's right,' Rose replied. 'It's very important that I get in touch with the owner.'

'There is something a little fishy about your interest in it,' Melanie said, sounding suspicious. 'You'd better tell me the truth.'

'Oh all right,' Rose said, trying desperately to find a more plausible explanation. But she couldn't think of anything. 'The thing is,' she started, 'I have a necklace that is identical to the one Penny owns. My necklace has been in my family for generations and it was made in eighteen eighty we think. So I wanted to find out where Penny got hers, and then include it in a vintage fashion show I'm running. I thought mine was unique, but then I saw the other one, so...' Rose stopped, wondering if this half-truth sounded plausible or like a pack of lies.

'Oh,' Melanie said, her voice softer. 'I see. Why didn't you say so?'

'Well, I felt it was too personal,' Rose explained. 'I didn't want to involve my family in this. But now...'

'Of course,' Melanie said, her voice sympathetic. 'I will get in touch with Penny and her family and ask them to call you. I'm sure they'd be interested to know how there can be two identical necklaces. And I'm sorry if I was a bit snarky with you before.'

'That's okay,' Rose mumbled. 'I'm sure I came across as very pushy.'

'Very understandable under the circumstances,' Melanie soothed. 'I'll call them right away, I'm sure they'll contact you very soon.'

Rose heaved a sigh of relief and thanked Melanie. She started going through her emails, but couldn't stop thinking about the promise of the call.

It didn't take long for the phone to ring. Rose snatched it up. 'Hello, Rose Fleury here.'

'Oh hello, Rose,' a man's voice said. 'My name is Philip Lincoln. I heard from Melanie Blennerhassett about the necklace and the duplicate you have. Or whatever it is,' he added.

'Thank you for calling me,' Rose replied. 'It's a little hard to explain like this on the phone.' She paused for a moment. 'I know this is going to sound strange, but I think our families, and the necklaces, are connected.'

'Yes, you might be right,' Philip replied. 'But I'm not sure how.'

'Maybe we could talk about this in person?' Rose suggested. 'I'd love to meet you and Penny, and explain, if that's possible.'

'Of course,' Philip said. 'We live in West Cork, just outside Kinsale.'

'In Willowbrook House?' Rose asked, her heart beating.

'No, sadly,' he replied. 'That house was sold a few years ago. We live in a bungalow nearby. I'll text you the address.'

'Oh great. When could I come and see you?'

'How about next Saturday?' Philip suggested. 'Whatever time suits you. It's a long drive from Dingle, I suspect.'

'How did you know I live in Dingle?' Rose asked.

'Your name,' he said. 'You're right, our families were connected long ago. We can talk about that when we meet. See you then, Rose Fleury.'

He hung up without waiting for a reply, leaving Rose more confused than ever. So this Philip Lincoln knew something. Maybe the truth about the necklace would finally be revealed...

## 21

Rose tried her best to concentrate on her research, despite the fact that she no longer had Noel by her side to help her. She had asked Vicky what was going on with him, but she said she didn't know. Apparently, he was the same as always in the office, but seemed a little preoccupied and distant at times. 'He also leaves a lot earlier and seems to rush off home or wherever he goes after work these days,' Vicky added. 'I'll tell him you were asking about him.'

'Just say I'm fine and he can give me a call when it's convenient,' Rose said.

Vicky promised to pass on the message, and then they discussed their plans for the fashion show. Vicky had offered to help out with the selection and they had had great fun choosing who would wear what. They had ten models lined up for the event.

'All fabulous women of all ages and sizes,' Vicky said. 'They're all helping out with the arrangements too. We're saying prayers for good weather because it would be so lovely to have the event in the garden.'

'That would be perfect,' Rose said, sitting on her stool in the storeroom. She glanced out the window and noticed it was raining. 'I hope the rain holds off. But it's a few weeks away, so hopefully all will be well.'

'Fingers and everything else crossed,' Vicky said. 'Hey, he's back,' she suddenly whispered, 'so I'd better get typing. We have a complicated court case coming up so, until that's over, things will be hectic around here. Thank goodness my models are so helpful with all the planning and organising. It's such fun and a great break from work. I'll call you soon. Bye.'

Rose hung up feeling a little better about Noel and his disappearance. He was obviously very busy and had probably little time to spare. He might also be seeing that old girlfriend in whatever free moments he had. There wouldn't be much opportunity to help Rose with her research, she assumed. *Oh well*, she thought, turning back to the photos, diaries and letters. *I can't expect anyone to be as invested in this as me. Noel was a huge help at the beginning, and what's left isn't as difficult.* She resigned herself to working on her own, slowly getting used to the idea, even if she missed Noel by her side, always there with helpful suggestions. In any case, she had high hopes to solve the riddle of the necklace, now that she had made arrangements to call on the Lincoln family. It would be a long drive to Kinsale, that little coastal town in West Cork, but she looked forward to the break from everything at Magnolia Manor.

And then there was another thing to look forward to: her outing to Great Blasket Island with Henri. It would be good to get away from thoughts of Noel, from trying to figure out her feelings for him. Lily had guessed Rose was attracted to him and said she was sure it was mutual. *Lily might be right, but even if she isn't, I need to work it out on my own*, Rose said to herself. But if he was seeing another woman, she'd back away and leave him alone. It would be hard, but she couldn't interfere if he was falling for someone else. It all seemed so complicated and confusing. It would be best to concentrate on the research about Iseult and the necklace. She had to solve that mystery first of all.

Rose set off on Friday afternoon dressed in jeans, a navy top and a windproof jacket. She had been told to meet Henri at the Fungie statue in the harbour and then they'd 'go on from there', as he'd put it. *This trip across the bay will clear the cobwebs from my mind*, she thought as she set off on her bike.

The bicycle helmet didn't do her sleek hairdo any favours, but she decided that she wouldn't worry too much about her hair. Henri was just a friend and not a man she needed to impress. In fact, Noel wasn't fussy about appearances either, which was an added bonus for Rose. Gavin had been very demanding when it came to her appearance, encouraging her to buy expensive outfits for events and booking hair appointments at fancy salons. She didn't want to put up with that kind of pressure from any man ever again.

Rose parked her bike at the stand beside the tourist office and locked it carefully. Not that her old pink bike would be something anyone would want to steal, but better to be safe than sorry. Then she walked the short distance to the little bronze statue of Fungie, the nearly tame dolphin that had lived in Dingle Bay for over forty years, delighting tourists by swimming around their boats. Then he had mysteriously disappeared and everyone in the town had supposed he'd died. There had been great sadness, and a lot of searching with small boats in the bay, but there had been no sign of him. As forty years is a long life for a dolphin, everyone had slowly accepted that Fungie was gone. The statue was a reminder of the dear creature that had brought so much fun to anyone travelling by boat in Dingle Bay.

Rose spotted Henri standing by the statue and hastened her steps to join him. As she came closer, she saw he was wearing a light cotton bomber jacket, jeans, a black sweater and a safety vest around his neck.

'Hi,' she said when she was by his side. 'You look as if you've been out to sea already.'

'Not yet, but I'm ready to go,' he replied, handing her another safety vest. 'Put this around your neck. It will inflate automatically if you fall into the water. Follow me,' he said and started to walk to the quayside. 'The rib is just here.'

'What? Oh, okay,' Rose said and walked behind him. Then, when they reached the edge of the pier, she saw a large rib tied to the side.

Henri hopped down into the rib and held out his hand. 'Jump in.'

Rose climbed carefully into the rib. 'This is amazing.'

'I thought you'd like it,' Henri said.

'I certainly do,' Rose said, laughing. 'Lucky it's a lovely evening, or you'd be in trouble. Where did you get this thing? And do you know how to drive it?'

'One of my surfer mates lent it to me,' Henri replied. 'And yes, I do know how to drive it. Dinner is over there,' he said, nodding at a basket sticking out from under one of the seats. He started the engine. 'Ready to go?' he shouted over the roar.

'Yes,' she shouted back. 'Do you want me to untie the ropes?' But then she noticed a man on the pier doing just that. Once they were free, Henri pushed the throttle and they were away into the bay at speed.

Rose laughed out loud as the wind whipped her hair around her face, remembering her worries about how she looked. Well now she was completely messed up, as sprays of water hit her face – she was happy she had at least applied waterproof mascara. Not that Henri would notice, as he seemed absorbed with driving the rib as fast as he could, taking a route around the headlands so fast Rose feared they were going to capsize. It didn't take her long to see the Blasket Islands ahead of them as they rounded Slea Head. The island was Rose's most favourite place in the world, but she didn't often have a chance to take a trip there. It was impossible in bad weather, and in high season there were too many tourists for her liking. But this wonderful late spring evening was perfect for a visit, especially as they would be all alone and could stay as long as they wanted.

The crystal-clear water gave them a lovely view of the marine life below, as Henri slowed the engine and they glided near a beach with nearly white sand. Fish darted in and out between the rocks, and a large ray flapped away when they were nearly at the shore. Further out, Rose could see seals darting in and out of the translucent water. Farther still, where the water was deeper, there were large dark humps that emitted sprays of water from time to time, and Rose knew they were basking sharks filtering plankton. And then she saw dolphins at play nearby, their shiny backs glinting in the evening sunshine before they disappeared only to appear again, showing their smiling faces.

Rose was so absorbed by the spectacle that she didn't hear Henri telling her to get out. He had to repeat himself several times before she reacted. They had arrived and would have to wade in, pulling the rib onto the beach. Rose kicked off her shoes, folded up the legs of her trousers and jumped into the icy water. But as it was only up to her ankles, it wasn't long before the boat was secured. Henri took the basket with their picnic dinner, along with two foldable chairs that he quickly put on the sand.

'There,' he said. 'Now we can have dinner. You like the setting?'

Rose looked up at the cliffs that surrounded the little cove, and out across the endless ocean. Gannets hovered in the distance, diving in spectacularly from time to time to catch fish. 'Oh yes,' she said. 'This is heaven. What a glorious spot this is.'

'You've never been here before?' he asked.

'Yes, as I told you, I've been here, a long time ago. With Lily and Vi. We walked along the edge of the cliffs and looked at the seals and dolphins. But the weather wasn't as nice then. I've meant to come back but never had the time. So thank you for bringing me. A fantastic idea.'

'Thought you'd like it.' He pulled a bottle of white wine from the basket. 'I'm going to put this into the water for a while to chill it. Warm white wine is never a pleasure.' He handed her a small plastic bottle. 'But maybe you'd like some water while you're waiting?'

'Thanks.' Rose took the bottle and had a drink, while Henri walked to the water's edge and put the bottle of wine into the shallow pool the tide had left. 'Perfect,' he called. 'Should be chilled in a moment.'

'Great.' Rose smiled at him, thinking he looked happy standing there, his jeans rolled up, his hair damp from the sprays of salt water and his sunglasses perched on his nose. She felt grateful they were friends at last and that he had asked her to come with him. It was something a brother or cousin would do and that felt really good. Just as that thought hit her, a ping from her little tote bag woke her up from her musings. She glanced at Henri while she fished out her phone. It was a text message from Noel. At last. He hadn't been in touch for over ten days, but now here he was. She opened the message.

*Hi there, sorry for being so distant. Work and personal stuff took over. I didn't forget about our project and your search though, so now that I have a tiny window, I thought I'd pop over to see how you're getting on. I'll be there in a few minutes.*

'Oh, no,' Rose muttered to herself. She texted Noel back to say she was on an outing with Henri and wouldn't be home until late. Then she went on to tell him about her progress and that she was going to Kinsale tomorrow to meet the elusive Penny Lincoln. Noel texted back at once, asking if he could come with her. He had something on but could cancel that. *This is too exciting to miss*, he wrote. *I feel we have a very important clue at last.*

*Oh yes*, she texted back. *I'd love you to come.*

*What about Henri?* Noel asked. *Is he coming too?*

*No, of course not*, Rose replied. *Why would he?*

*But you're dating, aren't you?* Noel asked.

Rose stared at the last text. What did he mean? How could he have got that idea? *No, we're not*, she typed. *We're just friends. He had the loan of a rib and asked me to come along to the Great Blasket, so I said yes. A trip out to this lovely island was just what I needed.*

'Rose?' Henri asked as he arrived back. 'What's going on? Has something happened? You look upset.'

Rose looked up from her phone. 'Nothing to worry about. I just got an important message from Noel that I had to reply to straight away. Then he asked about you and...' She shook her head. 'I think he's overworked and stressed. I'll just tell him I'll talk to him later.' She turned back to her phone, finished the message to Noel about when she was heading off in the morning, then turned off her phone and put it back in her bag. 'There. Done. No more texting, I swear.'

'I don't mind. If you need to tell him something, go ahead. We can eat later. What did he want anyway?'

'It was about the research we're doing together,' Rose explained. 'But I told him I was on an outing with you and wouldn't be home until later. And that seemed to annoy him.'

'He wanted to check up on you,' Henri said, smiling. 'Sounds like he's jealous too.'

'What?' Rose stared at Henri. 'No of course not,' she protested. 'He's a friend and he's been very helpful. That's all.'

Henri's eyes twinkled. 'You're protesting too much, my dear. I have a feeling the two of you are trying to deny your feelings for each other. He looks at you as if he thinks you're the greatest thing since sliced bread. And you're always talking about him with these starry eyes.'

'What?' Rose protested. 'Starry eyes? What are you going on about?' She felt her face flush and thought for a moment. What was going on? She had been so happy to hear from Noel that she had forgotten everything else. She couldn't be in love with him. Could she? He wasn't her type, but more like a best friend; someone with the kindest heart, who was so on her wavelength, with whom she felt so relaxed and secure. He didn't have Gavin's gloss and glamour, or the money. But that didn't seem important at all. 'Okay, so maybe there's something going on,' she confessed. 'But I don't know what it is yet. Can we forget about it for now? Let's have our dinner and enjoy this amazing evening.'

Henri laughed. 'Finally. I thought you'd never admit it, even to yourself. I mean, your knight in shining armour rescued you from a thunderstorm on top of a mountain. You don't think that was a sign?'

Rose felt a tiny niggle in her heart as she thought about all the things Noel had done for her. 'I agree that rescuing me was impressive. And he is the kindest man I've ever met.' *But it was all the other little things too*, she thought, *starting at that wedding and him being by my side, supporting me at difficult moments, and all the times he helped me with my research...* Her eyes filled with tears as she thought about Noel. 'Even though I have feelings for him, nothing much will come of it,' she said. 'He doesn't feel the same about me. He's dating a girl he used to be in love with, you see. I'm sure he still is.'

'Oh. But that doesn't have to mean anything.' Henri sank down to the blanket and put his arms around her. 'But you're upset about it. What can I do to make you feel better?'

'Nothing,' Rose said with a sob and put her cheek against his chest for a moment, taken aback by his sudden sympathy. 'Except give me food and wine.'

'Of course,' Henri said, getting up. 'Food and wine coming up. I hope it will make you forget your sorrows for a while.'

'You know it won't,' Rose said. 'But I do need a shoulder to cry on and a friendly ear to listen.'

'As long as it isn't about Noel,' Henri remarked drily. 'I've had enough of his virtues for one night.'

'Okay,' Rose promised. 'I won't mention him again.'

Henri nodded. 'Good.'

Henri went to get the wine and they had their long-awaited supper on the beach. Henri was so nice to Rose while they prepared to go back, helping her into the rib and driving slowly across the calm water of Dingle Bay, so she could see the sun setting into the ocean in a riot of colours. He even promised to help her with the fashion show, adding little bit of money from the senior apartment funds to the kitty. A peace offering, he called it, saying he enjoyed working with her, because he valued her opinion and thought she had a great head for business, which cheered her up.

'I hope you're feeling better,' he said as he saw her off on her bike after a kiss on the cheek. 'I enjoyed the outing very much. Hope you did too.'

'Very much,' Rose said. 'Thank you for being so kind.' She cycled home slowly, thinking he was a good sport deep down and a very kind and considerate man. When he wanted to be.

Rose had kept her promise and not mentioned Noel during the rest of the evening, even if her mind was full of him and the realisation that she was truly in love with him. She wondered how she should behave the next day. She couldn't possibly let him guess her feelings. She had to find out what he felt about her first – if anything at all except friendship. It was a good thing that they were going on a quest together. The riddle of the necklace would keep her feelings in check and the conversation going. Noel was fascinated by the story and would be anxious to find any clue possible. Rose felt sure they would find out a lot from the Lincolns, whoever they were. The trail was getting hotter than ever.

# 22

Rose woke up early the next morning, after a restless night tossing and turning, thinking, worrying, her stomach churning. Then she had fallen asleep only to wake up again, stressed about the following day. What was she going to say to Noel? How should she act? Probably as she always had, but now this seemed impossible. She knew Henri was right and that she was truly in love with Noel; she couldn't get the thought out of her mind. She would have to try her best to concentrate on the reason they were going to Kinsale together, to keep thinking about the necklace, Iseult and the connection with the Lincoln family. Did this Penny Lincoln know the necklace really belonged to the Fleurys, or was it an identical piece that had been made at the same time for them? But it couldn't be. Iseult was a Fleury and she had once owned the necklace, and it was unique. Rose felt she was so close to the answer she could nearly touch it.

But now here she was in a tizzy, trying to gather her thoughts and get ready for the day ahead. Noel had texted her earlier saying he'd do the driving if she wanted, as he was more familiar with the road. *Let's make a day of it,* he wrote, *and have lunch somewhere nice on the way. Don't forget to bring the necklace and all the photos of Iseult you can find.*

After a hasty breakfast, Rose ran up to the attic room and rifled through the pile of photos, sticking the ones of the family group into the album that contained the early photos of Iseult. On her way down the stairs, she bumped into her grandmother, who was carrying a large box.

'I found some things I thought you'd like to sort through,' she said. 'Photos, a diary and a few bits and pieces. Good material for the history page on the website.'

'Oh, great,' Rose said. 'Do you want me to carry them up for you?'

'We could look through it all together,' Sylvia suggested. 'I have nothing on this morning.'

'Oh, Granny, not right now,' Rose said apologetically. 'I'm on my way to Kinsale with Noel. We have an appointment to meet the Lincoln family. You know, the ones in the photo at that country house in West Cork.'

Sylvia looked confused. 'The Lincoln family from that photo? Wouldn't they all be dead by now?'

'Yes, of course *they* must be,' Rose said, trying not to laugh. 'I mean their descendants. What's left of that family. I want to ask them...' She stopped. 'I thought they might know what happened to Iseult. They might even have photos of her.'

Sylvia laughed. 'Of course. How silly of me. That sounds interesting. A nice trip too. Are you going along the coast?'

'I think so. Noel said we should make a day of it.'

'Sounds perfect.' Sylvia eyed Rose's summer dress and newly washed hair. 'And you've gone to a lot of trouble to look nice. I'm glad to see you in something other than the jeans you always seem to wear.'

'Well, it's a warm day,' Rose said.

'And Noel is a nice lad,' Sylvia said with a wink. 'But I thought you and Henri...'

'We're good friends, that's all,' Rose said. 'If you were hoping we'd get together romantically, I'm afraid you'll be disappointed.'

'I'm not disappointed.' Sylvia's eyes softened. 'Maybe it was not to be. I have a feeling he would make you miserable in the end. I'm glad you're friends now though.' She paused and studied Rose for a moment. 'Do you love him?' she asked. 'Noel, I mean.'

Rose nodded, suddenly breathless. 'Oh yes, Granny, I think I do.'

'Then tell him. Life is so short. You never know what's going to happen. If you love someone, you have to tell them. You really do, believe me.'

'I know.' Rose kissed Sylvia's cheek. 'I will. When the moment feels right. Even though he probably doesn't love me at all.'

'Maybe he does and he's afraid to say it,' Sylvia suggested.

Rose shook her head. 'No. I think he might be interested in someone else. But I'll have a go anyway. What do I have to lose?'

'Nothing at all,' Sylvia said. 'Good luck. And be careful.'

Rose nodded. 'I will. In any case, we'll be finding out about the Lincolns and Iseult and all that, which will keep us from getting too emotional. But now I have to run.'

'Have a lovely day,' Sylvia said. 'And let me know if you find anything out that might be of interest.' She tapped the box she was carrying. 'We'll go through these things tomorrow.'

'Brilliant. See you tomorrow,' Rose said and ran down the rest of the stairs carrying the photo album.

She hurried back to the gatehouse and fetched the scuffed blue velvet box from its hiding place, then put it with the album into a canvas bag. When Noel tooted outside, she was ready to go. The sight of him standing there in the sunshine made her heart beat faster; she felt a sudden jolt of love as he smiled at her.

'Morning,' he said, opening the passenger door. 'Lovely morning. And you look so nice in that dress.'

'Thank you,' Rose said, suddenly shy.

'We'd better be off.' He banged the door shut. He drove off as soon as she had put her bag on the back seat. 'Sorry to be in a rush,' he said. 'But it's quite a long drive, and I thought we'd have lunch in Kenmare and then a coffee in Clonakilty. How about that?'

'Sounds great,' Rose said, smiling at his eagerness. 'Nice day for a drive.'

He nodded. 'Yes. Windy and warm.' He was dressed casually in jeans, a green polo shirt with the Kerry football team logo under a beige windcheater. Not very trendy but so very typical of Noel, which made Rose feel a strange tenderness towards him. What did clothes matter anyway?

'It was great you could get away,' she said. 'I'd have gone alone but your moral support will make it so much easier. Nice of you to cancel whatever it was.'

'Oh that.' Noel shrugged. 'I was going to meet Sally for coffee, but we'll do it tomorrow instead. No big deal.'

'Sally?' Rose asked. 'Is that the old flame you met up with?'

Noel nodded. 'That's right. We had such a good time at our date we decided to meet again to continue the stories of our lives since we parted. She's just been through a rather difficult divorce and I'm helping her with a few legal issues.'

'So she's single again,' Rose said. 'How do you feel about that?'

Noel glanced at Rose. 'Not sure. It's a bit strange to meet up after all these years. You can't expect to pick up where you left off, you know.'

'But what about the spark, the chemistry?' Rose asked,

anxious to know how he felt about this woman. 'Were they still there?'

Noel looked confused as he rounded a bend in the road. 'I'm not sure,' he said after a while. 'Maybe. She's changed, I thought.'

'For the better?' Rose asked, hungry for every detail.

'Just changed,' Noel said. 'Different. More mature. A little dented by life. But still as attractive as ever.'

'I see,' Rose replied, her voice flat. He sounded so enthusiastic, as if he was on the cusp of a new relationship. Was he falling in love with this Sally again?

'But tell me,' he continued. 'How did you manage to get in touch with the Lincoln family?'

'I pestered this Blennerhassett woman and told her a bit of a sob story,' Rose said. 'Half true, half lie. It softened her and made her want to help. And then this man called Philip Lincoln called me, said he knew something about the connection between our families. I told him about the necklaces. Not sure if he knows mine is fake and theirs is real, but whatever. I need to look at the one they have and then hear their story. And ask about Iseult and what they know about her.'

'That's great. Very cleverly done, even if you had to tell a fib here and there. What else did you find out about the Lincolns?'

'I asked Granny and she told me a bit more. Iseult married a man called Patrick Lincoln, who was a lot older than her. He had children by his first wife but, as far as we know, Iseult had no children of her own. The baby she is holding in the photo can't have been hers.'

'No, it can't have been. Not possible in many ways,' Noel said, as if he was talking to himself.

'In many ways?' Rose asked. 'What do you mean?' She stared at him, waiting for an answer, but he looked ahead, concentrating on the road, and didn't seem to want to reply.

'We'll take the road through the Ladies View and Moll's Gap

on the way to Kenmare,' Noel said when they drew closer to Killarney. 'It's a longer road but it would be a pity to miss those beautiful views.'

'Oh yes,' Rose said with a happy sigh. 'I love that road.' She glanced at him, noticing he looked apprehensive, as if there was something he wanted to tell her but was nervous about her reaction. 'What's going on, Noel?' she asked softly. 'I can tell something is worrying you. Do you want to talk about it?'

He shook his head. 'Not really. Could you see if my sunglasses are in the glove compartment? The sun is very bright.'

'Okay.' Rose found the sunglasses and handed them to Noel. Then she put on her own. They continued the journey in silence through the beautiful landscape, stopping for a moment at Ladies View to look at the stunning vista of lakes and mountains, and had a quick cup of coffee before they continued.

The narrow road up to the mountain pass called Moll's Gap was difficult even in good weather, but today it was shrouded in mist, making it even more challenging. When they reached the top, they were disappointed that the glorious views of the MacGillycuddy's Reeks were impossible to see. But instead of driving down the other side, Noel pulled up by the side of the road.

'Why are we stopping?' Rose asked. 'There's nothing to see in this weather. It'll be better when we get out of the clouds.'

'I know.' Noel turned to face her. 'It's just that I feel I have to tell you something.'

'Okay,' Rose said, startled by his troubled eyes.

Noel cleared his throat. 'This is going to shock you. But it's the truth and I have just figured it out. You remember that family photo of Iseult holding the baby?'

'Of course,' Rose said, staring at him. 'What about it?'

Noel swallowed noisily. 'I know who the baby was.'

'You mean the one in Iseult's arms? It was her baby?'

Noel shook his head. 'No, it wasn't. It was her husband's grandchild. His son's firstborn.'

'Oh. Of course. That makes sense. He was so much older than her. And she had no children. So how do you know this?' Rose asked, intrigued.

'Because that baby was my grandmother.'

## 23

Speechless, Rose stared at Noel. 'What do you mean?' she whispered. 'How is that even possible?'

'Of course it's possible,' he said. 'My grandmother was born in nineteen twenty-one and died ten years ago.'

'Yes, yes,' Rose said impatiently. 'I understand about the age of someone born in nineteen twenty-one, but how come... I mean, your grandmother and Iseult... It seems too strange to be true. When did you figure this out?'

'It came to me bit by bit,' he said, staring out at the swirling mist. 'I had forgotten that my grandmother's name was Lincoln before she was married. I always knew her as Adeline Quinn.'

'Adeline?' Rose said softly, as if tasting the name. 'That little baby was called Adeline?'

Noel nodded. 'Yes. She was Patrick Lincoln's granddaughter and she grew up in County Cork. She married my grandfather in nineteen fifty-four, and moved to Anascaul in Kerry. Then she had my father a few years after that. And two more children, my aunt and uncle.'

'I see. But then how come it didn't ring a bell when we

looked at the photo and I talked about the Lincoln connection? And Willowbrook House? You must have heard that mentioned sometime.'

Noel nodded, looking awkward. 'Yes, I had heard it, but didn't remember in what context. I told you it rang a bell. In fact it shook me to hear you say it. Everything seemed to fall into place at that moment. I asked my father when I came home to confirm my suspicions, and he said that my grandmother had spent her early years in that house but it was sold when Iseult's husband died. I think the family was in a lot of trouble money-wise. Many people were of course, it was the start of the Depression.'

'You asked your father when you came home?' Rose said, trying to understand. 'You mean you knew all this weeks ago and didn't tell me?' She suddenly felt as if she was looking at a different person to the Noel she knew and thought she had fallen in love with. Someone she couldn't trust. 'Why?' she asked, staring at him.

'I wanted to have all the facts before I told you,' he explained.

'You were thinking like a lawyer,' Rose stated. 'Not like a friend who was helping me to find out what happened to Iseult.' She looked accusingly at him. 'You knew how desperate I was to find out and you kept all that from me?'

'It didn't change anything, did it?' Noel argued. 'The fact that the baby was my grandmother still doesn't answer any questions about Iseult. It's just a curious detail.'

'It's an important detail,' Rose said. 'And you didn't share it with me.'

'I'm sorry,' Noel said quietly. 'I was wrong. But I didn't want to...' He shrugged. 'I don't know. I always have to be sure before I say anything about an important issue. And maybe I was afraid you'd look at me differently.'

'Why would I?' Rose asked. 'It's the fact that you kept that important fact from me that makes me look at you very differently. If you had told me straight away you'd be the same person to me. I feel we lost something there. Something to do with trust.'

'Maybe we did,' he said, looking miserable. 'And that's all my fault.'

Rose tried to pull herself together. Yes, she was disappointed in him, and it felt as if she had discovered her hero was less shiny and wonderful. But they were here together on a quest. She needed to put her feelings aside and continue her search. She was here in the car on top of a mountain with Noel and they had to move on. 'Okay,' she said after a long silence. 'We'll talk about all that later. Right now, we have to go on and try to solve the mystery.'

'You're right,' Noel said stiffly and started the car. 'Let's get going. Where were we in the research? The Lincolns and where they live now. Not in Willowbrook House, as far as we know.'

'No, this Philip Lincoln said they live in a bungalow near what was their family home.' Rose paused, trying to figure out Noel's connection with the family. 'So he must be – what? Your second cousin or something?'

'Yes, something like that,' Noel replied with a worried glance at Rose. 'But we never met. My father didn't have much to do with his mother's family. No idea why. Maybe because they were in Cork and the Quinns are so very rooted in Kerry. And we were so close to my mother's German relatives. You know how that can be with families.'

'Yes,' Rose said, thinking of her mother's family and how they had never been very close or even met much through the years. 'Some families seem to overpower everyone, or something. The Fleurys are certainly such a family. Probably because of all the strong women.'

'Matriarchal,' Noel said. 'The Quinns certainly were. Not my mother so much as she was from Germany, but my grandmother took on this Quinn persona very early on and became the ruling force. Her Cork roots seem to have disappeared when she married.'

'Yes, they probably did.'

They drove on for a while without speaking, both lost in thought, the tension between them easing a little. Then Noel turned to Rose. 'I don't want you to think I was deliberately keeping my Lincoln connections from you. It was just so confusing and I didn't believe it until I saw it in black and white in a document at our house.'

Rose nodded, still feeling hurt and angry, trying to keep her voice calm. She remembered Noel's initial reaction to the necklace all those months ago. Did he have a hidden agenda? She felt as if she was second guessing everything he did now: his kindness, his interest, their connection. 'I understand that it was very confusing, but you should have told me. Lincoln is a common name, so it might not have meant anything at all.'

'No, that's true. It didn't resonate with me at all at first.'

'What was it that made you realise your grandmother was one of *those* Lincolns?' Rose asked.

'The name of the house,' Noel replied. 'I had a vague memory of that name being mentioned sometime just before my granny died. I was going to tell you over lunch, before we met Penny Lincoln. But then I just couldn't hold it in any more.' He looked at Rose. 'There is something else I need to tell you. But that has to wait until the right moment.' He drove in silence for a moment and then pressed the accelerator, speeding up once they had reached the main road to Kenmare. 'We'd better hurry or we won't have time for lunch,' he said.

'Yes. It's getting a little late,' Rose agreed, wondering about that other thing he wanted to tell her. *Probably that he's in love with that old girlfriend Sally*, Rose thought bitterly. *And that he has finally found his true love and they are getting married...* She had a fleeting image of watching Noel walk down the aisle with some pretty woman, looking blissfully happy while Rose stood by and watched, fighting back tears. That image told her that she was still in love with him despite everything. Yes, he had kept his connection secret and that had disappointed her. She was still angry with him about that, and it would take a while before she could forgive him. But him being in love with another woman was another matter, and much harder to cope with.

Noel drove carefully down the steep, narrow road into Kenmare while Rose tried to shake off her feeling of impending doom. They had become close during the past weeks while they searched for clues, and now she began to understand his interest in the mystery. How strange that he was related to the Lincolns, and that Iseult had held his grandmother in her arms, probably doting on the baby as she had had none of her own.

Noel parked the car just off the main square and they walked to the restaurant he had picked. It had tables outside in a tiny front garden behind a low hedge. The cuisine was French and the menu had a mouthwatering array of dishes that made Rose hungry just reading the descriptions. She finally picked a salade niçoise, which was served with a freshly baked baguette and vinaigrette dressing. Noel ordered an omelette with chips and a green salad, all of which was served in record time, which suited them as they were in a hurry.

'So—' Rose put down her knife and fork, having eaten half her salad '—we should talk.'

'I thought we already did,' Noel said, taking a gulp of water. 'I told you about my grandmother and the Lincolns. I know you're upset with me for not telling you. And I'm truly sorry about that.'

'I know. I don't want to talk about that right now. But you have to fill in the gaps,' Rose explained. 'Whatever else you know.'

'There isn't much more,' Noel said, looking apprehensive. 'I know I should have told you when the name of the house came up. I knew then that I was somehow related to the family who owned it. But I didn't know how. I didn't want to stir up trouble or make you suspicious of me. I had to work out exactly what connection my grandmother had with this family. In any case, I never thought they might have anything to do with the necklace.'

'But now I think maybe they did,' Rose said. 'And that's what we have to find out.'

'We will of course,' Noel agreed. 'All will be clear once we meet Penny Lincoln. She's the one who would have all the clues, I'd say.'

'And the real necklace,' Rose said. 'I just want to see and touch it, even if I can't have it. I want to be able to tell Granny what happened to it, and where it is.'

'Of course you do,' Noel said, looking at her with sympathy. 'But don't be upset if you can't have it. There's no way you could prove you have more right to it than Penny Lincoln. It could be that Iseult herself gave it to her stepdaughter or stepson, then had the copy made, which was handed over to your family instead of the real one. And then it was handed down to their daughters and granddaughters. After all, the rule that it had to be given back to the Fleury family was never any kind of contract or law that was written down anywhere. It was just a family understanding, as far as I could gather.'

'I never saw anything like that in writing,' Rose said. 'So you must be right, even if it's disappointing.'

He smiled and touched her cheek. 'Don't be sad. It's just a piece of jewellery. You have so many other things to be proud of.'

'I'm not sad about that,' Rose said, the light touch of his hand on her cheek affecting her heartbeat, even though she was still hurt.

But when they were back in the car, he raised the subject again. 'Look, Rose, I know you're upset about me not telling you, but you're blowing it out of all proportion. Of course I should have told you everything but you know the reason why.'

'Yes,' she said, staring ahead. 'It's just that I hate secrets. I hate people not telling me things and keeping it to themselves. Granny did that to us the year before last, and we had to go through a lot of arguing and cajoling before she told us we might lose Magnolia Manor. Gavin, my ex, had a lot of secrets too, which I didn't find out about until recently.' She turned to face Noel. 'And now you. I feel kind of cheated and lied to when this happens. And then I wonder what else you haven't told me.'

Noel looked taken aback. 'Oh I see. Old traumas coming back to haunt you.'

'Something like that,' Rose admitted.

'I see. That's what I suspected. Secrets are a pain anyway. Hard to keep and difficult to tell.' Noel paused and looked into her eyes. 'Rose, please believe that I have told you everything that I know about Iseult and the Lincolns and my connection to them. There is nothing else, I swear.'

Rose nodded, touched by his sincere tone and the honesty in his eyes. 'All right. I believe you. I guess this trip is more emotional for you now. The Lincolns are your family.'

Noel looked relieved. 'I'm not really interested in distant relations. I'm sure I have a lot of second and third cousins all over the place, but if you've never met or have any shared memories, they don't mean much. It's the ones you've grown up with that count. Especially those you're fond of. Twin souls, kindred spirits, you know?'

'A twin soul is someone who sings a song only you can hear,' Rose said, so quietly it was barely audible above the noise of the engine. 'That's true friendship to me.'

'Lovely thought,' Noel said and quickly squeezed her hand.

They travelled through the lovely landscape in silence then, not speaking until they reached Clonakilty, a nice little town inside the Cork–Kerry border. Noel asked if Rose wanted to stop for tea but she wanted to keep going and not stop until they were in Kinsale. So they skipped through the lovely seaside village of Schull, with its beautiful views over Roaring Water Bay, and on down the country road until they reached Kinsale, the little fishing town with steep winding streets. It ended at the harbour, where sailing boats were moored and the sixteenth-century Charles Fort stood at the high point of the headland, guarding the entrance to the bay.

'What a magical place,' Rose remarked, looking at the old houses, pubs and restaurants that lined the harbour. 'The houses look so quaint and quirky.'

'It's a lovely spot to come for a weekend,' Noel agreed as they drove down the main street.

'I can imagine.' Rose picked up her phone. 'But we're here on a mission and we have to find that house. It's nearly three o'clock already.'

'Do you have the Eircode?' Noel asked. 'Then we can put it into Google Maps and it'll lead us there, no problem.'

'I just put it in,' Rose replied, her eyes on the screen. 'And I can see the house is only up the road from here, above the area called Summerhill. Look.' She held the phone out for Noel to see.

'Yes,' he agreed, glancing at the screen. 'We're very close. What views they must have from the top of that hill.'

'Breathtaking, I'd say.' Rose suddenly felt uneasy. What was she doing here? How were the Lincolns going to react when she told them the facts about the necklace? She had been so obsessed about finding the original that she had forgotten about everything else. Now she wasn't so sure about anything any more. As if Noel's secrets had put everything into question.

It didn't take them long to find the house, a long bungalow with a front garden full of flowering shrubs. A rambling rose with tiny pink blossoms climbed over the green front door, which had a knocker in the shape of a lion's head.

'Nice house,' Noel said.

'Yes,' Rose said, shaking with nerves. When Noel had parked the car beside the gate, she grabbed his arm to stop him getting out.

'What's the matter?' he asked. 'You're as white as a sheet.'

'I can't do this,' Rose whispered.

## 24

---

'What do you mean?' Noel asked, staring at her. 'Do what?'

'I can't just waltz in and tell them about the necklace. It's going to sound like I'm suggesting they stole it.' Rose looked at Noel, her eyes full of tears. 'What am I going to do?'

Noel frowned. 'I see. Well, I suppose in a way you're right. I understand why you feel that way, even if you do have the moral right to claim the real necklace. After all, it was stolen from the family.'

'Maybe, but we don't know who did it or why,' Rose argued.

'No, we don't. I think...' Noel paused for a moment, as if deep in thought. 'Go with your gut,' he suggested. 'Don't say anything about the fake necklace. See what happens. You're just here to find out more about Iseult because of your research.'

Rose nodded, feeling calmer. It was such a comfort to have him here by her side supporting her, and knowing exactly how she felt. 'Good idea. That's what I'll do.'

They walked together through the front garden, and then Rose knocked on the door using the lion's head knocker. They waited for a while and eventually heard footsteps. The door was opened by a tall dark-haired man with kind eyes behind dark-framed glasses. He smiled politely at them.

'Hello. Are you Rose Fleury?' he asked.

'I am,' Rose replied and shook his outstretched hand. 'And this is my friend Noel Quinn.'

'I'm Philip Lincoln,' the man said and shook Noel's hand as well. 'So nice to meet you. Welcome to Willowbrook Lodge.'

'Oh,' Rose exclaimed. 'How nice that you called your house after your ancestral home.'

Philip smiled. 'Yes, we felt we wanted the constant reminder both for us and for our children. Willowbrook House meant a lot to our family. It still does.' He held the door open. 'But come in. My wife is on the terrace at the back of the house with our daughter.'

Rose glanced at Noel, wondering if he would break the news that he was related to Philip, but then assumed he wanted to wait for the right moment. 'Thank you,' she said, stepping into a bright hall.

'Go through the door to the left and you'll come into the living room,' Philip instructed. 'The doors to the terrace are open. I'll go and make some coffee. Or would you prefer tea?'

'Coffee for me,' Rose said.

'Me too,' Noel chimed in. 'Do you need any help?'

'Oh, eh, not really,' Philip said. 'I can manage. You go out to the terrace. The view from there is quite nice.'

It was more than 'quite nice', Rose realised, even when she was inside the living room door. The picture windows revealed a panorama of the bay and the ocean. The blue water was dotted with white sails as a little armada of sailing dinghies headed out to sea. 'Must be the sailing school on an outing,' she said to Noel. 'What a spectacular view.'

'Stunning,' he said behind her.

They walked through the bright, airy living room and out onto the terrace, where a woman sat with a little girl on her lap on a garden sofa. She looked up as they arrived. 'Hello. You must be Rose.' She got up, putting the little girl down and holding out her hand. 'I'm Kathleen. So lovely to meet you at last.'

Rose shook Kathleen's hand, feeling confused. 'Hi, Kathleen. Yes, I'm Rose and this is my friend Noel Quinn.' She looked around the beautiful terrace, with its large pots of flowers and stone balustrade. 'But I thought I was going to meet someone called Penny Lincoln?'

Kathleen smiled and pushed the little girl forward. 'Here she is. My daughter Penny. Say hello to Rose, Penny.'

'Hello, Rose,' the little girl said, and held out her hand. 'Howdodo.'

Rose did her best to hide her confusion and shook the tiny hand. 'Hello, Penny. How nice to meet you. How old are you?'

'Free,' Penny said and held up three fingers. 'How old are you?'

'Thirty-five,' Rose said, and crouched down so she was level with this enchanting little girl. She had brown curly hair and enormous hazel eyes with long eyelashes. 'That's a very pretty dress. Did your mummy make it?'

'No,' Penny said with a giggle. 'She bought it in the shop. She can't make dresses.'

'Oh, well,' Rose said, getting back up. 'I'm sure she can do a lot of other things.' She glanced at Kathleen. 'Sorry, but I thought *you*'d be Penny. Melanie said...'

'Melanie is Penny's godmother,' Kathleen explained. 'She probably didn't make that clear. Or she was joking. Of course, it's Penny who inherited the necklace. It's been in my husband's family for over a hundred years.' Kathleen paused. 'I believe you have an identical one?'

'Oh, eh, yes,' Rose said. 'I do. I'll show it to you in a minute. But first, I'd like to hear what you can tell me about Iseult, who I believe was the stepmother to your husband's...' She paused, trying to figure out the relationship. 'I don't really know the details of the family.'

'It's a little complicated,' Kathleen agreed. 'But here is Philip now,' she added as he came out on the terrace carrying a tray. 'Philip, could you tell Rose what you know about Iseult? I have always found the ins and outs of the relationship with her difficult to remember. She married your great-great-grandfather, is that right?'

'Yes.' Philip put the tray on a table and pulled out a chair. 'It's quite fascinating. She's a legend in our family.' He handed Rose a steaming cup of coffee.

'Thank you.' Rose sat down on a chair and Noel settled beside her on another. Philip joined his wife on the garden sofa while little Penny played with a doll's house beside them.

Philip offered Rose and Noel a plate with ginger snaps. 'So,' he said, once they all had coffee and a biscuit, 'I'll tell you about Iseult, who I believe was your great-aunt or something, Rose?'

'She was my great-grandfather's sister,' Rose replied. 'My father's great-aunt. But she seems to have run away from home or something because we know very little about her.'

Philip nodded. 'Yes, that's true. She did run away from home with my great-great-grandfather Patrick Lincoln, who was a lot older than her. Apparently, he was her father's friend from university. They both studied in Cork and became friends. Then Patrick married very young and had a son, my great-grandfather, who had two children, a son and daughter.'

'I have a photo of a family group taken at Willowbrook House,' Rose interrupted, picking up her tote bag. 'I have it here, if you want to have a look.' She pulled out the album and found the photo, which she showed to Philip.

He looked at it with great interest for a moment. 'Yes, that's Iseult with my grandfather's sister. Her name was Adeline.'

'Weirdly, that's my grandmother,' Noel cut in. 'I only discovered that recently, actually.'

'Wow, really?' Philip asked, looking at Noel incredulously. 'I believe Adeline married a lawyer and moved to Dingle.'

'Exactly,' Noel said, smiling. 'My grandfather. His name was Maurice Quinn.'

'So then we're second cousins?' Philip asked. 'How amazing.'

'Such a strange coincidence,' Kathleen remarked. 'All these connections.'

'Yes, really weird,' Rose said. 'I was researching into my family history, then I found Iseult in a few photographs and realised she was my great-grandfather's long-lost sister that we know nothing about. And then Noel was helping me sorting out the papers and photos in the family archives, and he found out that Iseult was his grandmother's... What?'

'Step-grandmother,' Philip filled in. 'And she was only thirty-nine when that baby was christened.'

'Must have been strange to become a granny at that age,' Kathleen mused. 'And nice for her, especially as she didn't have any children of her own.'

'That must have been a comfort to her,' Rose said. 'But what do you know about her earlier life? About how she fell out with her family and ran away from home? I heard something about her having been a debutante in London at the beginning of the last century. And then that she was involved with women's rights and the nineteen sixteen uprising in Dublin. Not sure if all that is true,' Rose concluded, looking at Philip.

'Most of it is,' Philip replied. 'She was a debutante in London when she was nineteen. I think she had an English godmother who took Iseult under her wing and had her presented at court. But then she was in touch with the suffragettes in London. She had to go back to Ireland in a hurry to avoid being arrested after a big protest. So nothing came of her being presented. She didn't fit in with the British upper classes of the time, and the connection with the women's movement didn't exactly make her popular.'

'What about the Easter Rising?' Rose asked.

'I believe she was involved, but then went home to Magnolia Manor to be with her family during that difficult time. The Fleurys, as you know, were not an Anglo-Irish family and were much loved in the area.'

'They still are,' Noel cut in.

'When did she marry this Patrick Lincoln?' Rose asked. 'I'm imagining it would have been around that time?'

'Yes, that right,' Philip replied. 'We don't have the exact date, but we know that Patrick Lincoln, our great-great-grandfather, lost his first wife in nineteen fifteen. And he met Iseult during a visit to Magnolia Manor a year or two after that. They were married in Cork in nineteen eighteen. Sadly, they only had eight years together before he died of a heart attack in nineteen twenty-six.'

'That's sad,' Rose remarked. 'And what happened to Iseult after her husband's death?'

'She lived in Willowbrook House until it was sold. That was around nineteen thirty or so. She moved into a small house nearby, and Patrick's son, our great-grandfather, built this house and moved here with his family.'

'So my granny Adeline grew up here?' Noel asked, looking moved. 'I had no idea. I just knew she grew up in County Cork.'

'Yes, that's right, she did grow up here,' Philip said. 'With her brother, who was my grandfather.' He looked curiously at Noel. 'How strange that we never met. But then my grandfather died before I was born, so much of his childhood was forgotten about.'

'But to come back to Iseult,' Rose said. 'She died quite young then?'

'In her early forties,' Philip confirmed. 'What do you know about her early life?'

'I only have a few photos to go by,' Rose replied. 'Nothing much else. What about you?'

'Only the family stories,' Philip said. 'What I just told you. But as she was not connected to Patrick's children by blood, the interest in her faded a little. Except for the necklace she left to my family for the eldest daughter. Penny is the first girl to inherit it.'

'I see,' Rose said, feeling a dart of frustration. Iseult had had no right to keep the necklace and give it to someone who was not a Fleury. Although, perhaps it was a silly rule. Why shouldn't she have been allowed to give it to someone she loved?

'We do have some photos in an old album,' Kathleen said. 'I'll go and get it.' She got up and held out her hand to Penny, who had interrupted her game with the doll's house and was yawning and rubbing her eyes. 'Come, Penny. We'll go and get the album for Rose. And then maybe you'd like to have your nap.'

'Okay,' Penny said and trotted after her mother. 'Naptime.'

'What a good girl,' Rose said when they had left.

'Usually not very eager for a nap,' Philip said with a smile. 'But she's tired after having been to the beach for the first time this season. It was such a warm day we went for a swim down at the beach near James Fort. Penny loved it.'

'I'm sure she did,' Rose said, sipping her coffee while they waited for Kathleen to come back. The story had made her even more interested in Iseult, a woman she hadn't known even existed until she had found out about the necklace. But that was a mystery still to be solved, even if Iseult's life story was now all but told. She seemed to have been a fascinating woman, brave and feisty and ready to take on any challenge that came her way, even marrying against her father's wishes. The fact that she was also very beautiful gave her an added gloss. But why had she cheated her family by having a copy made of the necklace, then giving the real one to her stepchildren? It seemed like a very sneaky thing to do, and not in line with the character of a woman who had fought so hard for her principles.

Kathleen came back with an old leather album a few moments later. She handed it to Rose. 'Here you are. There are some nice photos, starting with Iseult and Patrick's wedding in Cork, and then a few of their honeymoon in Paris. And then one or two of the family at Willowbrook House.'

Feeling excited, Rose opened the album and found the wedding photo on the very first page. Iseult was a beautiful young bride, dressed in a lacy wedding gown and long veil, a wreath of flowers on her head, her blonde hair in an elaborate updo. She looked adoringly at her new husband, a tall, handsome older man with a moustache, who looked back at her with an expression of pure love, even if there was a touch of sadness in his eyes.

Then there were the photos from their honeymoon, which were interesting as they depicted Paris in 1919. 'Wonderful vintage photos,' Rose exclaimed, looking at the ladies with large hats and sweeping skirts, including Iseult in the best Paris fashions. 'This must have been when they were still quite wealthy,' she remarked, turning the pages and looking at pictures of family groups and parties at the big house.

'Yes, the glory days,' Philip said. 'I'm sure they were all sad when the big house was sold and turned into a hotel. But I have to confess, I prefer this house, it's much easier to manage.'

'I'd say it is,' Rose agreed. 'Our ancestral home, Magnolia Manor, which is even larger than Willowbrook House, is being turned into apartments for older people. It is sad to see it rebuilt as something else, but it was becoming impossible to maintain. Now I'm happy that it wasn't demolished and a large part of it is being maintained as it was. And we don't have to worry about repairing the roof or rising damp and all that stuff that happens to old houses.'

'Magnolia Manor,' Kathleen said in a dreamy voice. 'I've seen it from the distance. It's a beautiful house. I was always intrigued that Iseult grew up there. Her necklace is a wonderful memento of her life at the manor.' She turned to Rose. 'I'd love to see yours just to compare it to ours. Could we take a look at it?'

'Of course,' Rose said, picking up her bag again. 'And I'd love to see the one you have.'

'Oh ours won't be a patch on yours,' Kathleen said.

'Why not?' Rose asked as she started to pull the velvet case out of her bag.

'Because,' Kathleen said, 'it's a copy. Yours is the real one, so it has to be twice as beautiful.'

---

## 25

Rose's hand with the velvet case froze – she felt suddenly dizzy. Had she heard correctly? 'Excuse me?' she stammered. 'What did you say?'

'Our necklace is a copy of the original,' Kathleen said. 'The one you have.'

'What?' Rose said, so hoarse she could hardly speak. 'I mean, how come you think I have the original?'

'Because, as you know, it had to be handed back to the Fleurys when Iseult died,' Philip cut in. 'But she gave the necklace back to her family when her husband passed away. She knew she wouldn't have any children, so it had to go back in order to be given to the next Fleury daughter in line. So she had a copy made, and stipulated in her will that this one would be given to the daughters of the Lincoln family. She thought it was a nice gesture to connect her husband's family with her own. It's a beautiful necklace, even as a copy, and we cherish it.'

'Oh,' Rose managed, her mind whirling. She glanced at Noel, who looked as shocked as she felt. Perhaps the two had been swapped, she wondered, looking at Noel for an answer. But he looked as bewildered as she felt. 'Before I show mine to you,' she started, 'could I see the other one? It would be interesting to see how alike they both are.'

'Of course,' Kathleen said and went into the living room, coming back a moment later with a scuffed leather box. 'Here it is.' She handed the box to Rose, who grabbed it and opened it, holding her breath. An identical necklace to hers was nestled against a bed of dark blue silk, the silver and glass glittering in the sunshine.

'It's... it's very like mine,' Rose said. 'Identical. When was it made, do you think?'

'In nineteen twenty,' Philip replied. 'There is a little "e" engraved at the back, which means it was made then, according to the hallmark directory.'

'Just like mine,' Rose said, pulling out her velvet box and opening it. 'This one is also a copy.' Her voice shaking, she stared at Philip. 'I thought yours was the real one, the one with the topazes and pearls, which is worth a lot of money.'

'We thought the same about yours,' Philip said, looking equally shaken.

'But now we know it's not,' Rose said. 'So...'

'Hold on a moment,' Noel said, startling them. 'Could we take a look at that hallmark?'

'Of course.' Kathleen handed Noel her box. He opened it and lifted the necklace out, peering at the back of it.

'Just what I thought,' he said, putting the necklace back. 'Let me have a look at yours, Rose.'

Rose handed him her case. He examined her necklace and then nodded, looking satisfied. 'Rose's necklace doesn't have the same hallmark. It looks like an "e", but it's a different kind. More elaborate and swirly. I have a feeling it was made a lot earlier than yours, Kathleen.'

'Oh,' Rose said. 'How strange.'

Noel picked up his phone. 'I can look up hallmarks on the internet. Hang on.'

They all looked at Noel in silence as he kept working the screen of his phone. Then he nodded and looked at them with excitement. 'Found it. Your necklace was made in nineteen hundred, Rose. I've found the hallmark from that year and it matches yours.'

Rose stared at him, then at the necklace in the open case. 'I don't understand anything now. Why were two copies made twenty years apart?'

'It's strange, but I'm guessing that Iseult didn't know hers was a copy,' Noel suggested.

'So where is the original?' Kathleen asked, her eyes wide with bewilderment as she looked at the necklace in Rose's case. 'We thought... We were sure you had it. Why wouldn't you?'

'I have no idea,' Rose whispered. 'None at all.'

'Someone went to a lot of trouble to have that first copy made,' Noel said very slowly. 'And then Iseult thought hers was the real one. Maybe it would be an idea to find out where her copy was made? It must be possible to find that out at least.'

'How?' Philip asked. 'It was over a hundred years ago. The craftsman in question would be long dead.'

'The shop might still exist,' Kathleen said. 'Could be around here or in Cork. We should look up silversmiths in the area.'

'A long shot,' Noel agreed. 'But it's worth a try, don't you think?'

'It says Weir&Sons on the silk lining in my case,' Rose remarked. 'I have a feeling it was the one the original necklace was kept in. It must have been swapped by whoever took the original.'

'Yes,' Philip said. 'You must be disappointed that the original is still missing.'

'Yes,' Rose confirmed. 'It's been hard losing the manor, and when I recently found out that the necklace was fake, I was keen to find the real one before my granny found out. She's been through so much, I didn't want her to lose a family heirloom as well as our family home... I feel dizzy,' she mumbled as she closed the case and put it back in her bag.

'You're still so pale,' Noel said, looking concerned. 'Maybe a drop of brandy would help?'

Philip got up. 'I have some inside. I'll bring it out. Kathleen, do you want some too?'

Kathleen shook her head. 'I'm fine. Noel?'

'Thanks, but I'm driving,' Noel replied.

The drop of brandy helped Rose feel more relaxed; she could take stock of what she had just learned. 'You know what I feel?' she said, putting her brandy glass on the table. 'I just realised that we're barking up the wrong tree. Trying to find out who made the copies won't help me find the real necklace. It'll just confirm what we already know. So why spend a lot of time and effort trying to find what jewellers or silversmiths made the copies? They were made at different times and for different reasons. I think I need to go back to Magnolia and the store-room. Someone somewhere must have made a note of what happened and why. Or there could be an old invoice for the work done.'

Kathleen nodded. 'I think you're right. We're not interested in whether the necklace is real or fake, so there's no need to dig further into it at this end. Our necklace is a memento of a kind lady who loved her husband's family and wanted them to remember her. She seemed to have been upfront about what it was she was passing on, a copy of a beautiful necklace that had been in the Fleury family for generations. That's enough for me, whatever about the real necklace, the other copy and what and when and why. That's not our mystery to solve. It's yours, and I hope you will find the answer.' She drew breath and smiled at Rose. 'In any case, it was lovely to meet you and your boyfriend, Rose.'

'It was so nice to meet you too, but we're not...' Rose started.

'We're not a couple,' Noel filled in. 'We're just very close friends, that's all.'

'That's very nice too,' Kathleen replied. 'Close friends should be treasured.'

Rose shot Noel a warm smile. 'Oh yes. And I do. Very much.'

Noel's cheeks turned pink. 'Ah, well, yeah, that's very good to know. I mean it's very special to me too.'

'But now we should really get going.' Rose picked up her bag and got up. 'It's a long drive back.'

Kathleen rose from her chair. 'Of course. I'll see you out. I would have liked to ask you to stay for dinner, but I think you want to get home.'

'Yes, we do.' Rose shook Kathleen's hand. 'Thank you so much for everything. It was lovely to meet you. You've been a great help.'

'Oh I don't think we did much,' Kathleen protested.

'You did a great deal,' Rose argued. 'You clarified a lot. Even if we didn't find what I was looking for, it made me realise that maybe finding the real necklace is not that important.' She glanced at Noel. 'It's been a long journey and it's not over yet. But along the way I've discovered a lot about myself and the people around me.'

'That's a treasure in itself, I suppose,' Kathleen said, smiling. She leaned forward and kissed Rose on the cheek. 'I'm so happy to have met you. Please keep in touch.'

'I will,' Rose promised. 'Come and see me in Kerry sometime. I'll give you my number.'

'We'd love to.' Philip stepped forward while Kathleen and Rose exchanged phone numbers. He shook Noel's hand. 'Hey, cousin. So great to find you at last. We'll have to keep in touch. I'd like to meet your father too. I mean, we're family, aren't we?'

Noel smiled broadly and squeezed Philip's hand back. 'Absolutely. So happy we connected. All thanks to Rose.'

Philip and Kathleen saw them to the front door and stood waving as they drove away.

'That was lovely,' Noel said as they drove through Kinsale. 'Sorry about the necklace and all that, but for me it was such a nice discovery. My father will be delighted that I've met my Lincoln cousins.'

'Yes,' Rose said without really listening. Her mind was too full of the mystery of the necklace for her to take anything in. 'That's terrific.'

'Sally was just saying that I should try to get out more and meet new people,' Noel continued. 'She thought I was a little stuck in the mud.'

'What?' Rose asked, staring at Noel. 'That wasn't very nice.'

'Oh she knows me since we were at college. We used to tease each other all the time.'

'What happened with her husband?' Rose asked. 'I mean, she's single now, you said.'

'Yes, that's right,' Noel replied. 'Single and free, she said. And now she's going to India on a voyage of spiritual awakening, she told me. She won't be back for a long time.'

'How do you feel about that?' Rose asked, studying Noel to gauge his mood.

'I'm happy for her,' he said after a moment's silence. 'I thought for a moment that we might... But then I realised there was too much water under the bridge, so to speak. Too much time and too many arguments in the past. She's quite a prickly person, really, and I find it hard to put up with that.'

'You mean she's easily offended?' Rose asked, feeling strangely happy to hear him say something negative about her perceived rival.

'Not only that, she imagines an insult where there is none. And then she is always analysing everyone and passing comments on how they should feel. It's very tedious. I had forgotten that bit about her.' Rose couldn't help but smile. Noel scanned the signposts. 'Hey, do you mind if we take the faster way home? The Cork–Killarney road inland is much quicker than the coast road.'

'Great idea,' Rose replied. 'I just want to get home. It's been such a tiring day.'

'In so many ways,' Noel agreed, and swung left onto the main road. 'Very emotional for you. I know you must be disappointed.'

'Yes.' Rose looked out at the rolling green hills as she tried to gather her thoughts and feelings. 'But I was relieved that I didn't have to convince them to give the real necklace back. That would have been awkward.'

'So was I,' Noel said. 'Especially as I'm related to them. That wouldn't have been a great introduction.' He started to laugh. 'Hey, imagine if they had the real necklace and then you'd said you'd sue them and that I was your lawyer and—' He stopped and shook his head. 'Thank goodness that didn't happen.'

Rose smiled. 'Or I swapped them back secretly. Would you have defended me in court if I was caught stealing?'

'No. You'd be on your own with that one.'

'I suppose I'd deserve it.'

'Definitely. I'd visit you in jail though,' he remarked.

'How kind,' Rose said, smiling. 'But it didn't happen. I might not have had the nerve to do it anyway.'

'I think you'd have chickened out at the last minute,' Noel agreed.

'You're right.' Rose looked at him as he drove, at his strong hands on the wheel, his blonde hair falling into his bright blue eyes, and felt a surge of something akin to love. He mightn't love her back, but at least there was a close bond between them. And she had found out he wasn't entering into some kind of relationship with his former girlfriend. As far as she knew anyway.

Rose's thoughts were interrupted by Noel suddenly pulling

up by the side of the road. 'Why are we stopping?' she asked, confused.

'I have to tell you something.' He took a deep breath. 'There's a black leather box in your grandmother's safe. She told me it contained some valuable items that were part of the late Caroline's estate.'

'Caroline? Cornelius's wife?'

Noel nodded. 'Yes. It was all kept in the strongroom of your grandmother's former solicitors in Tralee. When her files were moved from them to me, that box was with all the documents. Sylvia asked me to put it in her safe instead of keeping it in our big one in the office. The necklace could be there.'

'Why are you only just telling me this?' Rose asked, shocked.

'Sylvia made me promise not to tell anyone. I know there are some valuable pieces there,' Noel replied, looking awkward. 'But I haven't looked at them. Sylvia wanted to itemise everything so she could decide what to leave to whom in her will. And then I would draw it up once she had decided.'

'So this is the itemisation you first mentioned to me? Why didn't you tell me Granny has been worrying about her will?' Rose asked glumly. 'More secrets,' she muttered.

'Yes, but,' Noel started, 'I had to adhere to client confidentiality, Rose. I couldn't break that. And besides, you'd already found the second necklace when you told me yours was fake. I hoped we'd find the real one, and I wouldn't have to break Sylvia's trust in order to help you find it.'

'Have you told Sylvia anything about the necklace being fake?' Rose asked.

'No, of course not, Rose. I would never do that. And I'm probably going to get in trouble for divulging Sylvia's business to you.'

'I'll handle that,' Rose said. 'I just want to get home now. I don't want to talk about this.'

'Okay.' Noel started the car and pulled away from the edge of the road.

Rose tried to put it all into perspective while Noel drove. She knew it was difficult for him; he had now revealed something a client had told him in confidence, which had to make him feel bad. But he had kept important information from her, even though it might have solved the whole mystery a lot sooner. Now she didn't know how she would convince Sylvia to reveal what was in that box. She might have to tell her the necklace was fake after all.

Her thoughts were interrupted by her phone ringing, the sound jolting her back to reality. It was Vicky, sounding frantic.

'Rose, where are you?' she asked. 'I thought you would be here, helping out with the rehearsals for the fashion show.'

'I'm so sorry,' Rose said. 'I totally forgot about that. I had to go to Kinsale with Noel for something that came up during the week. Is there a problem?'

'Nothing but,' Vicky replied, sounding desperate. 'I think we might have to cancel the whole thing.'

## 26

'What's going on?' Rose asked, startled by the desperation in Vicky's voice.

'Everyone is fighting and two of the best models have dropped out,' Vicky said. 'Someone fell off the catwalk and is threatening to sue because the silly woman twisted her ankle, which wasn't because of the catwalk but because she doesn't know how to walk in high heels.' Vicky drew breath. 'I need you here as soon as possible. When are you coming back?'

'We're just going through Bandon,' Rose said after a quick look out the window. 'I'd say we should be back in about an hour and a half. What do you think, Noel?'

'Something like that,' Noel said. 'What's going on?'

'I'll tell you in a minute. I'll come straight to the ballroom when we're back,' Rose said to Vicky. 'See you then.'

'If I'm still alive,' Vicky muttered. 'That Mrs Moore is looking daggers at me because I told her she couldn't possibly get into a size ten dress. Can't wait for you come and sort everyone out.'

'Poor Vicky,' Rose said once she'd hung up. 'I shouldn't have left her holding that particular baby. I feel so guilty, I totally forgot about the rehearsal. I should have known there would be problems.'

'But you thought you were so close to finding the necklace,' Noel said. 'Understandable that you forgot everything else.'

'Yes, I...' Rose started, but then her phone pinged interrupting her. 'A message from Henri,' she said and opened it.

*Big problem. The chimney in one of the flats on the top floor has caved in. Needs urgent repairs before the building work can continue on that floor. What kind of insurance do we have?*

'Oh no,' Rose exclaimed. She turned to Noel. 'I have to call him. It's about a problem with the building work.'

'Of course you must call him,' Noel urged. 'No need to ask for permission.'

'Great.' Rose quickly found Henri's number. He answered straight away.

'Where are you?' he asked, sounding annoyed. 'I thought you said you'd be home at the weekend.'

'Well, I'm not, but never mind,' Rose snapped. 'Tell me about the chimney. What happened?'

'A recent rainstorm damaged the brickwork and all the mortar in the old chimney,' Henri explained. 'That part of the roof had been stripped back for repairs, but the tarpaulin blew off or something and all the rain got in. And the fireplace in one of the smaller flats has to be rebuilt. That will stall the work on the flats on the top floor.'

'I'll be back in an hour or two,' Rose said. 'And then we can look up the insurance and everything and see how much extra all that will cost.'

'Okay,' Henri said. 'I'll wait in Sylvia's study until you arrive.'
Rose hung up and placed the phone back into her bag.

'More bad news?' Noel asked.

'Yes, but it can be sorted.' Rose glanced at Noel. 'Can we

speed up a bit? I need to get back to sort out that mess with the fashion show. And everything else.'

'Not if you want to stay within the speed limit,' he said drily. 'But I can take a shortcut and see if we miss the traffic around Killarney.'

'Okay, great.' Rose stared straight ahead, feeling frustrated. The trip to Kinsale had been for nothing. Now she had this problem with the fashion show, which seemed to be falling apart. And the news from Henri about the chimney was annoying to say the least.

'I'd better get you back fast or you'll explode,' Noel said, as he suddenly sped up.

'Be careful,' Rose warned. 'You don't want to get penalty points.'

'Never mind the speed limit,' Noel snapped. 'We need to get back.'

'I know,' Rose agreed.

As Noel put his foot down, suddenly Rose felt sad and disconnected from him for the first time. He had been with her all through this search, but now something felt different. She wondered if the real necklace was in Sylvia's safe. That would be the end of their search and maybe help heal the rift between them. If she could ever get over the secrets he'd been keeping. Her thoughts drifted to the necklace and the question of who had had it copied. The answer to the riddle had to be in the manor. As they drove around the bend and Dingle town came into view, she had a strange sensation that the mystery was very close to being solved.

## 27

After Noel pulled up to the front of the manor in a shower of gravel, Rose threw open the door and jumped out, racing up the steps and in through the entrance. Then she raced up the two flights of stairs and arrived on the top landing, her heart pounding. 'Henri?' she called, fighting to regain her breath. There was no answer. She hurried down the narrow corridor to the last room and flung open the door, gasping at the sight of the fireplace, which was now just a pile of bricks and crumbled mortar.

The smell of dust and mould was so thick she had to run across the creaking floorboards to open the window. She took deep breaths of the fresh air as it gushed in, looking around the room, which was larger than the other servants' rooms on the top floor. This one had two windows and a sloping ceiling, which they had thought would be a charming feature once it was turned into a studio flat. The fireplace had been an added asset, but now Rose saw it would have to be rebuilt from scratch. 'Holy mother,' she mumbled, remembering Henri had said he'd wait for her in Sylvia's study. She ran out of the room, relieved to be away from the mess, and hurried downstairs, arriving in the study breathless.

Henri, sitting on the sofa looking at his phone, stood up when Rose arrived. 'There you are,' he said.

'Yes,' she said. 'Is everything okay with the chimney?'

'Not quite,' Henri replied. 'But there was something else too.'

'What else is wrong?' Rose asked with a resigned sigh.

'Not wrong but weird. Could be a good thing, actually,' Henri replied. 'You see there was stuff stuck up that chimney that fell down when it caved in. Something that must have been hidden there years ago.'

'Like what?' Rose asked.

'A lot of cash.'

'Old notes?' Rose asked.

'No.' Henri's voice took a lighter tone. 'Better than that. Much, much better. Gold coins. Sovereigns it looks like, so that could be worth a lot. Should pay for the repairs if the insurance company doesn't pay up.'

'Gold sovereigns?' Rose said.

'Yes, about twenty of them. Not sure what they're worth today, but I'd say a lot.'

'I'm sure you're right. Where are they?'

Henri pointed at the desk where Rose could see a dirty fabric bag.

'Great.' Rose went to the desk and lifted the bag. 'It's heavy,' she said, just as Noel peered in. 'Hey, you're just in time.'

'For what?' he asked.

'Henri found a bag with gold coins in one of the chimneys,' Rose explained. 'I suppose we'll have to give them to Granny and then she can decide what to do. After all, it's her property, as far as I know. What do you say, Noel?'

'Yes, it is,' Noel said after a moment's hesitation, his eyes on Rose. 'It'll have to be itemised with the rest of whatever is in the safe.'

'I suppose,' Rose said, looking at Noel, trying to guess what he was thinking. He looked at her glumly; she guessed he was upset about their argument. 'It's okay,' she said softly. 'I understand why you had to keep it from me. I'm sorry if I was being a pain earlier.'

Noel's eyes softened and he looked at her. 'I'm glad you understand. And I'm sorry if I upset you.'

Henri cleared his throat. 'Yes, well, that's all lovely. But enough of that. There's a real drama going on in the ballroom. I think your fashion show is falling apart, Rose. The models are fighting and the shops sent the wrong sizes or something and Vicky is about to have a nervous breakdown.'

'I'll see what's going on in a minute,' Rose said, still looking at Noel.

'Okay.' Henri looked exasperated. 'I think I'll leave you two to sort yourselves out. See you later, lads, as they say here.'

Rose burst out laughing. 'You're getting into the swing of Kerry at last. About time.'

Henri smiled. 'I know.' He walked out, closing the door behind him.

Rose stared at Noel. 'Sort yourselves out? What did he mean? Oh never mind,' she said, turning to leave. 'I have to go down and sort out the fashion mess.'

Noel put his hand on her arm to stop her. 'Hold on. I want to tell you what Henri meant.'

'What?' Rose asked, feeling suddenly breathless as she saw the expression on his face.

'He meant I should tell you how I feel about you,' Noel said, and stepped closer to Rose. 'How I've been in love with you ever since that night on top of Conor Pass.'

Rose felt her knees go weak as she saw the look in Noel's eyes. 'Oh, Noel,' she said, tears welling up in her eyes. 'That's so sweet.'

'Oh I know,' Noel said with a sad expression. 'I'm sweet, but you could never love someone like me. A tall nerd from the sticks.'

'You're wrong,' Rose said, standing on tiptoe to put her arms around his neck. 'That's exactly the kind of guy I can love. With all my heart. And if you don't kiss me, I'll never speak to you again, you tall, wonderful nerd from the sticks. The best sticks in the world, actually.'

Noel's eyes lit up – his arms went around Rose's waist, picking her up, swinging her around and then kissing her long and hard. Then he let her go and looked at her, his bright blue eyes shining. 'I had no idea. I thought you were still moping after Gavin.'

'Is that why you never asked me on a date?' Rose asked.

'I was trying my best not to show how I felt.'

'And I thought you were in love with that ex-girlfriend, Sally. You were talking about her all the time until I wanted to scream.'

'I was just making conversation. And maybe trying to make you jealous.' Noel leaned over and kissed Rose again.

She closed her eyes and leaned back in his arms. She wanted to stay there for a very long time, to just feel the joy of being loved by this man, so honest and kind and true. Someone she could trust and who would always be there for her. She just knew that, this time, it was going to last. 'I think I loved you even before you rescued me. But it wasn't until I was on the outing with Henri that I really knew. He was the one who told me. I laughed off the idea but then...'

'Then?' he asked.

'Then you were so sweet and came with me to Kinsale. It was when I walked out of the house that morning. You were standing there in the sunshine beside your car waiting for me, and I saw the light. I mean I felt that bolt of lightning they talk about.'

'Amazing.' Noel looked as if he had just won a million euros in the lottery.

'And you know what?' Rose continued. 'At that moment, I didn't really care about the necklace or if we would ever find it. I just wanted to be with you.'

'Why didn't you tell me?'

Rose sighed and stepped away from him. 'Because you started talking about Sally. So I thought...'

'But I told you what I felt about her, which is precisely nothing,' Noel protested. 'It was just fun to catch up.'

'I know that now.' Rose picked up the bag with the gold coins. 'This has to be put away in the safe. Do you know the combination?'

'No, why would I?'

'As Granny's special confidant, I thought you might,' Rose said with a slight edge in her voice.

'Rose,' he pleaded. 'Please don't start that again. You said—'

'I know.' Rose put her arms around his waist. 'Sorry. I'm just a little raw after your revelation. And these gold coins make me feel funny. We'll just put them in the desk for now and then Granny can deal with it.'

'Good,' Noel said, giving her a little squeeze. 'We have to put all that behind us. We might never find the necklace, you know.'

Rose sighed. 'You're right. And I'm just going to have to come to terms with telling Granny.'

Rose smiled all the way down the corridor, until she reached the double doors that led into the ballroom. She stopped for a moment to collect herself, preparing what she was going to say to calm the troubled waters. But then she heard that someone had stepped in already. Someone who was trying to make herself heard in the din of arguments and angry voices. Then, when nothing else seemed to work, there was a piercing whistle that stopped everyone in their tracks.

## 28

Rose laughed and walked into the ballroom. She knew that shrill whistle. When she was a small girl climbing trees in the garden, she had pretended not to hear her grandmother calling her in. But then Sylvia would put two fingers in her mouth and let out a whistle that could be heard all the way down to the shore. Rose had known she'd better behave and come at once, or there would trouble. Even now it brought her back, and she felt like she had to obey or else. She tiptoed in, not wanting to attract attention, and smiled as she saw what was going on.

Sylvia, a pen stuck in her hair, holding a clipboard, was standing on the catwalk beside a distraught Vicky. After the showstopping whistle, Sylvia was now talking loudly to the group of women standing just below her. 'Now listen, girls,' she said sternly. 'Stop arguing at once. We have to row this boat ashore, and pull together. Eileen Moore, I heard you were going on about a size issue? I have spoken to the boutique and they will change the size ten dress to a size sixteen, which I believe will fit you better.'

'How do you know what size I am?' Eileen asked, looking angry.

'My expert eye,' Sylvia said in a tone that didn't allow argument. 'You're a grand, statuesque woman, Eileen, not a slip of a girl. Just go with it and move on. Be proud of yourself and who you are.'

'Okay. Thank you, Sylvia,' Eileen said, sounding chastened.

'No problem.' Sylvia consulted her clipboard and breezed on. 'I have also made a list of clothes for each one of you to model, and got in touch with the two ladies who dropped out, telling them to come back and behave. We don't like quitters, do we? Also, I might add that walking in high heels is a skill that not everyone possesses. But you do it at your own risk. We will make you sign a disclaimer that you have understood this. Ballet flats will be provided for those who feel they don't want to risk their ankles. In any case, the vintage fashion doesn't demand very high heels. And finally, please remember why we're here. This show is about raising enough money for the lovely new garden that you will all be able to enjoy, and also for the wonderful café in the orangery that will also contain mementoes from the glorious past of Magnolia Manor. You should all be proud to be part of creating these additions to the new manor.' Sylvia drew breath and looked at the assembled women. 'Any questions?'

They all shook their heads. 'Good.' Sylvia gave the clipboard to Vicky. 'There you go. All done. You can take over now, but let me know if there's any trouble from anyone.'

Vicky laughed. 'After that delivery? Nobody would dare. Thank you, Sylvia, you're a star.'

'My pleasure.' Sylvia suddenly noticed Rose standing just inside the door. 'Hello, Rose. Glad you could join us at last.'

'Hi, Granny,' Rose said, walking into the ballroom. 'I thought you had gone out.'

'I did, but I came back when I heard about all the trouble here.' Sylvia held out her hand. 'Help me down, please, pet. Catwalks were never part of my comfort zone. All that strutting around in high heels. I'd be the worst model in the world.'

Rose laughed and helped her grandmother down from the catwalk. 'There you go. I'm so glad you managed to calm everyone. It'll be easy from now on.'

'They needed to be told to behave and pull together as a team,' Sylvia said. 'Everyone seemed to think it was all about them. That's the problem nowadays. It's all me, me, me.'

'You're so right.' Rose took Sylvia by the arm, steering her out of the room. 'But now, Granny, I want you to come to your study. I have something to show you. And there is something else I have to ask you,' she added. 'Something important.'

'Good or bad?' Sylvia asked, looking worried.

'Could be good,' Rose replied. 'I'm not sure yet.'

Sylvia let herself be led down the corridor by Rose while they talked about the fashion show, the new garden and the café that was nearly ready to open. 'Lily is all excited and has set up a schedule for the babysitters,' Sylvia began. 'She's also organised deliveries from the bakery in Ventry and ordered a barista coffee machine. She's buying crockery from charity shops too. She's such a trooper, doing all this with a new baby,' she said proudly.

'I know,' Rose said. 'She's amazing. I'll get started on the marketing as soon as I can. But it could take a little while yet. The fashion show has to come first. When that's over, I'll get going. The website is coming along great, and we'll have a show flat ready to visit soon. So I haven't been idle.'

Sylvia nodded. 'I know you haven't. Henri is beginning to pull his weight too, and I have a feeling that's all your doing.'

'I think he's finally growing up, that's all,' Rose remarked as they arrived at Sylvia's study.

'So what is it you wanted to show me?' Sylvia asked once they had walked into the room.

'It's in here.' Rose went to the desk, pulling out the bag with the gold coins from the drawer. 'Henri found these, they'd been stuck up the chimney in the big room on the attic floor. The chimney had been damaged by a recent rain storm, you see.'

'What? I had no idea,' Sylvia said and sank down on the sofa. 'Is the damage bad?'

'Yes, but I think the insurance will cover it. If not—' Rose put the bag in Sylvia's lap '—this will help pay for it.'

Sylvia recoiled slightly at the dirty bag. 'What is it?'

'Open it,' Rose said.

Sylvia did as she was told and peered inside, gasping at what it was. She took out one of the coins. 'A gold sovereign. How amazing. How many are there?'

'About twenty or so,' Rose replied.

'And they were stuck up that chimney? How extraordinary.' Sylvia put the gold coin back in the bag. 'This is wonderful. What a find.' She stopped and looked at Rose. 'You said you wanted to tell me something. Was this it? Or is there something else?'

Rose got her bag that she had left on the floor and took out the velvet case with the necklace. 'It's about this,' she started.

'Your necklace? What about it?' Sylvia asked.

'I don't know how to put it, so I'll just tell you the way it is,' Rose said, opening the case. 'A while back, just before that wedding, I found out that this necklace is fake.'

Sylvia stared at the necklace. 'Fake? What do you mean?'

'It's not white gold but silver and the stones are not real topazes.'

'What?' Sylvia stared incredulously at the necklace. 'But that's impossible.'

Rose nodded. 'Sadly, no. It's true.'

'But...' Sylvia stared at Rose. 'How could this be? You've been wearing it at parties ever since I gave it to you nearly two years ago. How can it be fake?'

'It's a long story,' Rose said.

'Tell me,' Sylvia ordered. 'I'm not moving from this spot until I know everything, even if it takes hours.'

'Of course,' Rose said. She went on to tell Sylvia all that had happened since the jeweller had told her the necklace was a copy.

'Why didn't you tell me?' Sylvia chided when Rose drew breath.

'I didn't want to upset you. There were so many things going on. I wanted to spare you this problem. I thought I'd be able to solve it on my own.'

'With Noel's help,' Sylvia said.

Rose felt her cheeks go pink. 'Yes. He's been wonderful. We didn't find the real necklace though.'

'You poor thing. It must have been so frustrating to learn that the Lincolns' necklace was also a copy,' Sylvia said.

'It was a huge shock,' Rose agreed. 'But now I don't know much more. We think Iseult didn't know about it either. She had a copy made of the fake one she had. Or at least that's what we think.'

'You're probably right,' Sylvia said, touching the necklace. 'But why did someone have this made in the first place? And when?'

'Around nineteen hundred, according to the hallmark,' Rose replied.

'Nineteen hundred...' Sylvia mumbled, deep in thought. 'Who could have... It couldn't have been Iseult. She was only eighteen, and she must have been given this fake one.'

Rose nodded. 'Yes, that's what we think.'

'This is so strange,' Sylvia said. 'I find it difficult to figure out.'

Rose tried to gather up the courage to mention what might be in Sylvia's safe. 'Granny,' she said, putting her hand on her grandmother's arm. 'Please don't get cross, but I know about the box in your safe. The one with some valuables from Caroline's estate.'

'The box?' Sylvia frowned. 'Who... Did Noel tell you about it?'

'Yes, but he was desperate. Don't worry, he only told me, nobody else.'

'He shouldn't have,' Sylvia said, looking annoyed. 'That was confidential.' Then she sighed. 'I understand the circumstances all the same. He thought the real necklace might be in there.'

'Is it?' Rose asked.

'No,' Sylvia replied. 'I've gone through it and made a list that Noel will put in my new will. There's a gold watch and a few bits and pieces of jewellery, some of it valuable. But the necklace isn't there. I'd have told you if it had been, of course.'

'Oh,' Rose said, feeling disappointed. 'That was our last resort. Now we'll never know what happened to it. I'm so sorry, Granny, you must be so disappointed. What with losing the manor, and—'

'Is this why you didn't tell me?' Sylvia interrupted.

Rose nodded.

'I'm completely at peace with the family home being renovated,' Sylvia declared. 'Don't forget that the senior apartments were my idea,' she continued.

Rose looked up into Sylvia's eyes and felt relieved. Had she been worrying over nothing? 'Are you sure?' she asked.

'Oh yes. Very sure. You see, now I feel that the house will be used in a very good way. It will be full of people again. I feel my life has turned a corner, and now I can look at a future without worry, living with Arnaud and being close to you all at the same time. I'm not worried about material things any more. I'm only sorry if the fake necklace upset you.'

'I'm coming to terms with it,' Rose said. 'And I'm learning to love it, because it belonged to Iseult, who seems to have been an extraordinary woman.'

'I'm so glad to hear that.' Sylvia looked thoughtful. 'And anyway, I might know where the real necklace is. I was going through the old papers and diaries that I found the other day, just before you left for Kinsale. There was a note in one of the little diaries that belonged to Maria Fleury. It said something about receiving payment for a secret sale. I thought nothing of it, but now I have a feeling...'

'Where is that little diary?' Rose asked.

'I left it up there. We should go and have a look.'

'If you feel up to it,' Rose said, noticing that Sylvia was looking a little pale. 'But I can go and bring them down here if you like.'

Sylvia nodded. 'Yes. Maybe that's best. I feel tired after my performance in the ballroom. I'll put the coins away in the safe while you're upstairs.'

Rose ran up the stairs to the storeroom, where she found the stack of papers and two small leather diaries. She brought them down to Sylvia as she was just closing the safe.

'Here they are,' Rose said, putting them on the desk. 'We can go through them together.'

Sylvia pulled out a chair and sat down at the desk, taking one of the diaries that Rose handed her. 'I'll look through this one,' Sylvia said, 'you go through the other one and then look through the stack of papers. I think they're just bills and invoices. The diaries seem to be the kind where they put in appointments and such. This one is from eighteen ninety-eight.'

Rose sat down on a stool beside Sylvia and picked up a diary, excited to find that it had belonged to Maria Fleury. The diary was from 1900, which made her heart beat faster. 'The year that first copy was made,' she mumbled, going through each page and studying every item carefully. '"*Mother very ill*", it says here. "*Tuberculosis... Must get her to a sanatorium...*"' Rose looked at Sylvia. 'How awful. Maria's mother must have been quite old in nineteen hundred.'

'Around seventy or so, I'd say,' Sylvia suggested. 'That was old in those days. And TB was prevalent.'

'Ugh, how horrible.' Rose turned the page. '"*Doctor recommends a few months in the sun*", it says here. But then she says, "*How can we afford that? There must be a way. Mother is all I have.*" How sad she must have been.' Rose turned a few pages and stared in excitement. 'Here it is!' she exclaimed. '"*Had piece copied. Sale of original arranged discreetly. Money to be paid to me in gold sovereigns.*"' She looked at her grandmother, grinning. 'I've found it! Maria Fleury had the necklace copied in order to sell the original so she could send her mother to the Riviera to recover from TB.'

Sylvia looked confused. 'But the money was here, hidden in the chimney. Why didn't she do what she said for her mother?'

'Because her mother died shortly after that,' Rose said, turning the pages of the diary. '"*Mama too ill to travel*", it says on February twenty-first, then, a week later, February twenty-eighth, "*Mama gone to the angels. Funeral on March first.*"' Rose flicked through the next pages. 'Nothing after that. I'd say Maria was devasted to lose her mother, just after she managed to get some money for that trip that might have saved her. How sad. Poor Maria.'

'So that's the story,' Sylvia remarked. 'I'd say Maria hid the money because she was ashamed of what she had done. Except the necklace was hers. But she may not have wanted anyone to know what she did with it, as it had been a gift on her wedding day.'

Rose nodded. 'That sounds believable. Let's assume that was the case and not go crazy looking for anyone else. It's Maria's secret, and her gift to us, in a way.'

'Yes, that's true,' Sylvia agreed. 'It will pay for repairs and part of the roof. So all is well. Except you don't have the real necklace and you probably never will.'

'Oh, I don't care,' Rose said. 'It was Iseult's necklace. I'll wear the copy with great pride now that I know what happened.'

'Good girl.' Sylvia patted Rose's arm. 'This has been hard work for you. But it brought you a lot of happiness too. I have never seen that light in your eyes before.'

'What light?' Rose asked.

'That sparkle in your eyes whenever you mention Noel,' Sylvia explained. 'I can see how much you love him. And I'm guessing he loves you too just as much.'

'Yes, Granny,' Rose said in a near whisper. 'That's what I was going to tell you. We're in love and it has never felt like this before.'

'That's the best news, apart from finding the buried treasure up a chimney. Pity we'll have to pay dearly for the repairs, but it was worth it in the end to find it, don't you think?'

'Yes, I think it was.' Rose smiled and got up. 'I'll go back with these and then we can close the chapter.'

Sylvia nodded. 'Grand. Now we can go through the material in the archives at a more leisurely pace. I found a few more things you might want to go through. Some old letters and an appointment book from the time Maria Fleury came to Magnolia, a calendar with appointments and reminders, but interesting all the same.'

'I'd say that would be fascinating,' Rose said, feeling excited. 'A great insight into life here in the eighteen eighties. Dinners and outings and all the kinds of appointments and visits that they did in those days.'

'You can include that in your history page on the website,' Sylvia suggested.

'That's a great idea. We'll go through it together.' Rose let out a deep sigh. 'I'm going to take a break during what's left of the weekend. Spend time with Noel and make some plans. This is so new, we don't really know where we're at yet.'

'Take your time,' Sylvia advised. 'Just enjoy the moment and the rest will sort itself out.'

'I know,' Rose said, and kissed her grandmother on the cheek. 'I feel both excited and calm at the same time, isn't that funny?'

'It's the best feeling,' Sylvia declared. 'It means that you've finally come home.'


Later that evening, when she hadn't heard from Noel, Rose picked up her phone and called him. 'Hi there,' she said when he answered. 'It's only me.'

'Not so only,' he said with a smile in his voice. 'I was just telling my dad about you. Well, of course he's met you from time to time, so you're no stranger to him. Except now he has to think of you differently.'

'How did he take it?' Rose asked.

'He was delighted. He likes you a lot, but also sad because he assumes this means I'll be moving out eventually.' Noel chuckled. 'I was going to call you later but you beat me to it. Has anything happened?'

Rose smiled, warmed by the sound of Noel's soft happy voice. 'Not really, except I told Granny everything. And then we found out, nearly by accident, how the necklace was copied through an old diary from nineteen hundred. It appears that Maria Fleury needed money to pay for her mother to go somewhere sunny when she was suffering from TB. But her mother died before she could go, and then Maria hid the money in the chimney. We just guessed that last bit, but it has to be what happened.'

'What?' Noel gasped. 'Incredible. And amazing detective work, of course. How did your granny take it?'

'Granny was shocked and happy at the same time. Shocked

that the necklace had been copied, and happy about us. She's very fond of you.'

'That's mutual, of course,' Noel said. 'She's an amazing woman.'

'She is. And then I thought I'd be bold and ask you out for a date.'

Noel laughed. 'How very forward of you. What did you have in mind?'

'Dinner on my tiny patio tomorrow. Birdsong and lovely sunset guaranteed. At least the birdsong. The lovely sunset is in the lap of the weather gods. I'm not the best cook in the world, to put it mildly. But if you're willing to take the risk, and don't mind some burned steak, oven chips and salad, I'd love to see you.'

'I'll bring dessert,' Noel offered.

'Perfect. See you at six tomorrow evening. Don't dress up.'

'Yes, ma'am. See you then.'

'See ya.' Then Rose hung up with a happy smile. There had been no endearments or talk of love in their conversation, but there was no need for that. She knew what was in his heart, and he in hers.

# EPILOGUE

A year later, nearly on the anniversary of the fashion show, there was another event that was the high point of the year – the inauguration of Magnolia Senior Apartments. As it was the first of its kind, and because of the location and family history, it had attracted a huge amount of attention in the media and would even be broadcast on national TV. After a lot of discussion and arguments, the board had decided against asking a celebrity or a local politician to officially open the apartment complex. Sylvia was the obvious choice. She had been at the helm of the Magnolia project from the start, and had come up with the idea in the first place. She had worked hard to get the project off the ground and, if it were not for her, it would never have happened. Plus, she was quite well known in the local area, of course.

The fashion show had been a huge success and it helped raise a lot of money, far above expectations. There were enough funds to get the garden project started, and the café in the orangery would be ready in a few months. It had been so popular they'd decided to hold a fashion show every year; it would pay for the maintenance of the gardens and raise a little extra for charity donations. They hoped that the residents would be models in the future.

The manor looked magnificent, all replastered and painted, the moss and damp patches gone from the façade, the roof and chimneys repaired, partly paid for by the gold sovereigns, and all the apartments were now beautifully decorated and ready to receive their first tenants. Rose had worked hard on the interiors and done most of the designs herself, including choosing wall-paper, curtains and carpets. All the flats were decorated in blues and greens with lovely animal and floral print curtains. It all went so well with the views of the gardens and the sea, making the interiors blend with the exterior in a subtle and harmonious way.

'Superb,' Henri had declared, kissing his fingers as they were all walking around the flats the day before the launch.

'Sublime,' Arnaud agreed, applauding as he inspected the finished apartments.

'Perfection,' Sylvia had exclaimed.

'You're a genius,' Lily had said, hugging Rose.

The best accolade had come from Noel, however. 'Every single flat feels like a home,' he said when she showed him around that evening. 'A true home with a heart. How did you do it?'

'I just imagined myself living here,' Rose explained. 'I wanted to keep the homely feel of Magnolia that has always been there for me.'

'You succeeded with flying colours.' Noel kissed her cheek. 'I'm so proud of you.'

'That means a lot to me,' Rose said and kissed him back.

'You know, my dad would be interested to move in here,' Noel announced as he stood looking out at the view from the top floor. 'Not straight away, but when the time comes and he feels he wants to live somewhere that's easier to run than our old house.'

'Maybe he should wait until the new lift has been installed?' Rose suggested.

'I think you're right.' Noel turned from the window. 'But what about us? We need to decide where we want to live. We've been together for a year now, and I'm practically living with you in the gatehouse. But that doesn't feel permanent to me.'

Rose put her arms around him and pressed her cheek against his chest. 'I know. I feel the same. But I needed this year to get the Magnolia project off the ground and the museum started. Now that everything is nearly in place, I'm ready to get on with our life. And our home. The gatehouse isn't really ideal if...' She stopped.

'If what?' he asked tenderly.

'If we want to have a family and a real home that's ours and not just mine,' Rose continued. 'We have to look around for a place of our own, with a garden and enough bedrooms. I have seen a few houses that might suit us. We could start looking soon.'

Noel nodded, looking pleased. 'Terrific. It'll be fun to go house hunting together.'

'It'll be fabulous,' Rose agreed. 'I'm so glad you agree with me.'

'Of course I do. But I want us to do it properly. We should get engaged,' Noel said. 'I thought we'd go to Killarney after the launch and pick a ring. Then we should get married as soon as possible. I mean...' He paused, took her hand and kissed it. 'I should propose, but I'm not sure what to say.'

'Let me say it.' Rose laughed and hugged him. 'Noel, my darling, will you marry me? As soon as possible?'

Noel grinned and squeezed her tight. 'Yes, my darling, my most wonderful Rose. I will marry you and live with you wherever you choose.'

'Can we be married here, under the magnolia tree? We could

have the reception in the orangery as the museum isn't ready yet. I think it would be fabulous.'

'That would be perfect,' Noel declared. 'But when?'

'In about three weeks?' Rose asked. 'Or is that too soon?'

'Not soon enough,' Noel declared. 'I'd marry you tomorrow if I could. But we have to have the launch first, of course.'

'Absolutely. It'll be such a grand event.' Rose looked out over the gardens and heaved a big sigh. 'Finally all is finished and ready to go. I can't believe it, after all the hard work. It's Granny's big day. She's so excited about it.'

'She's been such a trooper all through this year,' Noel said. 'You'd think that, at her age, she'd be ready to retire. But I don't think she ever will.'

'Not as long as she's alive and kicking,' Rose declared. 'It's her life's work, and she would never hand over the reins to anyone.'

'You're very alike,' Noel remarked. 'I'm trying to decide if that's good or bad.'

'It's good, of course,' Rose said, pulling away from him. 'But come on, we have to go down to Granny's place for dinner. Everyone's there. Even your father. I saw his car coming up the drive just now. And Lily and Dominic and little Naomi are already here.'

'Oh good. All my favourite people together for dinner.'

'Even Henri?' Rose teased.

'Even him. He's turning into quite a grand lad.'

'He has a way to go yet, but yeah, not bad,' Rose agreed.

They went down to dinner and joined everyone at the big table in Sylvia's kitchen. Rose looked around at them all: Sylvia, Arnaud, Henri, Lily, Dominic and little Naomi in her high chair, and Noel's father, Maurice, who she was already very fond of. Violet, the youngest Fleury sister, had also arrived for one of her rare visits while on a break from filming. They felt like a big family, even if they weren't all related by blood.

The year and a half that had passed since she came back to Kerry had been eventful and full of surprises, both good and bad. The best thing was finding love that she knew would last all her life. As Noel passed her a big platter of sliced roast beef and French beans, she smiled at him and felt a surge of happiness. How lovely it was to have come home at last.

# A LETTER FROM SUSANNE

I want to say a huge thank you for choosing to read *The Granddaughter's Irish Secret*. If you enjoyed it, and want to keep up to date with all my latest releases, just sign up at the following link. Your email address will never be shared and you can unsubscribe at any time.

*www.bookouture.com/susanne-oleary*

I hope you enjoyed *The Granddaughter's Irish Secret* and felt you were transported to this beautiful part of Ireland. I love the Dingle Peninsula and I'm always sad to leave and so happy every time I come back. I created the Fleury family as I wanted to write about strong, smart women who face life's ups and downs with great courage. They are not always perfect or as well behaved as they should be, but characters with flaws are more interesting and make a better story. I also want to write about women of all ages – young, old, middle-aged – and mix up their life experiences and situations.

If you did love the story, I would be very grateful if you could write a review. I'd love to hear what you think, and it makes such a difference helping new readers to discover one of my books for the first time.

I love hearing from my readers – you can get in touch on social media or my website.

Thanks, Susanne

# KEEP IN TOUCH WITH SUSANNE

www.susanne-oleary.co.uk

facebook.com/authoroleary

x.com/susl

goodreads.com/susanneol

# ACKNOWLEDGEMENTS

As always, huge, enormous thanks to my brilliant editor, Jennifer Hunt, who is so in tune with my writing and always knows what I want to say and shows me the way when I get a little muddled. Also, many, many thanks to Becca Allen, proofreader extraordinaire, whose eagle eye spots all the inconsistencies in the story, along with incorrect place names, typos and other howlers. And, of course, many, many thanks to the rest of the team at Bookouture who make an author's life easier. Family and friends who are there for me and cheer me on are the best, so please take a bow and accept my deepest gratitude. Last but not least I must thank my readers for your support and enthusiasm and all those wonderful emails and messages that mean so much to me.

# PUBLISHING TEAM

Turning a manuscript into a book requires the efforts of many people. The publishing team at Bookouture would like to acknowledge everyone who contributed to this publication.

**Commercial**
Lauren Morrissette
Hannah Richmond
Imogen Allport

**Cover design**
Debbie Clement

**Data and analysis**
Mark Alder
Mohamed Bussuri

**Editorial**
Jennifer Hunt
Sinead O'Connor

**Copyeditor**
Faith Marsland

**Proofreader**
Becca Allen

Printed in Great Britain
by Amazon

45529559R00142